# THE
# BEAUTY
# BENEATH

## by Daniel Welch Kelly

WESTBOW
PRESS®
A DIVISION OF THOMAS NELSON
& ZONDERVAN

WestBow Press books may be ordered through booksellers or by contacting:

WestBow Press
A Division of Thomas Nelson & Zondervan
1663 Liberty Drive
Bloomington, IN 47403
www.westbowpress.com
1 (866) 928-1240

ISBN: 978-1-5127-7732-1 (sc)
ISBN: 978-1-5127-7733-8 (hc)
ISBN: 978-1-5127-7731-4 (e)

Library of Congress Control Number: 2017903037

Printed by Bookmasters in the United States of America.

WestBow Press rev. date: 08/07/2017

# DEDICATION

To those who see the Creator in each of His human creations.

# ACKNOWLEDGEMENTS

A number of people contributed to getting this project completed. First of all, I want to thank the painstaking work of my editor, Marguerite Hufford. She made a number of helpful suggestions and, to the extent that there are remaining imperfections, those are my responsibility alone. Also, I have always been awed by the artistic ability of my brother, James C. Kelly, of Madlab Studio. James, who is the artist of the "Famous Hoosiers" display on Georgia Street in downtown Indianapolis, created the cover art for my book. The staff at Westbow Press has been accessible and helpful in getting my story into print. I also want to thank my loving wife, Jamie, for her patience and understanding as I focused on getting this book completed and my kids, who I began talking to about this concept around the year 2000. Finally, I want to thank all who read this book. I hope you derive half as much enjoyment and inspiration from reading it as I did from writing it.

# THE BEAUTY BENEATH

**1**

Margaret Millington left the offices of Copeland, Rogerson & Zenhaus on the fourteenth floor of the Windy City Commercial Center, having concluded the fifth day of the mediation of her divorce proceedings. She knew she should have been relieved. After all, her divorce had been pending in the Cook County Superior Court for two and a half years. She exited the meeting with the attorneys after signing an agreement that made her the sole owner of $128.4 million in a wide variety of investments that represented her share of the marital estate. She thought she was long past being emotional about the demise of her marriage, yet as she descended the elevator alone, she was struck by a chilling depth of loneliness she had never before experienced.

Fifty-five years old, childless and loaded. To any objective observer, Margaret was still a striking woman. She possessed sharp features: a thin, straight nose that came to a slight upward point, a small chin and high, angled and symmetrical cheekbones. Her wide-set eyes were a deep and penetrating shade of blue. She was five feet nine inches and 135 pounds. Although she didn't exercise much anymore, Margaret was genetically blessed with good muscle tone and long, thin bones. Her infrequent smiles revealed sparkling white teeth that were perfectly aligned, contrasting with her hair, a purchased dark brown, cut short and stylish. Margaret spent freely on her wardrobe, and her gait and overall presentation suggested a connection to aristocracy from another land and time.

At times, this noble bearing was reinforced by a cold and impatient manner in her interactions with others and a practiced condescension. Despite all of this, Margaret had always been painfully self-conscious and was her own harshest critic. Her arrogant demeanor actually masked a deep-seated insecurity that Margaret recognized and dated back to her childhood.

When the elevator came to a stop, Margaret stepped out without pausing to notice whether she was on the main floor. It was a warm, sunny day and Margaret shielded her eyes from the sun. She quickly hailed a cab and had it take her to her high-rise apartment building.

The cab pulled to an abrupt stop outside of Margaret's apartment on Lakeshore Drive. "Thirteen dollars, ma'am," grumbled the cabbie with a thick, Arabic accent. She pulled out a twenty, paused momentarily and handed it to the cabbie as she grabbed her purse and stepped onto the sidewalk. Margaret stopped before the front entrance to the apartment building as though unsure that she wanted to go inside. She still felt lonely and lost. She took the elevator to her twenty-third-floor apartment and unlocked the door to her suite.

Margaret's spiked heels clicked across the tiles of the entryway of her apartment and she quickly removed each with the other foot and left them where they lie. The apartment itself was spacious, with ten-foot ceilings and a wall of windows from a foot above the floor to within inches of the ceiling that offered a breathtaking view of the southwest shore of Lake Michigan and downtown Chicago. Margaret's gaze scanned all before her critically. Although her apartment was expensively furnished and contained several pieces of original artwork, there were no pictures of family or friends. "Would anyone notice if I weren't here tomorrow?" she wondered with despair. The thought trailed off as she became enveloped by her loneliness. She phoned to have pasta delivered from an Italian restaurant around the corner, then turned on the stereo and listened to soft music as she ran water into her Jacuzzi bath. Margaret slowly removed her clothes and carelessly dropped them to the floor.

She climbed into the tub and slowly slid down until the warm water covered her shoulders. She rested her head and neck on the back of the tub and closed her eyes as her tired body was relaxed by the warmth and the droning sound of the running water. As the water filled the tub, Margaret lifted and dropped her hips slowly and rhythmically, causing the bubbling water to wash over her tanned, flat belly and then cascade off the sides of the tub. She picked up a bar of soap and lathered her chest and abdomen, rubbing her hand gently across the front of her body.

A hint of a sneer crept across Margaret's face as she thought about how she had confronted Alfred each day of the mediation wearing a different piece of expensive jewelry that she had purchased over the years in revenge for his philandering. For a fleeting moment, it felt good to revel in her hatred. But then Margaret started thinking about what a despicable, self-loathing person she must be to have put up with it for so long.

In an effort to push these thoughts from her head, Margaret sat up in the bathtub and washed and rinsed her hair. She then picked up her razor and began shaving her legs. When she was halfway finished with the second leg, her hand trembled. She looked at her shaking hand as though it were a foreign object, beyond the control of her brain. When the tremor increased, Margaret rose from the bath and walked over to the bar at the near end of her living room. She poured herself a glass of scotch and returned to her bath, where she took small sips as the water continued to flow.

As she sipped her drink, Margaret looked at the razor on the edge of the tub. The loneliness she had been feeling evanesced like the steam from her bath and was replaced by an indescribable emptiness. Margaret wished she could cry, perhaps to reassure herself of her humanity, but the tears wouldn't come. She hadn't cried for herself in years. She used to be angry with Alfred and angry about her life, but her anger was also spent long ago. Margaret had become numb.

She looked back down at the razor and picked it up with her left hand, after setting the glass of scotch on the side of the tub. She re-lathered her lower leg and resumed shaving, this time with renewed vigor. Margaret finished shaving her leg and looked down at her arms. She looked at her left forearm and then at her razor, and back at her forearm down to the wrist. She put the razor down again and picked up her drink, which was still nearly full. She raised the glass to her lips and poured the scotch down in one long and continuous gulp.

Looking down at her empty glass, Margaret held the crystal by the base and swung it against the outside of the tub, scattering broken glass across the bathroom floor. Margaret leaned partway out of the tub and, with a bloodied hand, reached out and picked up a long shard of glass. She plunged it deep into her left wrist as she screamed. Margaret's head fell against the back of the tub, and she closed her eyes as the water took on the color of a rose wine.

The water continued to flow from the bathtub faucet, pouring over the sides of the tub onto the bathroom floor. At about this time, the delivery boy from the restaurant stepped off the elevator with his package, leaving a smell of garlic behind him. As he approached Margaret's suite he looked down at his package to read the apartment number that had been scribbled down when the order came in just twenty-four minutes earlier. He rang the doorbell and waited. No answer. He rang the doorbell again. Still no answer. The boy then pounded on the door. Finally, he put his ear to the door to see if he could hear anything. The bathroom was just inside the apartment and he could hear music and the sound of running water. He knocked again, more loudly this time. "Ms. Millington! Ms. Millington!"

Once again he put his ear to the door and just as he did so, he noticed that water was beginning to run onto the tile from under the door. The delivery boy ran to the elevator to get the assistance of the porter.

**2**

As the young man stepped out of the shower, he continued to towel off in front of the bathroom mirror. Cleanly shaven and thirty-one years old, he had a thick crop of curly brown, closely cut hair that required little attention from its unselfconscious owner. Standing thusly, the man, whose mind was lost in meditation, could see the familiar square patches, symmetrically located on each of his upper thighs, where skin had been removed before he could remember, to be grafted onto other areas where the burns over his body were of greater cosmetic concern.

Crossing the small bedroom to the closet, the man donned his standard black dress slacks, black shirt and black dress loafers. He took two steps to his left and placed his right hand on the feet of the crucifix that was on the wall at eye level in front of him. He audibly mumbled a short prayer that would have been incoherent to any person who may have been in this room which had, in fact, never known a visitor.

The young man stole a quick glance out of his bedroom window and was grateful that the clouds that had hung over the city for two weeks before finally dispersing yesterday had not returned. It promised to be the first sunny Sunday in many weeks. Within minutes, Fr. Peter Kearns was in the seven-year-old Ford Taurus that had been given to him by the parish that was his first assignment in central Illinois upon his ordination to the priesthood. Fr. Kearns did not consider himself worthy of such a generous gift before he had begun serving, and seven years and two parishes later the car still looked new due to the conscientious care of its owner.

Fr. Kearns always squeezed in a visit or two to the sick and shut-ins before the ten o'clock mass. Today, his first stop was Whispering Willows Convalescent Center, where he planned to visit a few of the residents there who eagerly awaited his regular visits. As the priest walked by the front desk at Whispering Willows he received a warm smile from the woman on duty.

"How are you today, Grace?" asked the priest, as he met her eyes and returned her smile.

"I'm fine, Father. You might want to stop in Mr. Addison's room pretty quickly though. We don't expect him to make it much longer."

Sylvester Addison was eighty-three years old and was succumbing to a combination of old-age ailments, including emphysema, glaucoma, diabetes and, lately, Alzheimer's disease. He also had an unspecified mental illness, characterized by unpredictable emotional outbursts. The nursing home was never provided with any useful information about his mental health history, but the amateur diagnoses offered in conversations among the nurses and aides ranged from simple dementia to some type of personality disorder. Addison was widowed and his two grown sons lived on separate coasts with their families, who tried to stop in for visits a couple of times each year. Although he wasn't counting, this was Fr. Kearns' fortieth visit to Sylvester Addison since he became a resident of Whispering Willows sixteen months earlier.

As he entered the elderly man's room, the priest was struck by how much thinner and frailer Addison had become in the last couple of weeks. The older man was sweating and his breathing was labored as Fr. Kearns approached his bed, which was raised about three quarters to upright.

"Hello Sylvester." Fr. Kearns tried to get on a first-name basis with those to whom he ministered, forcing his natural deference to the elderly to yield to his desire to befriend the people he visited.

Addison wore a blank expression as he turned his head in the priest's direction. It was obvious to Peter that he had continued to deteriorate since the priest's last visit. Fr. Kearns leaned over the old man's bed and addressed him again.

"It's me. Fr. Peter. Can you see me Sylvester?"

"Fr. Peter. Good to see you," replied the elderly man.

"I understand you are suffering, Sylvester."

"Yes Father, … didn't recognize you… glad you came."

After a brief conversation in which the elderly man appeared distracted, he caught the priest off guard when he put the following question to him: "Will you hear my confession?"

Sylvester Addison was not a Catholic. In fact, he claimed to be an atheist when Fr. Kearns first visited him at Whispering Willows, and therefore quickly became a priority for the priest. Over the course of the past year, the staff had noticed a gradual improvement in Addison's temperament prior to the recent decline in his health. He was no longer screaming obscenities at the frightened nurses' aides when he was hungry, and he had almost entirely deleted the once-common, profane exclamations from his occasional, remaining outbursts. Fr. Kearns appreciated the efforts of his elderly friend, but was still caught off guard by the man's request.

"Sylvester, I'd be happy to hear your confession."

"How does this start?"

The young priest patted the man's shoulder gently, squeezing it in a reassuring manner.

"I know you're not Catholic, Sylvester, and that is fine. But I take it that you've never been to confession before. Is that right?"

"No Father, I haven't. What do I need to do?"

"Well," replied the priest. "Let me begin by asking you if you have had a chance to think about the ways in which you feel you may have disappointed our Lord."

"Yes, Father. I sure have."

"Good," said the priest smiling warmly. Peter then gave a quick history of the Sacrament of Penance to his friend.

"Jesus actually established the sacrament after he rose from the dead and revealed himself to his disciples. He knew he wouldn't be staying on earth for long, and he wanted men to be aware of their sinful nature and of their need for the Lord's abundant mercy. So he told his apostles, 'Just as the Father has sent me, I also send you.' He breathed on them and told the apostles, 'Receive the Holy Spirit. If you forgive the sins of any, they are forgiven; if you retain the sins of any, they are retained.'"[1]

"In the Sacrament of Penance, although you will be telling your sins to me, and I'm just a man, my ordination into the priesthood allows me to perform the seven sacraments of the Church. So try to just close your eyes and tell me what you'd like to say if our loving Lord Jesus, who forgives all of our sins, were sitting here beside you instead of me."

The old man then spoke in a voice just above a whisper for the better part of an hour. Halfway through his soul-cleansing monologue, tears began streaming down the face of the elderly penitent. When he had finished talking, Peter blessed the man and recited a brief prayer, as Addison regained his composure. Fr. Kearns told Addison that for his penance he would like for him to say or do three kind things for his nurses before the day was over. He tenderly held the older man's hand as he told his friend good-bye. Addison looked the very picture of serenity as the priest left his room for what was to be the last time and headed to the next room.

---

[1] John 20:21, 23 **NET**

**3**

"Ms. Millington? Ms. Millington? Can you hear me?" As Margaret awoke, she looked up and saw a nurse leaning over her bed. Behind her was a face that, while familiar, didn't immediately register. She ran her eyes around her surroundings and realized that she was in a hospital room, looking into the eyes of Dr. Frederick Blair, her physician. She then immediately remembered the events at her apartment and understood why she was here.

Fred Blair was the ex-husband of one of Margaret's friends, Elena Blair. The Blairs and the Millingtons were roughly the same age and were once active in the same country club, where the men frequently drank and golfed, while their wives often drank and played tennis. On many other occasions they just drank. Elena Blair divorced her husband a decade ago, which ended the couples' friendship, though Dr. Blair remained the primary care physician for both of the Millingtons.

"Margaret, you're awake. How do you feel?" The caressing voice of Fred Blair was pleasant, but she was heavily sedated and didn't answer right away. She felt herself thinking of her answer before she gave voice to it.

"I guess I'm still here, Fred. How long have I been here?"

"At St. Francis? A couple of days. Do you want to talk about it?"

"No thanks. I think I'd just like to rest. How much longer will I be staying here?"

"Probably not long, Margaret. But you know you're going to have to get some further help in our stress unit until you're out of the woods. I'll let you get that rest right now. If you need anything, push this button and it'll light up at the nurse's station just down the hall, okay?"

"That'll be fine. Thank you, Fred."

Dr. Blair smiled at his patient and gently patted her hand. "It's going to be alright. I'll be checking on you again in the morning." He quietly slipped out of the room and left Margaret alone again.

Margaret looked down at her left arm. Just below the elbow an IV tube connected her to two different solutions. She figured one was nutrients and the other one was probably some sort of medication. Further down her arm, her wrist was completely covered by a gauze wrap, with only the ends of her fingers protruding. She wiggled the fingers on her left hand. Having satisfied the full extent of her curiosity about her circumstances, she closed her eyes with a sense of indifference and fell back asleep in the dimly lit room.

When she next awoke, it was morning, and Margaret saw a stranger sitting next to her bed. When she first looked at her male visitor, she was taken aback at the sight of him. He looked to be in his early thirties. He had dark-brown hair, cut short, and a thin, narrow face. He smiled somewhat crookedly and there was a slight irregularity in his face that Margaret couldn't quite identify. But the predominant feature of the stranger that Margaret actually found somewhat startling was what appeared to be a large burn across the right side of his face, from his hairline just left of the center of the forehead, down to his cheekbone, then at an irregular path back to the bottom of his right ear.

Margaret noticed that her visitor was wearing a cleric's collar and appeared to be some sort of a minister or priest. He saw that she was now awake.

"Good morning. You must be Ms. Millington," he said as a broad smile flashed across his disfigured face. "I'm Fr. Peter Kearns. I hope you don't mind me stopping by."

Being devoid of sympathy for her uninvited visitor's rather tragic appearance, Margaret did not bother to feign interest in his mission to her room.

"Are you a man of God?" she asked with a slight tilt of the head.

"Why, yes. I'm a Catholic priest. Do you have a religious preference?"

"Listen to me, man of God. The last thing that I need right now is your superstitious preaching."

If Margaret's icy reaction was designed to shock the clergyman, it was clear by his undiminished smile that her effort had fallen short.

"Don't you believe in God, Ms. Millington?"

Margaret fixed her gaze evenly on the priest and responded sarcastically.

"My ex used to think *he* was God, and he was actually a lying slime ball. So I guess I don't really know what to think." As she was speaking, Margaret pushed the button to the nurse's station. She had apparently reached the very short limits of her patience.

Within moments a thin, young nurse with a tan complexion who appeared to be mixed race entered the room. She acted somewhat timid and had a soft voice. "Can I get something for you Ms. Millington?"

"Yes. Please take Fr. Kearns to a Catholic room. He's wasting his time in here."

"That won't be necessary Ms. Millington. I'll see myself out. I hope you have a speedy recovery." With a smile undimmed by the frosty response to his visit, the priest bowed his head slightly and backed away from the bed and exited the room.

Before the priest had completely removed himself from earshot of the patient, Ms. Millington demanded of the young nurse: "Who is that poor ugly soul?"

The nurse visibly cringed at her patient's rudeness. "Fr. Kearns is a priest from St. Michael's Church, downtown. He stops by to visit patients all the time. He's really a good guy."

"What is your name?" Margaret asked the nurse.

"I'm Janeen."

"Well listen Janeen. You tell Fr. Kearns for me that he can skip this room if he comes by any more while I'm still here. The last thing I am in the mood for right now is for somebody to tell me how I've got to find Jesus. You hear?"

"Whatever you say, Ms. Millington. Can I get anything for you while I'm here?"

"No thank you."

The hospital door closed. Margaret was once again alone. Her thoughts returned to the priest and from there to the various churches that she and her husband had attended off and on over the years of their marriage. Although she was raised in a Methodist home, Margaret was never devout, and when she became an adult and married, she came to view church primarily as a social club, and their selection of churches varied, depending upon which one offered the most social opportunities at any given time. She was aware that as she had aged, her feelings about religion had degenerated from a rather indifferent tolerance to a near hostility. In recent weeks her faith had sunk to an all-time nadir. Since she first awoke in the presence of Dr. Blair, she was certain that people were going to be making judgments about her mental state. And yet, as disconcerting as that thought was to her, she was even less ready to be the object of moral judgments by people possessed of a faith she did not share.

Ending several hours of solitude, Dr. Blair returned to Margaret's room.

"How are you feeling today, Ms. Millington?" asked the doctor.

Margaret realized that more time had passed than she'd realized and it was now evidently the next morning, but with the room-darkening shades drawn, it could have been nighttime for all Margaret could tell. Feeling somewhat disoriented, Margaret replied.

"I feel a little light-headed. And sore," she added as she looked down at her arm.

"Well, we're going to move you upstairs sometime this afternoon. I think you'll find your new room a bit homier than this."

"Is that the nut ward you're moving me to?" Margaret asked, as she envisioned rooms with wild-eyed roommates.

"It is our psychiatric unit. I don't know if we have any 'nuts' right now for you though," answered the doctor with a half-smile. "You'll be seen by a good friend of mine, Dr. Emil Sankar. I know you'll like him. He'll take good care of you. In a few days, we'll get those stitches out of your arm."

Margaret sensed that Fred Blair's formality was now, ironically, leaving her feeling cold and distant, as she was beginning to experience genuine apprehension about her predicament at the hospital. Margaret softened in response.

"How bad was my arm, Fred?"

The doctor picked up on the new tone from his old friend and spoke more warmly in reply.

"Well, the wound was serious, but it will heal. You really did a number on yourself though, Margaret. If the cut had been a quarter of an inch over, you wouldn't be here right now. As it was, we had to give you several units of blood to get you stabilized. You'll be on antibiotics for about a week too. Are you ready to talk about it yet, Margaret?"

The doctor was no longer smiling and looked sincerely concerned for his patient and friend. Margaret was not comfortable being the beneficiary of what she perceived as the doctor's officious concern. She answered him with barely suppressed anger and a hint of panic in her voice.

"No, I'm not. I really don't want to think about it. I am not up to any of this, including being seen by your shrink friend. I want you to leave me down here and when my cut has healed sufficiently, I want to be released to my home. If I feel like talking later, I'll find a counselor or something."

"Well, I'm afraid that's not possible. You are going to be staying here a couple more days under what's called an 'emergency detention order.' That's an order from a judge. Then Dr. Sankar will see you and he'll decide whether he thinks you ought to stay for a while longer. Under the circumstances, I think he'll recommend that you spend some time here."

"And if I refuse?"

Doctor Blair finally dropped the friendly tone in his voice and answered her factually and without emotion.

"You'll be entitled to a hearing before a judge. If Dr. Sankar believes you are suffering from a mental condition that makes you a danger to yourself or others, the judge can order you detained for psychiatric care for up to ninety days."

Although Margaret understood that she had come close to killing herself, she had not fully appreciated the complications she had created for herself beyond the damage to her health. As this realization began to sink in, she looked down at the foot of her bed and remained silent. Dr. Blair excused himself abruptly and left the room.

**4**

"All rise. Cook County Superior Court Number Twenty-four is now in session, the Honorable Gail Lee presiding." The bailiff entered just ahead of the judge and then quietly disappeared into the high-ceilinged courtroom. Judge Lee opened the morning's proceedings by inviting the few persons present to be seated. In accordance with Illinois state law, the room had been cleared of all but those directly participating in the mental health commitment hearing.

Margaret Millington felt an unnerving degree of self-consciousness. As the judge made a few introductory remarks about the nature of commitment hearings and the rights of the patient, now the "Respondent," Margaret was awash in feelings of shame, embarrassment, and trepidation. She understood that, depending upon the outcome of the hearing that was about to take place, she could find herself involuntarily placed in a locked unit of a psychiatric hospital for many weeks.

The first witness to testify was Dr. Sankar, the psychiatrist who had been appointed to evaluate Margaret at the hospital. After reciting his educational and professional qualifications with what seemed to Margaret to be a total sense of self-satisfaction, Dr. Sankar turned in his chair toward Margaret and began discussing his new patient.

"My initial consultation with Ms. Millington occurred on March 14 at St. Francis Hospital. I found Ms. Millington to be oriented as to person, place, time, and event. Her appearance was unremarkable and her manner was somewhat impatient and suspicious. Nevertheless, I did find the patient to be a reasonably credible reporter of the facts and circumstances that led to her admission to the hospital."

Approximately ten minutes into his testimony, Dr. Sankar got to the heart of the matter. "Based upon all of the foregoing, it is my professional opinion that the patient suffers from a severe depression and, that as a result of her depression, she is presently a danger to herself. I therefore recommend to the court that Margaret Millington be committed for a period not exceeding ninety days for mental health care."

Although her attorney had warned her about the doctor's likely recommendation, the words sent Margaret reeling. She was allowed to testify in her own behalf, and made a feeble attempt to do so. Though she tried to follow her lawyer's questions, she remained stunned and distracted, reinforcing the impression left by the psychiatrist that Margaret was an unstable woman.

Approximately twenty minutes after the hearing began, Margaret was led out of the courtroom by her attorney, followed by Dr. Sankar and the sheriff's deputy who would escort her back to the stress unit at St. Francis Hospital: her home for the indefinite future.

**5**

St. Francis Hospital was founded in Chicago at the turn of the previous century by an order of Catholic sisters, whose numbers had now dwindled to the point that their influence in the hospital, once so pervasive, was but a memory to the residents of this upper middle-class neighborhood in the city's downtown. The staffing of the hospital was now comprised entirely of laypersons, and the uniforms of nurses had replaced the habits of nuns.

The one religious relic that remained at the hospital were the crucifixes that still adorned the walls of each of the rooms. The crosses in most of the rooms of the hospital were made of wood and pointed at the top and bottom. And yet it was the appearance of this one small room decoration in this now modern hospital that led the astute observer to know he had passed into the stress unit of the hospital. For on the walls in this section of the hospital, in the place of an actual crucifix was a mere painting of one. As one considered this distinguishing characteristic of this part of the hospital, it was difficult not to contemplate the sort of hideous incident that may have occurred in the past and led to this modification to the hospital's decor.

Unit 5, as the hospital's stress unit was more commonly known, was comprised of eighteen patient rooms; a large, formal conference room and two smaller, informal ones; a dining room; three therapy rooms; three intensively monitored rooms and a combination lounge and rec room. In addition to these rooms, all accessible to the patients, were the nurses' station, situated in the middle of the unit, and staff offices.

A full-time psychiatrist, a part-time psychiatrist, a psychologist, two counselors, several psych techs, nurses, and security staff were the personnel of Unit 5. All of them walked freely between the patient rooms and the rest of the unit. The entire unit was "secure" in that a key was required to enter or exit the unit. All staff members had keys. The patients had free access to all of these areas except for the staff offices. The liberality of the patients' visiting privileges between rooms as well as their freedom to use the lounge depended upon the current merit level of each patient. This in turn was based upon a point system devised to reward effort in therapy and generally good behavior.

The psychologist on the unit was Dr. Melanie Sekorski. She was a mid-fortyish, married mother of two college-age daughters, who often served as subjects in the real-life examples used by Dr. Sekorski to illustrate points she was trying to make in therapy. Dr. Sekorski was devoted to her patients and they generally responded well to her as she helped them explore the depths of their thoughts and experiences.

Soon after Margaret's arrival in Unit 5, Dr. Sekorski led a group therapy discussion on trust. She went around the room and asked the six patients before her to share their experiences of a trust that was kept and one that was betrayed. Two of the six were new patients who were participating in their first group therapy session. Sekorski had the other patients share their stories first and finally came to the two new patients. The first of the new patients was Roger, a schizophrenic who functioned well on the outside as a printer, as long as he took his medication. Occasionally, Roger would attempt to wean himself from his meds, which he complained clouded his thinking. These efforts invariably failed, and his latest attempt at pharmaceutical independence landed him in Unit 5 on the Friday night before this Monday morning session.

"Mr. Colson, can you tell us about an event that stands out in your mind as a time when your trust in someone was betrayed?"

Roger started out nervously in a voice so low it was nearly inaudible. "I had a co-worker who agreed to work my shift one time so that I could go to a family get-together."

The words "get together" were pronounced at a more normal volume, as Roger Colson told Dr. Sekorski and the other patients about how the untrustworthy co-worker intentionally failed to show, causing Roger trouble with his superiors at "Double Image Copy Shop."

"Did that experience make you question the relationship that you thought you had with your co-worker before this incident?" pressed the psychologist.

"Yes. I thought that my co-worker respected me and valued our friendship. Obviously, he didn't think anything of the problems he caused me," said Roger, again picking up steam vocally as he went.

Dr. Sekorski followed up on this point with a story of her own about a similar betrayal and then looked at the final patient in the group. "Margaret, can you tell us about a person you have known that you can trust without question?"

Margaret was suddenly flooded with a torrent of emotions. She hesitated for several seconds and finally responded:

"Trust is a concept I'm not real familiar with. I'd prefer to wait and bare my soul to all of you strangers when you're discussing something I can relate to." She then stood up and walked out of the room. Deciding that this may not be the ideal time to confront her, Dr. Sekorski made no attempt to stop Margaret. But she did make a mental note that Margaret was likely going to be a challenging patient to treat.

Back in her room, Margaret looked around, then remembered she had not yet earned telephone privileges, other than for emergencies. She went out to the nurse's station and asked if she could use the phone.

"Ms. Millington, I'm sorry, but I do not have authority to give you telephone access today. Is there something else I could do to help you?"

Exasperated, Margaret summoned all of her remaining self-control and responded politely to the nurse, "Yes, thank you. Could you please call my attorney?" Margaret gave her the telephone number. The nurse looked at the number and then looked back up at Margaret.

"Well, I don't suppose one *short* phone call would hurt anything." The nurse dialed the phone. When she heard it was ringing she handed the phone to Margaret and busied herself with some papers on her desk, pretending not to pay attention to the ensuing telephone conversation.

"Hello, Marvin Zenhaus please." Margaret tapped her nails impatiently on the counter by the nurses' desk.

"Marvin. This is Margaret Millington. I need you to get me out of here today."

The nurse stole a peek at Margaret's expression as the latter awaited her attorney's reply.

"Listen Marvin. There has to be something you can do. I ...."

It was apparent that Margaret was not encouraged by what her attorney was telling her. The nurse watched as Margaret's stance and demeanor changed from proud and erect to slouching and forlorn.

"But.... Yes, I understand that, but, if you don't get me out of here I really am going to go crazy!"

Margaret appeared to be listening for another ten to fifteen seconds. She then started to hand the phone back to the nurse, but at the last instant tried a different approach.

"Apparently we were disconnected. Could you please dial that number for me one more time? This should only take a minute." The nurse smiled and complied with Margaret's request.

"Marvin Zenhaus, please. This is Margaret Millington again. Thank you."

Within seconds, Margaret's attorney was back on the phone. Immediately Margaret got to the point: "Marvin. I have fifty thousand dollars for the competent attorney who can get me out of here. Do you know anyone that fits the bill, or will I have to call another attorney?"

Margaret paused for Zenhaus' answer. She then burst into tears and dropped the phone on the counter. She turned around and, pressing her back to the counter, allowed herself to slide to the floor, where she remained seated. Margaret leaned over her knees and sobbed until she was escorted back to her room by a husky security staffer with a deep and soothing voice.

Later that evening, Margaret sat in the dining room at dinner. Two other patients joined her at her table. One of them was a very large and heavy, ebony-skinned woman who introduced herself as "Fannie". The other was a small, mousey, pale-white woman Fannie called "Diane".

Becoming resigned to her fate for what she knew would be at least the next several weeks, Margaret decided to be cordial to her dinner companions. Fannie explained that she had been on Unit 5 for two months and was expecting to be released in another month to the Cook County Jail. As it turned out, Fannie had beaten her live-in boyfriend with a ball bat. For a while they thought he was going to die, in which case she could have been facing a charge of murder. Eventually, he pulled through and the charge remained one of aggravated battery. After receiving an ambiguous report from a court-ordered psychological evaluation, Fannie was committed until it was determined that she was competent to assist in her defense and stand trial.

Diane was a very sad-appearing woman who looked sixty, but was actually thirty-seven years old. She was in the hospital on her eighth commitment in the past ten years for depression. Upon learning this part of Diane's history, Margaret wondered what sort of missteps might lead her down a similar path. Although she was far from sold on the necessity of her hospitalization, and still less on her own prospects to be "cured," Margaret made a silent vow that this would not be her fate; she would either "get better," or would make sure that she was successful in any future attempt to do herself in.

As the trio ate their dinner together and became acquainted, a broad-shouldered woman of approximately thirty came and set her tray down next to Diane. The woman, who did not introduce herself, but whom Margaret later learned was "Keisha," had a square jaw and a generally brooding disposition. As the other three continued to talk, Keisha maintained a disinterested expression, occasionally looking at the others, but primarily focusing on her food.

Margaret sat across the table from Keisha and Fannie sat across from Diane. At one point during the meal of fried chicken and mashed potatoes, Keisha reached over to Diane's plate and, without saying a word, picked up a leg off the frail-looking woman's plate and raised it to her own open mouth. Fannie's arm shot across the table and grabbed the poacher's wrist. Without raising her voice Fannie spoke to the woman in an even tone:

"You take one bite out of that and I swear I'm gonna snap your neck like they done to that chicken. You hear me?"

Keisha made fleeting eye contact with the larger woman, and, evidently not liking what she saw, gently placed the chicken leg back on Diane's plate and got up with her tray to leave the dining room. No further incidents transpired during the meal.

After dinner, Margaret was in her room and had a visit from the psychiatrist, Dr. Manuel Gonzales.

Dr. Gonzales introduced himself upon entering the room and pulled out a chair from the desk opposite Margaret's bed, where she had been sitting and watching television. Dr. Gonzales straddled the chair as it faced backward, and with a large grin and a heavy Spanish accent addressed his new patient.

"How did you sleep last night, Ms. Millington?"

"Very poorly, thank-you."

"Would you like something to help you sleep tonight?"

"I guess my own bed would be out of the question?"

The friendly doctor laughed aloud. "We hope to have you back in your own bed as soon as possible, Ms. Millington. For now, I can offer you a sedative."

Margaret accepted the doctor's offer and thanked him.

"I will be meeting with you tomorrow morning at eleven. We will see if we can prescribe something else to help you feel better during the day, okay?"

"Whatever you say, Doc," replied Margaret, as she dismissed the psychiatrist with a wave of her hand.

Before she turned out her light to go to sleep, Margaret Millington looked at a framed poster on the wall of her room and read the caption below. "Attitude: the difference between a good day and a bad day." As she drifted off to sleep with the help of Dr. Gonzales' sedative, Margaret skeptically pondered the simplicity of these words. She wondered if she would ever enjoy a truly good day again. She did not feel optimistic.

**6**

On the third day of her commitment, as she was reading a magazine in the lounge, a man in a long black coat approached Margaret. When she spotted the clerical collar, a look of recognition flashed across her face.

"Good afternoon, Ms. Millington. I don't know if you remember me; I'm ..."

"You're the young man who presumes to possess all of the answers to life's most important questions, aren't you?"

"I'm Peter Kearns. Can we start with that?"

"Let's end with that. I have no interest in continuing this conversation."

"Certainly, as you wish, Ms. Millington. But could you do me a simple favor before I leave?"

"What do you want of me?" asked Margaret, allowing a bit of desperation in her voice to weaken her defiant posture.

"I would like the honor of giving you a blessing."

Margaret hesitated, then resignedly shrugged her shoulders. Finally, she nodded her head. The young priest approached her and placed both hands just over her head. He then looked down toward the floor and softly said the following prayer:

"May God the Father, Son and Holy Spirit descend upon you and cure you of every ailment of the body, mind and spirit and bring you happiness in this life and in His eternal kingdom in heaven."

These unexpected words caught Margaret by surprise. She felt a lump in her throat and before she could decide what, if anything, to say, the priest hurried out the door and down the hall.

At the end of her first week in the stress unit, Dr. Sekorski confronted Ms. Millington with her lack of effort in therapy and her general resistance to the program.

"What benefits do you hope to get from your stay here, Margaret?"

"I am not here expecting to get any benefits, doctor. I am here as a prisoner of the court. In fact, I think this is completely ridiculous. Can the judge make me pay for this treatment, even though I don't want it?"

"Yes, he can. Are you concerned about the cost?"

"Do you know anything about me, doctor?"

"The social worker from the hospital provided some basic biographical information on you, but since you've refused to open up in counseling, I really know very little beyond your name, age, and marital status. And that you have been depressed and very nearly killed yourself."

"What is all of this skillful insight costing me each week?" asked Margaret scornfully.

"Ms. Millington, we want to help you. If you don't care about helping yourself, about all we'll be able to do for you is to give you medications to help your general mood a bit. But I would like to try to do better than that. All I'm asking is for a chance to help you."

"Well, maybe you're going to have to do something with my generally foul mood first. Can you really dope me out of my misery?"

"I'm going to speak with Dr. Gonzales and discuss our lack of progress. I think we might temporarily get you something to help you relax. Would that be all right with you?"

"What difference does it make what I think? Nobody cared about my wishes when they locked me up in here!"

"Well, that may be, but you don't seem to be a candidate for forced meds," replied the psychologist with a frown as she peered over her glasses. "I'll speak with Dr. Gonzales and see what he wants to do."

That same day, Margaret was placed on an anti-depressant. Still, there was only a marginal improvement in her mood and little progress was being made in counseling. During her third week in the unit, Margaret was watching television alone in her room when there was a knock on the door.

Fr. Kearns entered the room. He looked around and saw that, although the sun outside was shining, the louvered blinds in the room were closed and the lights were dimmed. The greatest source of light in the room was coming from the television set. The priest's eyes met the patient's. She wore a vacant expression.

"Ms. Millington. I have received permission from the staff to escort you out to the patio. Would you join me outside for a little while?"

Since she quickly calculated that it would take more energy to fight him than to give in, Margaret reluctantly agreed. She slipped into the hospital-issue shoes and accompanied the priest out into the hall and then through a back door onto a raised concrete patio overlooking a neatly groomed lawn. A number of tables and chairs and patio loungers were sprinkled across the patio. Several patients were outside enjoying the weather. Margaret pulled a chair away from a patio table and sat down. The priest followed suit.

"It really is a beautiful day, isn't it?" asked Fr. Kearns with a smile.

The warmth of the afternoon sun was tempered by a cool, springtime breeze and seemed to ameliorate Margaret's cranky disposition as she found herself audibly agreeing with her persistent visitor's indisputable observation.

"Yes, it is. I guess spring is finally here."

"I'm sorry that I haven't been in to check on you for a while," replied Fr. Kearns. "It's been pretty hectic around church with Holy Week and Easter and everything. How are you getting along here?"

Margaret opted not to quibble with the priest's implied

assumption that his presence at the hospital was desired and answered him frankly. "I think they're trying to wear me down. They evidently plan on keeping me here until I play along and tell everyone how wonderful it is."

"Is it really all that bad?" asked Fr. Kearns.

"I guess not. I'm doing a lot of relaxing: reading, watching TV, talking, listening to everyone's problems."

"Some might say you've just described a pretty fair vacation!" laughed the priest.

"I think I could use a little of that myself."

"Do you stay pretty busy?" asked Margaret with a degree of interest that was encouraging to the young priest.

"Oh, yes. I know a lot of people think that all priests do is to say a couple of masses on Sunday and otherwise sit around chanting hymns with other priests."

Margaret looked at the priest and a smile forced its way to her face. The priest seized this opening and asked, "How did things become so bad for you?"

In the instant following this question, the priest half expected to be told to leave for the third time. He was relieved when Margaret responded in a calm tone,

"I haven't figured that out yet. I guess that's what the shrinks are here for. But I'm afraid I haven't offered them many clues yet either." Margaret smiled again, but the smile faded quickly and she continued, "I guess I basically feel alone and worthless. I think it may be as simple as that."

"I know you don't want to hear this from me, but I have to tell you that from an outsider's point of view, you seem to have a lot going for you. Why do you feel this way?"

For the first time since she was admitted to the hospital, Margaret told the story of her unhappy marriage to Alfred Millington and her recent divorce. She explained that she devoted most of her life to a man who ultimately rejected her, and that although she had wanted children, she and Alfred never had any. Later in their marriage, they had tried to have children, but had no luck conceiving. Margaret felt that, although he never explicitly said so, Alfred blamed her for failing to give him an heir. "I know I'm no longer beautiful, and I really am too old and angry to want to be attractive to anyone. Instead, I'm just old. And, I guess, lonely." Margaret didn't know what had impelled her to open up to the young, disfigured priest, but if he was surprised, his expression didn't betray it.

"First of all, you are still a very attractive woman, whether you care to believe it or not. But no matter. You are really so much more than your physical appearance. You have a soul. You have much to offer."

She shook her head and began to protest, but before she could interrupt him, Fr. Kearns continued,

"*God does not view things the way men do. People look on the outward appearance, but the Lord looks at the heart.*"[2]

Margaret sat quietly and looked out across the lawn. No one spoke for the next several seconds. Then Fr. Kearns rephrased this passage from scripture that they had both been contemplating.

"It is true that we often notice the superficial aspects of a person, isn't it? But we are fortunate that God sees the beauty beneath. That is what matters."

With these words, Margaret caught herself staring at the young priest's severely scarred face. She noticed that one side of his face was relatively smooth, while the other side, which appeared to have received some efforts at cosmetic improvement, still had a rough and leathery appearance. It occurred to Margaret that the young priest would have been a fairly handsome man if it weren't for this facial disfigurement. Not seeming to notice her inadvertent gaze, the priest looked at his watch and quickly rose to his feet. "Ms. Millington, it was very nice to have someone to share this beautiful afternoon with. I have got to get back to a meeting this evening, but I hope you don't mind if I stop by from time to time to see how you're getting along?"

---

[2]  1 Samuel 16:7 NET

Ms. Millington stood up and offered her hand to the priest. "Sure. That would be fine."

Margaret wasn't sure what it was about this man, but she felt drawn to him, in spite of his unpleasant appearance and her usual disdain for people and things religious. She found herself hoping that Fr. Kearns would indeed return again.

**7**

Ginger Wolfe drove her 1994 Buick Regal west on I-74. The setting sun was a ball of fire just above the road on the horizon. Although wearing sunglasses, she adjusted the visor in an effort to shield her eyes from the sun's blinding rays. Her husband had decided against accompanying her on this trip from west central Indiana into Illinois. As she drove alone into the sun, her mind drifted back to the not-so-sunny meetings she had had with her sister the past few times they had been together.

Ginger had gently suggested to her older sister that she consider getting help to stop drinking a couple of years earlier. Then, when her brother-in-law filed for divorce against her sister, she suggested counseling because she was concerned about her sister's state of mind. On both occasions, Margaret scornfully rebuffed her tender solicitations. On both occasions, her intoxicated sister said hurtful things to her and failed to apologize. So as she approached her Chicago destination, she anxiously wondered how she would be greeted by Margaret, whom she had not seen since her recent suicide attempt and involuntary commitment.

An hour and a half later, Ginger pulled into a parking garage adjacent to St. Francis Hospital. She made a mental note of her parking space and walked to the elevator in the parking garage. She glanced at her watch as she was greeted by the opening of the elevator doors. 7:45 p.m. Visiting hours ended at nine. Ginger had timed the beginning of her visit near the end of the visiting hours in anticipation of another uncomfortable meeting with her sister. As Ginger rode the elevator inside the hospital up to Unit 5, she nervously bit her lip and tapped her foot.

As the elevator doors opened, Ginger did her best to shake off the nervousness to present a calm appearance to her sister. Ginger signed her name in the guest register and was given a name badge which conspicuously identified her as "VISITOR." The attendant at the visitor's station gave her Margaret's room number and buzzed her through a reinforced, double-glass door. She was now in the stress unit of St. Francis Hospital.

Ginger nervously smiled as she feigned delight at seeing her sister in these surroundings. Margaret played along and smiled back. Although she truly was happy to see her sister, Margaret's overarching emotion was one of embarrassment. As soon as their eyes met, Ginger hoped that her expression did not convey to Margaret an "I-told-you-so" greeting. Margaret saw nothing of the kind in her sister's warm smile, but sheepishly considered that her sister would be justified in entertaining such a thought.

"You look well, Margaret."

"Thanks. So do you. How was the drive over?"

"The traffic was pretty light. It was really a good day for a drive."

Silence ensued. For Ginger it was a painful silence. Margaret detected her younger sister's discomfiture and stepped closer to her. Margaret opened her arms and Ginger stepped into them and returned the embrace. Ginger was suddenly overwhelmed with emotion and her eyes filled with tears. Still holding her sister, Margaret pulled her head back to face her. Ginger saw a combination of affection and deep-seated sadness in her sister's pale, blue eyes. As though reading her sister's thoughts, Margaret finally broke the silence.

"I guess I need to get a grip on things, on my life. Maybe all of this will work out for the best," she added without conviction."

"How *are* you getting along, Margaret?"

"I don't know. I'm a terrible patient. Unfortunately, I don't think they're going to kick me out of here."

They both laughed and Ginger shook her head.

"I'll bet the doctors and nurses are really earning their money with you in the unit."

"Well, maybe if I had listened to some advice from my little sister, it wouldn't have come to this."

Margaret tilted her head and looked apologetically at Ginger.

"I probably should have shut my mouth once in a while and been a better listener," offered Ginger, picking up on Margaret's conciliatory tone.

The two sisters caught up on each other's lives and were talking as though they had been good friends forever, when their conversation was interrupted by a soft gong.

"That means visiting hours are over. I'm sorry that you can't stay longer. It's really great seeing you."

"I'm glad to see you too, Margaret. I hope that you can go along with the program so you can get out of here as soon as possible."

"Give my best to Carl and the boys," said Margaret, as she kissed her younger sister on the cheek.

Ginger was glad she had come to Chicago and was relieved that she had found her sister in relatively good spirits. She hoped that Margaret was resolved to addressing her mental health and alcohol problems, which Ginger had seen growing over the past several years.

**8**

"Why did they let her out of her room?!" Fannie screamed.

Margaret, who had just taken her morning shower, exited her room to see what all the commotion was about. Two psych techs were leading Fannie, now completely hysterical, down the hall, away from the small group of staff and onlookers that had gathered outside one of the patient's rooms. The buzz in the hall quickly informed Margaret about what had taken place. Evidently, Diane, the perpetually depressed woman whom Fannie had befriended in the hospital, had been allowed out of her monitored "suicide room" to use the always-monitored rec room. From there she stopped at another patient's unmonitored room where she had asked to use the restroom. When Diane failed to emerge after fifteen to twenty minutes, the occupant of the room checked on her. The door was locked and Diane didn't respond to her knocking. A security staffer was called to unlock the bathroom door. Diane was hanging from the shower head with the shower curtain affixed tightly about her neck.

By the time Margaret arrived on the scene, Diane had been rushed to the emergency room, where she was promptly pronounced dead. Word spread immediately throughout Unit 5 of the inability of the medical personnel to detect a pulse, and this shocking event cast a pall over the entire unit. Fannie refused to participate in therapy for the next week. Eventually, Fannie resumed her involvement in therapy. The only lasting changed that Margaret noticed was that Fannie's language acquired more religious references. She increasingly mentioned "Jesus" and "Lord" in her everyday speech. Margaret later learned that as a child, Fannie was reared in a devout Baptist home and spent a lot of time in church. She had only strayed from her faith gradually in recent years. Diane's death served as a catalyst to bring Fannie back to her spiritual roots.

Although they had not become particularly close, Margaret too was struck profoundly by Diane's death. They had lived in close proximity to one another for weeks. They regularly shared stories in group therapy sessions. But to Margaret, the aspect of Diane's life and tragic death that struck closest to home was that both of them were being treated for severe depression following suicide attempts. Margaret knew that she herself had come within minutes of being found dead in her bathroom. The thought now caused her to shudder.

Diane's suicide became a central issue for discussion in both individual and group therapy sessions in the unit. Dr. Gonzales doubled the amount of sedatives he was prescribing to help patients in the unit sleep at night. Margaret herself began to experience occasional nightmares associated with her own attempted suicide.

In one recurring dream that haunted Margaret, she floated above the bathtub in her apartment and looked down to see her own completely dismembered body in the tub, which was filled with scotch rather than water. Dr. Sekorski confronted the dream with Margaret in individual therapy sessions. The conclusion that they settled upon was that Margaret was simply horrified by what she had done to herself and in suppressing the thought during the day, dealt with it in an exaggerated manner in her subconscious. Still, the frequency of the dream interfered with Margaret's sleep, as she became fearful of being haunted by the revolting images from the recurring dream.

While Margaret had begun to open up to both her therapist and psychiatrist even before Diane's death, the trauma of this event accelerated the process of her introspection, and she came to be one of the most open and forthright members of her group therapy sessions. She also began to be in regular contact with Fr. Peter Kearns, both through his continuing visits to the hospital as well as by telephone.

Margaret knew that Fr. Kearns ministered to many other people at St. Francis Hospital, including a few of the others in Unit 5. However, she also suspected that for a reason that was inexplicable to her, Fr. Kearns had been especially kind and solicitous to her. By the beginning of her third and final month in the unit, she was in daily contact with the man whose initial offers of friendship she had so brusquely spurned.

One evening Margaret and Fr. Kearns, whom she now simply called, "Peter," became engaged in an unusually long and intimate conversation about their lives before the fortuitous circumstances that led to their meeting at the hospital. Peter explained that he was raised in a series of foster homes in the near north side of Chicago. He knew nothing of his birth parents, except that they had negligently allowed him to become severely burned as an infant over his face and body. He had had a series of skin grafts during the first few years of his life. He later came to learn that his physical appearance had probably been the reason that this bright boy with a winsome smile was never adopted.

From age ten to sixteen, when Peter entered St. Ignatius Seminary, he lived in the home of Sam and Barbara Curtis. Mr. and Mrs. Curtis were devout Catholics. They lived in a middle-class neighborhood and had three grown children of their own at the time Peter was placed with them. In addition to Peter, one to three other foster children were always living in the Curtis home.

It was from Sam and Barbara Curtis that Peter first learned about God and the Catholic faith. Along with the other children in the home, Peter attended Catholic schools from the time of his arrival in the fourth grade through his sophomore year of high school, when he decided to enter the seminary. The family honored all the rituals of a traditional Catholic family: grace before meals, bedtime prayers, monthly confession, strict observance of Holy Days of Obligation and the fasting and abstinence of Lent.

Sam Curtis died unexpectedly of a heart attack when Peter was twenty-one. Barbara died after a long bout with breast cancer shortly after Peter's ordination. Though Peter initially maintained contact with the Curtis children and his foster brothers and sisters through letters and occasional phone calls, the contact eventually dwindled with the passage of time. Peter and his foster family grew distant once the unifying presence of Mr. and Mrs. Curtis was gone.

Margaret told Peter of her own childhood in New Hampshire. She was one of five children of successful dairy farmers. She was a cheerleader in high school and made straight A's. Following high school, Margaret attended the University of Chicago, where she met Alfred Millington, a tall, handsome and very ambitious son of an owner of a small chain of hardware stores in Chicago.

Alfred studied business and finance in college, and upon graduation, quickly became a successful manager for a succession of different business interests. The only real pattern to his job moves was that each new position paid substantially more than the one before. When Alfred's father passed away in 1980, Alfred took over the chain of hardware stores, greatly increasing their profitability and doubling the number of stores by the time he sold the business eight years later. He invested the millions that he received from the sale of the business in a number of different ventures, running all of his enterprises from the thirty-fifth floor of a Chicago skyscraper overlooking Lake Michigan.

Margaret wanted to have children with Alfred; however, before they were married, she unexpectedly became pregnant. To Margaret's surprise, Alfred was unwilling to interrupt his education and marry her before graduation. She hoped that he would change his mind and continued to carry the child until she was in her seventh month, when finally, Alfred drove her to an abortion clinic.

A year later, they were married. However, due to scarring that was a by-product of the abortion procedure, Margaret was never able to conceive. As the years went by and Alfred was busying himself with his work, Margaret became lonely and depressed and began to drink. When Margaret came to be suspicious of Alfred's infidelities, her drinking increased, both in frequency and in amount. Margaret's drinking caused her gradually to lose most of her true friends, who were replaced by other alcoholics and otherwise troubled and unhappy women.

"Did you ever try to get help with your drinking when you and Alfred were married?"

"Oh, I entered a few different programs to get Alfred off my back, but I actually loved my scotch more than I loved Alfred by that time, so I was never really committed to quitting," said Margaret with a slight smile.

"How about now?"

"Oh I definitely love scotch more than Alfred now," laughed Margaret.

"You have an unusually sharp wit, Margaret. I think you could learn to use your sense of humor instead of alcohol to take the edge off of things that are hurtful to you."

"Boy Peter, you really *do* sound like a shrink."

"I don't know anything at all about psychiatry, but I do know a bit about alcoholism."

"Somehow you don't strike me as a drinker."

"No, I never really was a drinker. But I saw what it did to my foster father, who was otherwise a wonderful man. I also have seen it take its toll on untold numbers of parishioners and their families and loved ones. I have worked with an AA group now for several years. In fact, when you are released from your treatment here, I would like to get you to join us."

Margaret looked at the priest pensively for several seconds.

"You never quit, do you Peter?"

"I've been told I'm stubborn to a fault, to which I'll have to plead guilty."

"Stubborn! I'd call that an understatement."

"You know Margaret, I think we're a lot alike on that score."

"Who, me?" replied Margaret with a grin.

"I have to confess to a streak of that myself. When you put up such a giant wall when we first met, I saw you as a challenge. I was determined not to let you win."

"You're still determined to bend me, aren't you?"

The priest turned serious. "I don't want to bend you. I want to save you." Margaret said nothing. "Just think about AA. You would be a tremendous asset to our group."

"I'll think about it. That's the best I can do right now."

"That's all I ask."

**9**

It was 8:15 in the evening. Juanita Montoya was finishing the dinner dishes as her three pre-school-aged children sat on the floor of their small, sparsely furnished living room and watched TV. Antonio Montoya was a laborer at the steel mill. When the work didn't get finished at the end of the normal work day, Antonio sometimes had to work an hour or so of overtime. Even with traffic, though, Juanita knew Antonio should have been home by now.

After Juanita dried the last dish and set it down on the counter, she pulled her long, black hair back off her shoulders, looked up at the clock and slowly sighed. Another night for the twenty-three-year old convenience store clerk to eat without her husband. Another night for her to clean up the dinner dishes alone. Another night for the Montoya children to be bathed and put to bed without seeing their father.

Three blocks from the parking lot where Antonio Montoya left his car to catch the subway to and from work each day sat the "Golden Keg" tavern. And two seats from the door up at the bar sat Antonio Montoya, sipping his fourth beer and watching ESPN with the sound of the hockey game on the screen drowned out by the country music tunes that were being played on the jukebox. A stranger sat on the barstool at the end of the bar, next to Antonio. They occasionally spoke about the game and about how the Blackhawks should be better next year. Beyond this minimal conversation, each man was lost in his own thoughts, grasping their draft mugs and staring at the TV.

At 9:30, after saying bedtime prayers with her two young sons and young daughter, Juanita collapsed in the only upholstered chair in the house - the one that sat in front of the TV. She closed her eyes and was soon asleep.

Juanita was awoken by the sound of the back door being closed. She opened her eyes and watched Antonio, once again intoxicated, stumble his way back to the bedroom. Antonio knew that Juanita would be hurt and angry. Anticipating her angry words and not wishing to endure them, Antonio simply ignored his wife, thereby hurting her further. When they would wake up in the morning, Juanita knew that the next day would be much the same as this day had been, and that there was pretty much an even chance that Antonio would come home late and drunk again.

He worked hard at the steel mill and was respected by his superiors as well as his co-workers. When he was home, Antonio truly loved his family. He wrestled and played catch with his little boys, and he often held his young daughter's hand when the family was walking together in a nearby park. He kept pictures of Juanita and his kids in his well-worn billfold. He went to St. Michael's Church with the family on Sunday and, although he preferred to sit near the back of the Church, he was willing to help around the parish in a number of volunteer capacities. In short, he was a good man with a serious drinking problem.

Antonio's drinking, an occasional source of arguments during the first couple years of the Montoyas' marriage, had become worse in the past year or so. It seemed to Juanita that Antonio was choosing the bar over what he should have seen as precious time with his family. Her resentment over this was building. As she lay in bed that night next to the man she continued to love, Juanita wondered if she and the children could get by without him.

A few days later, Juanita dropped off the kids at the daycare a couple of blocks from their home as she did six days a week and went to work at the "Gas-N-Shop". On this particular morning, Juanita was running the cash register when the bread deliveryman walked into the store.

"Good morning, Beautiful," said Mark Slover as he pushed a cart of bread past the counter, resuming the harmless, flirtatious banter that had become their custom over the past year or so since the Gas-N-Shop became part of Slover's route.

Juanita smiled at the deliveryman and said nothing. After unloading the bread onto the shelves, Slover poured himself a cup of coffee and took it up to the counter to pay for it. As Slover reached over the counter with a dollar bill, Juanita pushed his hand away and said:

"This one's on the house."

"Well, if you're going to buy me coffee, you've got to let me buy you dinner sometime. How about Friday?"

Juanita was taken aback by the minimal encouragement Slover required to take his flirtation to another level. Still, to her own surprise, Juanita found herself replying without thinking.

"Depends on what you have in mind."

"Dinner, for starters."

"I mean, where would we go?"

"I'll let you pick. Write your number on my cup and I'll give you a call."

Juanita hesitated and then said, "Give me your number. I need to check my calendar."

Slover grabbed a napkin and scribbled his phone number on it. After a few parting comments, he was out the door. Juanita wondered what she was getting herself into.

**10**

Margaret felt that today's individual therapy session with Dr. Sekorski went well even by recent standards. She had actually come to enjoy individual therapy, now realizing its cathartic effect. As Dr. Sekorski finished her notes and closed Margaret's patient file, she looked at Margaret and announced in an understated tone,

"We staffed you this morning Margaret. We all agree that you have made tremendous progress. If you'll promise to see us for a few months on an out-patient basis, we think you're ready to be discharged."

Margaret knew that she was nearing the end of her ninety-day commitment. By the feedback she had been receiving, she also knew that she would be recommended for discharge rather than an extended commitment. Still, to actually hear these words caused Margaret's pulse to quicken. Although the first few weeks of her stay in Unit 5 seemed to be interminable, Margaret felt that the last eight weeks or so went by surprisingly quickly.

"How do you feel about that," asked the psychologist?

"I feel good about it. I'm ready."

"I think you are too. We're going to miss you around here. Your leadership in group is going to be especially missed."

"I'll bet you didn't expect to be saying that two and a half months ago," replied Margaret with a sheepish grin.

"It's a credit to you and your hard work. While we expect to be able to help most patients make some progress, your turnaround has truly been remarkable."

"I do feel so much better. Thanks to you and everyone here…." She paused momentarily and then added, "And thanks to Peter Kearns."

The staff in Unit 5 was very familiar with Fr. Kearns from long before Margaret's stay. Dr. Sekorski had also become aware of the friendship that he had developed with Margaret and suspected that he merited at least some of the credit for Margaret's new outlook on life.

"Fr. Kearns is such a fixture around here that I sometimes think he should be on our payroll."

When Margaret finished her conversation with Dr. Sekorski, she went back to her room and called the friend about whom she had been speaking to tell him that she would be discharged from the hospital at the end of the week.

## 11

Juanita Montoya sat on the edge of her bed and pulled the crumpled up napkin from her purse. She trembled as she picked up her phone and punched in the number. The conversation was very short. Juanita realized that she was shaking after she hung up the phone. She poured herself a tall glass of cheap wine and slugged it down like a shot of whiskey.

Because she needed an excuse to be picked up away from her house, Juanita had told Mark Slover that she had to pick up something at work and asked him to meet her out in the parking lot. When she pulled into the lot outside the Gas-N-Shop, she saw the deliveryman without the familiar uniform, sitting on the hood of a navy blue Sunbird. She drove to the other end of the parking lot, pretending not to see him yet, and quickly exited her car and went into the store.

Juanita asked the clerk, her friend Angie, for a pack of Marlboro Lights from behind the counter. As she started to reach into her purse to get some money, a hand came from behind her and gently held her hand down. Juanita heard the deliveryman's voice come softly from just behind her ear.

"This one's on me."

Immediately, Juanita realized she had made a mistake by meeting Slover at her store. In an instant she saw Angie reading the situation and wondered how obvious it was that she was about to betray her family.

Juanita clumsily tried to cover, not sure what Angie may have been thinking.

"Oh, hi. That's nice of you. You're not in uniform."

"Neither are you," replied Slover sardonically.

Juanita walked away from the counter towards the door.

"See you Angie."

"See you Nita."

She hoped that Slover realized she was trying to make it appear to the clerk that they were not together. At the same time she was hoping not to offend him. Slover evidently took the hint and let Juanita walk out ahead of him. When they got into the parking lot, Slover took her arm.

"You're really nervous, aren't you?"

As Juanita struggled with what to tell him under these very awkward circumstances, Slover spoke up again.

"I know you're worried about your husband finding out. Don't worry about it."

"You know about my husband?" Juanita finally said to him.

"I kind of figured it out just now," laughed Slover.

"Oh."

"Like I said, don't worry about it. This is strictly a business meeting as far as I'm concerned," Slover said with a straight face.

He opened the passenger door to his Sunbird and Juanita slid into the car. In the short seconds she was alone while Slover walked around to the driver's side of the car, Juanita shook her feelings of guilt by thinking of Antonio sitting in a bar. She forced out of her mind all thoughts of her children, whom she had taken to her sister's apartment for the evening. Slover climbed in behind the wheel and drove away from the Gas-N-Shop. Juanita looked in the side view mirror and saw her own car in the parking lot fading into the distance.

# 12

Ginger and Carl Wolfe, Margaret's sister and brother-in-law, with the aid of their two teenage sons, Matt, sixteen, and Jeremy, fourteen, had spent untold hours on recent weekends setting up the new home that Margaret had purchased during her stay in the hospital. Before that, Carl had supplemented the available photos of the prospective homes on the internet real estate listings with additional photos and videos that he took. These were then e-mailed to Margaret. She passed many long hours in the hospital studying the assortment of homes and townhouses that made it through Ginger's critical analysis of the Chicago-area real estate market. Margaret ultimately settled on a relatively modest townhouse which, coincidentally, was only a ten-minute drive from Fr. Kearns' church.

Unfortunately, she ran into an unexpected impediment to her consummation of the purchase: the seller's attorney refused to accept Margaret's signature on the purchase documents due to the usual concerns about the legal competence of a patient in the stress unit of a hospital. Margaret's attorneys eventually obtained affidavits from Margaret's family physician and her psychiatrist at St. Francis, both of whom attested to Margaret's grasp of the legal documents and thereby, to her legal capacity to enter into the real estate transaction.

After the Wolfes closed the deal with the power of attorney that Margaret had executed, they began the time-consuming process of decorating the home to Margaret's tastes and of getting the home repainted and carpeted. Finally they oversaw the transfer of such furnishings as would fit into the new home. Although Margaret had seen pictures of the completed project, she was thrilled to be getting to finally see her new home in person.

The weather on this summer day cooperated completely with the Wolfes' combination house-warming/welcome-back-to-society party. It was sunny and seventy-two degrees. The air was dry and cool. The sky was blue and cloudless. It was the type of day that would make any person happy to be alive, let alone a person who was being released from a ninety-day mental health commitment with a new home and a new lease on life.

Ginger had picked up Margaret at St. Francis Hospital and drove her to her new home. As they pulled up in front of the townhouse, Margaret was mildly surprised at the size of the home, which appeared larger than it had in the photos she had seen. Still, the home was far less palatial than what Margaret had become accustomed to in her life with Alfred Millington. But Margaret had insisted that she was going to live a simpler life upon her release, which she hoped would be less stressful.

When the two sisters walked through the front door, they were immediately greeted by Ginger's husband, Carl, and their two sons. Carl was smiling broadly. This was a change from the past few times Margaret had seen Carl, and it occurred to her that this apparent change in Carl's visage was probably due more to Margaret's own outlook than to any real change in Carl himself.

For years, Carl felt that Margaret was a self-absorbed drunk, with whom he had precious little in common, other than their tie to Ginger. Carl often thought that Margaret failed to appreciate or reciprocate Ginger's kindness and loyalty to her older sister. But Carl knew from his recent telephone conversations with Margaret and from Ginger's reports that Margaret had acquired a more outward-looking view of life as a result of her sobriety and therapy. And Carl's warm reception reflected his pleasure at this improvement in Margaret's personality.

Matt and Jeremy Wolfe joined their father and mother in welcoming their Aunt Margaret to her new home. As Margaret surveyed her new surroundings she was struck by the fact that, while most of the furnishings and knick-knacks had come from her downtown apartment, they seemed newer to her and, in a sense, different, in this home.

Margaret passed the day with the Wolfes and enjoyed them, and life itself, more than she remembered doing in many years. She thought back to Dr. Sekorski's oft-repeated theme in group therapy sessions of the purer happiness brought by sobriety and at this moment she was certain that Dr. Sekorski was correct.

"This is really wonderful," Margaret gushed uncharacteristically. "I can't believe all the work that you put into this place. It is absolutely beautiful! I will never be able to thank you enough."

"Wait til you get our bill," Carl teased.

The Wolfes and Margaret enjoyed a dinner of grilled salmon together that Ginger had seasoned ahead of time and that Carl grilled out back. While Matt and Jeremy did the dishes and Carl was cleaning off the grill, the sisters had a bit of time alone in Margaret's new living room. Margaret opened up to Ginger regarding her recent realization about the emotional toll that Alfred's demeaning behavior had taken on her self-esteem. As a result, Margaret confessed that she had grown to place a childlike priority on her physical appearance, because it was the one aspect of herself in which she had retained a measure of pride.

As dusk approached and the small party wound down, Carl and Ginger bade Margaret a good first night in her new home and left for their hotel. Margaret wasn't sure exactly how her new life was going to unfold, but she was grateful to have another chance.

**13**

The next morning, Margaret woke up and looked outside. Apparently, the previous day's beautiful weather was going to continue for a while. Margaret put on her robe and walked into the kitchen. She sliced a bagel and put it in the toaster. While the bagel was toasting, Margaret peeled an orange. She then sat down at her kitchen table and ate her breakfast while scanning the morning paper.

An article on the front page of the "City" section caught Margaret's eye. A drunk driver was in an accident and killed two teenage girls who were on their way home from a friend's house. She shook her head and thought of the promise that she had made to Fr. Peter to try out the AA group that he was involved with. Margaret made a mental note to call Peter sometime that day and find out when and where the group met.

Just then, Margaret's phone rang. It was her telepathic friend, Peter Kearns.

"Good morning, Margaret. How're things going in your new house?"

"Couldn't be better. I think I'm going to like it here even more than I had expected."

"How did the housewarming party go yesterday?"

"It was very nice. I'm sorry you couldn't be here with us."

"I'm sorry too. But I don't think the young couple that I married

51

yesterday would have been very understanding if I had gone to your party instead."

Finally, they got around to the subject Margaret had been thinking about at the time of his call.

"Peter, I think I'd better get hooked up with an AA group right away, to keep building on the progress I made at St. Francis."

"That's a good idea."

"Well, when does your group meet?"

"We meet every Tuesday at eight p.m. in the upstairs lounge area at the YMCA over by church. I make it to most, but not all of the meetings. You want to come tonight?"

"I don't see why not. I think I can fit it into my busy social schedule," replied Margaret, dripping with good-natured sarcasm.

"Why don't you let me pick you up and take you this first time?" Peter suggested, hoping to ease any anxiety Margaret may have been feeling.

"Fine. I'll see you this evening a little before eight then."

"Okay. See you then."

**14**

The night of Margaret's housewarming party was not a good night for the Montoya family. Juanita went with Mark Slover to a small neighborhood tavern that was near his apartment. In earlier years, Juanita had gone to bars with Antonio pretty often. As Antonio's drinking got worse, though, Juanita's own interest in alcohol had diminished greatly.

To her surprise, Juanita felt guilty about being with another man. She felt so guilty, in fact, that she found she really was not able to enjoy herself with this man who had become a common object of her daydreams. While Juanita was fiddling with her drink and half listening to Slover talking at length about his life, she got a call on her cell phone. It was her sister, Vada.

"Nita. Oh God, Nita. Something terrible's happened," sputtered Vada, nearly incoherently. "It's Tony!"

Juanita instantly felt sick. "Vada, what's going on? What about Tony? Did something happen to him?"

"Tony wrecked his car. He's in jail, Nita…But he's okay."

"Oh no. Was he drunk?"

"Yes, Juanita. But that's not the worst of it."

Vada hesitated for what seemed an eternity to Juanita. Then she continued.

"Nita, there were two girls in the other car that was involved in the accident." She paused. "They're dead."

Juanita was momentarily speechless.

"Is everything okay?" asked Slover with feigned concern.

"I've gotta go right now," said Juanita, who stood up and began walking dazedly toward the door of the bar. Juanita suddenly felt ill. They climbed into Slover's Sunbird and in a few short minutes, they were back at the Gas-N-Shop, where Slover, utterly clueless as to what was going on, dropped Juanita off by her car.

She mechanically put her key in the ignition and started the car. Before shifting the car into gear, Juanita paused and wondered where she should go first. Her mind began to race. She thought about her children, the innocents of the family, who had spent the evening with Vada and were doubtless in bed and unaware of the tragedy that had befallen their family. She then thought of her drunken husband. He was probably in the drunk tank at the county jail. He may still be too drunk to know what he'd done. Then she thought of the victims: two young girls with their whole lives ahead of them; now gone forever. Gone because of Antonio.

Guilt started to creep into the confusing picture that was developing in Juanita's mind. "What if I hadn't planned this stupid night away from home?" she wondered. "Antonio might have stayed home tonight and those girls might be alive right now." Juanita gripped the steering wheel of her still-parked car and closed her eyes. She began to sob uncontrollably.

Eventually, Juanita regained control of her emotions and drove to the jail. After passing through the main doors, Juanita was buzzed through another set of doors that separated the lobby of the jail from the reception area. Juanita walked up to the reception desk and was rather confronted more than received by a large, masculine-looking woman who appeared to be in her early fifties. She had her hair pulled back tightly and pinned to the back of her head. The hair was unnaturally dark for the woman's age. She had on grey slacks with a vertical black line running down the outside of each leg. Juanita observed that the pants looked as though they could have been taken from a mailman. Her blouse was a light-blue, short-sleeved dress shirt with a collar that fit loosely over the woman's muscular torso.

"What dah ya need?" growled the receptionist, in a tone that made her question sound like a dare.

"I believe my husband is in here," offered Juanita relatively meekly.

"Name?" replied the receptionist, who coughed and then rubbed her nose vigorously with the back of her hand.

"Antonio Montoya."

The woman peered over the papers she was holding and sized up Juanita.

"Jesus, lady. He can't have any visitors for a while. He just got here a couple hours ago and ...." The woman's words trailed off and she shook her head sadly. "He's due in court tomorrow morning at eleven. Visiting hours are Wednesdays, four to eight."

The woman's use of the plural form of "Wednesday" forced Juanita to think more about the possibility that Antonio could be behind bars for quite a long time. She thanked the woman for the information and left the jail, shuddering this time as she was buzzed back out to the lobby.

Juanita drove to her sister Vada's home. The house was dark, except for a small kitchen light. Juanita walked around to the back door and peeked into the kitchen through the window in the back door. Vada sat at the kitchen table sipping a cup of coffee and staring straight ahead. Juanita rapped lightly on the door window, causing Vada to be visibly startled from her reverie. Vada jumped up from her chair and let her sister in.

"Oh Nita," began Vada in a voice filled with pity. "I can't believe this."

"Do any of the kids know?" asked Juanita.

"No. They've been asleep since eleven. I thought I'd better let them sleep. I know it's going to be bad enough to deal with after a good night's rest."

Juanita and Vada talked for about an hour, together wondering what was going to come of all of this. At last, realizing that there was nothing further that she could do that night, Juanita decided to go to bed on the sofa in the living room. After her first few fitful minutes on the couch, Juanita knew that tomorrow she, unlike her children, would be dealing with this tragedy without the benefit of a good night's rest.

**15**

The Young Men's Christian Association building was built shortly after the First World War. The building had been allowed to deteriorate throughout the sixties and seventies, but a capital improvement drive in the community in the late eighties provided a comprehensive, modernized fitness facility inside the aging shell of this YMCA.

Fr. Peter sat quietly, listening attentively to the group members' varied stories of dealing with their addictions. Margaret sat beside him, initially constrained by her notions of propriety as the new member to keep from doing much talking. But by the end of the hour-long meeting, Margaret was showing signs of the form she had acquired at St. Francis as a leading contributor to such sessions.

Peter had introduced his friend to the group at the beginning of the meeting, and all of the regular members of the group went out of their way to make her feel welcome. Upon being introduced to Margaret, two or three of the members made comments about the priest that made it clear to Margaret that her friend was universally held in high esteem by these people.

To Margaret it was amazing how the members of this group, with such disparate backgrounds, had dealt with strikingly similar problems resulting from their abuse of alcohol. For instance, Melvin was a thirty-two-year-old mechanical engineer who had grown up in an affluent neighborhood near Boston. Jake was a forty-eight-year-old electrician. Both of them had lost jobs, had been divorced, and had belatedly come to realize that their alcoholism was at the center of much of the upheaval in their lives.

A key element of any twelve-step program based on the model of Alcoholics Anonymous is to acknowledge one's dependence on a higher being. Fr. Kearns' primary role in the group was to help the members, individually and as a group, to become acquainted with that higher being. And while Fr. Kearns was unabashedly Christian and Catholic, he embraced those of all persuasions, as well as those who came to the group with no religious or spiritual background. Although she wasn't there tonight, an alcoholic Unitarian minister often came to the same group and filled a similar role.

Chelsea, a twenty-something girl whose eyes alone belied the hard journeys of her young life, expressed her difficulty believing that there was a God listening to her silent prayers for assistance.

"How could someone hear my heart's desires? A lot of times, I'm confused about what I'm even trying to say in my prayers."

Peter gently answered his young friend.

"How could people be created so that physical and even mental characteristics are passed down from one generation to the next for centuries, keeping these traits intact? And yet we know with scientifically provable certainty that this is the case. If our Creator can set this sort of miracle in motion, so greatly surpassing our ability to comprehend, why could He not read the very minds that He Himself created?"

"In the Book of Judith, we are chastised for presuming that we should be able to comprehend the awesome and limitless capacities of our Father: 'You cannot plumb the depths of the human heart or grasp the workings of the human mind; how then can you fathom God, who has made all these things, discern his mind, and understand his plan?'"

The young priest, with reverence filling his being, continued.

"So often, I think we are *afraid* to believe. We overlook many of the positive proofs of our Father's greatness and of His love for

58

us and content ourselves with a comfortable skepticism, probably borne of our earthly experiences of having our trust in other humans betrayed. But God is the Alpha and the Omega. He is Goodness, Truth and Life itself. Don't be afraid to believe. Just trust Him and keep praying. He will gradually reveal Himself to you in His time, strengthening your faith and helping you accomplish His will. Just remember, as long as it is *your* will that is the object of your prayers, you may feel that your prayers aren't being answered. But when you come to Him in humility, seeking His will, He will give you the strength to accomplish anything."

"St. Augustine, one of the great saints of the early church, prayerfully confessing his transformation into a faith-filled disciple of Jesus, made the same observation: 'This was the sum of it: not to will what I willed and to will what you willed.'"

The young woman nodded her head slowly, pondering the priest's words in silence. Margaret felt proud of Fr. Kearns, as though her special friendship with this impressive man gave her a bit of a share in the aura of goodness that surrounded him.

As was the group's custom, the meeting was closed with a prayer. Margaret added her own silent addendum to the prayer, thanking God for helping so quickly to find these people who could relate to her struggles. From what she had learned in therapy, she knew that finding a group such as this was indispensable to deal with her daily and permanent struggle with alcoholism.

# 16

Antonio Montoya wrestled with his own demons in his cell in the Cook County Jail. He lay on what the jailer referred to as his bed, a one-inch mattress on a wooden board. His head was throbbing from behind his eyes up into the top of his skull. His throat was dry and his tongue felt thick and heavy. Miraculously, Antonio suffered no injuries in the accident the night before. He declined medical treatment at the scene, and as he displayed no apparent signs of injury, he had been taken directly to the jail, where he tested .26% BAC: more than three times the standard for intoxication in the State of Illinois.

Antonio was exhausted but slept little as the alcohol played its dirty trick of stimulating his mind while his body ached for sleep. A few hours earlier, at the scene of the deadly collision, the arresting officer had informed Antonio about the fatal consequences of his drunken driving. However, due to his state of intoxication, he neither understood the officer's words at that time, nor remembered them now. He did recall being involved in a collision and remembered that he vomited in the presence of a couple of state troopers at the scene.

When breakfast was served to the inmates, Antonio turned away from the tray of food placed before him, sickened by the smell of the fried eggs and slightly burnt toast. In spite of his condition, the jailer forced Antonio off his bed and made him take a shower and don the orange jumpsuit that was the inmates' required attire.

Shortly after he was dressed, Antonio was led to an area of the jail outside of his cell and chained to a group of eight other inmates. He was then informed that they were being taken to the courthouse to be arraigned.

Antonio assumed that he was being charged with Driving While Intoxicated. This would be his second time for being charged with this offense, as he faced a similar charge eight years earlier. As the two cases before his were called up, Antonio paid little attention. He looked down at his jail-issue slippers and wondered whether anyone had told Juanita what had happened to him.

At about that time, Antonio heard the booming voice of the bailiff:

"State of Illinois versus Antonio Montoya."

As Antonio was disconnected from the rest of the chain gang to approach the defense table and face the judge, a jailer handed him a sheet of paper that contained the written charges against him. In the instant between being handed the charging paper and looking down at it, Antonio's eyes wandered into the gallery where they met those of his distressed wife, whom he hadn't notice until just then.

Antonio was horror-stricken as he read Juanita's expression. Although he wasn't sure what exactly was going on, he was beginning to understand that he was in more serious trouble than he had previously considered. He looked down at the charging paper as the judge began to read the preliminary charges on which he was being held.

"You have been charged by the State of Illinois with Count I, Reckless Homicide in the death of Vickie Bunch and Count II, Reckless Homicide in the death of Erica Benning."

Antonio heard nothing more after those words which struck him with the force of a sledgehammer. He thought he heard the words repeated during the course of his arraignment, but he was trying to convince himself that this was all a bad dream and that he'd wake soon. When the judge asked Antonio whether he wanted an attorney, he fought an urge to retch and simply nodded his head affirmatively. Since Antonio was employed, the judge said he would give him ten days to hire an attorney and the case was reset for further proceedings at the end of that ten-day period. Antonio then heard the judge tell him that bond would remain set at fifty thousand dollars cash for the time being. As he was re-chained to the other prisoners on the bench in the courtroom, Antonio looked back at Juanita whose tired-looking eyes were filled with tears.

When Juanita arrived back at her house, it was just after noon and her children were eating lunch. A neighbor had come over to stay with the kids while she went to the courthouse. Antonio, Jr., five, who was known to the family as "A.J." was the oldest of the Montoya's three children. The spitting image of his father, A.J. was playful and outgoing. The middle child was Johnnie, who at three already looked up to his big brother and loved to help his mother with his baby sister, Inez, who was just over a year old.

Although Juanita had taken her children home before going to her husband's arraignment, she had not said anything to them about what had happened. When she walked in the door, A.J. looked over from the lunch counter in the kitchen where he was eating a peanut-butter and jelly sandwich and arched an eyebrow as though questioning his mother about what was going on. He obviously sensed that something was amiss.

Juanita pulled a chair from the kitchen table and positioned herself among her young diners. She knew she had to tell them something, but what should she say? How much did they need to know? How much could they handle at such tender years? Finally, she just came out with it.

"Kids, your daddy got into trouble last night for drinking too much. He's in jail and is going to have to stay there for a while."

"How long, Mommy?" queried A.J. immediately.

"Well, I really don't know. But it could be a pretty long time."

Johnnie didn't comprehend much about the situation, but he caught the part about his dad being gone for a long time and started crying. In her blissful innocence, Inez simply sat and continued drinking milk from a sippy cup without pause.

"Will we get to see Daddy while he's in jail?" asked A.J.

Juanita hesitated momentarily and then answered him honestly. "I hope so, but I don't know if the jail allows children to visit or not. We'll find out soon, I'm sure."

As her two older children began to absorb the reality of their father's absence from the home, Juanita began to contemplate the financial impact of the previous night's events. Her job at the Gas-N-Shop paid nine dollars an hour and helped pay some of the bills, but Antonio's job at the steel mill was the primary source of household income. With Antonio in jail and unable to provide for his family, Juanita wondered how they were going to even survive, particularly if Antonio really was going to be gone for a long time. It occurred to her that she might have to look to public assistance to help her get through this. But even with that, how could she pay the rent and buy groceries? They also had a three hundred and fifty dollars-a-month car payment.

Juanita put on her best face to communicate an attitude of "*c'est la vie*" for the benefit of her children. This expressed a confidence that she did not truly embrace. In reality she was terrified.

**17**

Over the course of Margaret Millington's first several weeks out of the hospital, her friendship with Peter Kearns continued to grow. She saw him about three nights a week at the AA meeings at the YMCA. Although not a Catholic, Margaret began attending the ten o'clock Sunday mass at St. Michael's Church where Fr. Kearns served as pastor. In a sense, she was following her typical form of finding a church that met her social needs at the time. But this time she was drawn to something much deeper than social circles. Fr. Kearns made her feel better about herself and forced her to see herself as a person who could truly contribute to the well-being of others.

He was continuing to find ways of busying Margaret with activities around the church. Besides helping to keep Margaret's mind off drinking, this was giving her a sense of self-worth that she didn't remember feeling for a very long time. One Saturday afternoon, after stuffing the church bulletins with an insert about an upcoming mission appeal, Fr. Kearns approached Margaret about yet another new activity.

"You know, Margaret, you have a gift of speaking. You are eloquent, witty, and people like you."

"Shame on you, Peter! Don't you think I've been around long enough to know when I'm being set up for something with that kind of flattery?"

"It's not flattery to make an honest observation about someone's talents. And I'm serious," he said as he laughed.

"Okay, what is it? Your maintenance man can't make it next week and you need the church floors swept?"

"No. I would like for you to help me from time to time at the hospital. You could visit patients."

"Oh, now I get it," Margaret said with a devilish grin. "The shrinks at St. Francis want to see what kind of progress I'm making, and you're going to help them do it so that I won't even know I'm being watched!"

"Yeah. You're on to our plan. But since I was paid in advance for my role in this conspiracy, couldn't you just play along for a little while so I don't have to forfeit my fee?"

Margaret's smile eased a bit as she replied more seriously, "I'm not sure that I can handle *that* assignment, Peter."

"I know I'm abusing our friendship, Margaret. But I only have so many friends that I can pester. Just think about it, would you?"

"Here we go again," Margaret sighed with a smile that signaled to Fr. Kearns that she had not closed the door completely on his latest proposition. Margaret knew that Peter had not steered her wrong yet, but at times she was almost frightened by how quickly her life had changed. But almost before she could pause to think about it, there was Peter Kearns pushing her yet again.

Two days later, Margaret and Fr. Kearns were back together at the YMCA for another AA meeting. Margaret brought up the auto accident she had recently read about in which the drunk driver had killed two teenage girls. The group started talking about the pain that this man inflicted on the families of the two young girls. This was a somewhat sensitive subject for the group members, about half of whom had at least initially been court ordered into the group as the result of driving while intoxicated. Nevertheless, the consensus that quickly developed was that this was the sort of drinker that really needs to be kept off the road. There was little sympathy for him even among this group of alcoholics.

At the end of the meeting as the group was breaking up, Fr. Kearns pulled Margaret aside and spoke to her quietly.

"Margaret, you know the man you were speaking about a little bit ago who ran into the girls?"

"Yes," Margaret replied.

"He and his family are parishioners at St. Michaels. He doesn't come as regularly as the rest of his family, but I have known him for several years."

"What's his name?" Margaret asked.

"Antonio Montoya. He has three young children himself."

"I guess it's kind of easy to forget that the families of the girls aren't the only victims in a situation like this. Those poor kids!"

"Yes. And his wife, Juanita, is really a good person too. I am sure that she is having a very hard time these days."

"Have you spoken to her since the accident?" Margaret queried.

"No I haven't. That is actually something I need to do soon though."

"Peter, I would like to help with your ministry. Do you think I could go with you?"

Fr. Kearns looked at his friend, filled with pride at her decision. "Of course you can. I have a stop to make later this evening if you'd like to accompany me."

"Well, you know the old saying: There's no time like the present."

"Fine. Why don't you leave your car here and I'll drive us over to the Montoya's home. I'll drop you off back here afterwards."

And with that brief exchange, Margaret Millington, without realizing it, was about to take a giant leap forward into the world of Fr. Kearns' ministry.

Fifteen minutes later, Fr. Kearns pulled his Ford Taurus up in the front of the Montoya's modest, but well-kept, ranch-style home, which was sandwiched between a couple of similar-looking homes in the middle of the block. Fr. Kearns helped Margaret out of the car and spoke to her as they walked toward the front door.

"Do you mind if I tell Mrs. Montoya about your involvement in AA if the subject comes up?" the priest asked thoughtfully.

"Sure. Anytime to anyone. I'm really past being ashamed about being a drunk. I am so grateful to this organization, you have my permission to use my name in connection to AA whenever it suits your fancy."

Fr. Kearns smiled and said nothing further until a young boy, who appeared to be around five, answered the door. He had big brown eyes and wore a serious, business-like expression. He looked first at Margaret, almost suspiciously, and then looked up at Fr. Kearns. When A.J. Montoya realized who it was he called to his mother who was just a few steps behind him,

"Mommy, our priest is here! But he's wearing people clothes."

Juanita Montoya then appeared in the doorway and greeted her unexpected visitors.

"Hello Father. Would you like to come in?"

"Well, if it's not too late, yes."

Juanita let Fr. Kearns and the unknown visitor into her house and led them out of the entryway into the small living room, where several toys were strewn across the floor. Suddenly aware of the unkempt condition of her house, Juanita offered her apologies to her guests.

"I'm sorry about the mess. It's been a little nuts around here lately."

"Oh that's fine. I'm sorry for coming unannounced," Fr. Kearns replied, hoping to put his hostess at ease.

"Can I get you anything to drink?" Juanita offered.

"No, not me, thank you," said the young priest, extending both hands with his palms down and outward.

Margaret followed the lead of her companion and declined the offer.

"Juanita, I'd like you to meet a very good friend of mine. This is Margaret Millington. Margaret, this is Juanita Montoya."

Juanita looked kindly at Margaret and smiled, reaching out to shake her hand.

Fr. Kearns, seated next to Margaret and just a few feet away from Juanita sitting across from them, reached out and put Juanita's hand between his hands and held it that way as he addressed her.

"Juanita, I'm so sorry about what your family is going through. We just wanted to let you know that you're all in our thoughts and prayers."

"Oh, thank you, Father. We could use all the prayers we can get," she replied in a voice that began to break at the end of her sentence.

"Do you need anything?" asked the priest, without missing a beat in the conversation.

Margaret saw desperation in the younger woman's face. She sensed that the honest answer that Juanita would have given if she had the courage to voice it was that she needed *everything*. Instead, Juanita had a simpler response.

"We need Antonio, Father. The children miss him terribly. They don't understand why he isn't coming home. I have explained that their father loves them very much and wants to come home, but that he can't right now. There is just no way to make kids this age really understand that their dad can't come home even though he wants to. A.J. is getting mad at his father. I've explained that he's in trouble with the law, but they just don't get it."

"You have beautiful children, Mrs. Montoya," Margaret said earnestly to her despondent hostess.

"Thank you. They have a lot of their father in them, so I can't take all the credit."

"Juanita," said Fr. Kearns, getting back into the conversation, "I imagine money is going to be getting tight while Antonio's not working. If you need anything, please let me know."

Juanita smiled meekly, looking rather embarrassed. "Money was tight when Antonio was here. I don't know what we're going to do now," Juanita confessed.

"Well, we usually try to use at least ten percent of our Sunday offerings for the needs of our community in these sort of circumstances, so we should be able to help a little. Besides, you and Antonio have done so much for St. Michael's."

Margaret smiled, noticing that even while bestowing gifts on others, Peter had a way of being humble and lifting up the recipient. Nevertheless, Margaret was certain that Fr. Kearns was sincere in his gratitude to the Montoyas.

A short while later, Fr. Kearns and Margaret bid farewell to Juanita Montoya and her children.

"Please keep us in your prayers, Father."

"Always," replied the priest as he hugged Juanita at the front door.

"How are we gonna pay for stuff?" asked A.J., who had been listening to the grown-ups' conversation.

"We'll just have to have faith, A.J." The boy, looking at his mother in the light of the small lamp that illuminated the living room, saw that his mother, though smiling faintly, had tears welling up in her eyes. He climbed up on her lap, wrapped both arms around his mother and squeezed her tight.

As Fr. Kearns and Margaret drove back to the YMCA so Margaret could get her car, they both reflected silently until they had almost reached their destination. Margaret broke the silence by posing a question to the priest.

"Do you have a special account at church to help people like the Montoyas?"

"We usually come up with money on an as-needed basis," he replied.

"Well, would you permit me to help set up an endowment for parishioners in need?"

Fr. Kearns knew from some of their conversations that Margaret had some money, though she had never gone into any detail about the amount of her wealth. Before the priest could answer Margaret's first question, she quickly followed with a second.

"How much do you use in an average year for special purposes like this?" Margaret pressed.

"Oh, let's see, I'd say between five thousand and ten thousand dollars. It's not something that's budgeted, so that's why I say it's raised on an as-needed basis."

They pulled up behind Margaret's car that was parked on the street at the side of the YMCA. "Thanks for coming with me, Margaret." Fr. Peter paused and then continued.

"By the way, Margaret, I'd be thrilled to death for you to help us with an endowment. That would be incredibly kind and generous of you."

"Okay, well, I'll be speaking about it with you more in the next few days. Thanks for bringing me along." As she exited the priest's car, Margaret thought about the unintended double meaning of her words and about how on-the-mark they really were.

**18**

Antonio Montoya sat in his cell with a heavy, anxious heart. While some of the inmates talked non-stop, Antonio kept to himself. He had been in the jail for six days and figured he had slept a total of four or five hours. He ate little and had no thoughts of food except for when it was placed before him at mealtime. Many of the inmates spoke of getting their bonds lowered or discussed the terms of the plea agreements that their public defenders were proposing to them. Still others whined about the effects of their present incarceration on their employment, finances and families.

For his part, Antonio had thought very little about any of these relatively mundane matters. What had been haunting him morning, noon and night since his arraignment hearing was what he had done to his two young victims and their families. He also worried constantly about his own young family that he had abandoned by his own stupidity. Even in his worst moments, Antonio Montoya cared about others, particularly children. His own children were the center of his world when sober. That he carelessly, stupidly and criminally took the lives of two innocent girls was literally torturing Antonio. The thought was taking away his appetite, depriving him of sleep and racking his very soul.

Bernard Jackson was one of the talkers in Antonio's cell block. He had a lengthy record of thefts and drug offenses. He had an opinion, which he typically expressed as *the* opinion on any issue that came up. Most of the issues themselves were brought up by this twenty-eight-year-old career con whom Antonio viewed as obnoxious in the extreme. One day, as Bernard was expounding on what he saw as the fundamentally racist nature of the criminal justice system, he turned unexpectedly to Antonio for assent.

"Ain't that right, man?" Bernard asked with a challenging tone as he turned and faced Antonio. Antonio simply shrugged his shoulders without uttering a word.

Bernard had invited Antonio to speak and felt rebuffed and offended by Antonio's silence.

"What's the matter with you, man? You never learn to talk?"

This direct challenge to Antonio could hardly have been more poorly timed. Unrestrained by any considerations of self-preservation and sick of his cellmate's mouth, Antonio looked squarely at Bernard and finally answered him.

"You've got all the answers. Why are you asking me? If you say so, it must be right."

Bernard uncharacteristically paused before speaking, considering whether he wanted to push this verbal dispute to the next level. He looked at the others who had been listening, trying to gauge their reactions to the scene that was playing out before them. Looking back at Antonio, Bernard noticed that Antonio had fixed his gaze on him and had a frightening look in his eyes. Finally, Bernard turned to one of his other cellmates and posed the question originally directed at Antonio to him.

With the potentially explosive confrontation thus defused, Antonio walked back to his corner of the cell block and reassumed his disinterested posture. As his blood pressure returned to its pre-confrontation level, Antonio's thoughts returned to his own violent act of the previous week.

The paperwork that he had seen concerning his case indicated that the teenagers he killed were Vickie Bunch, seventeen, and Erica Benning, sixteen. Antonio wondered what his victims had looked like, what activities they had been involved in, whether they had brothers and sisters. He thought about the suffering that the girls' parents were experiencing, and how he might feel if someone had done something similar to one of his children. He was overwhelmed by his powerlessness to undo any of the damage that he had done. He felt as though he were living a nightmare from which he could not awaken.

Antonio knew that he should get an attorney. He had been around long enough to know that the money paid to a good lawyer was nearly always worth the cost. But this time he didn't feel right taking any action on his own behalf. He knew that Vickie Bunch and Erica Benning weren't going to have the luxury of hiring an attorney to improve their situations. His conscience wouldn't allow him to do more for himself.

As these thoughts were passing through his head, Antonio's reverie was interrupted by one of the jailers who walked up to his cell.

"Montoya. You've got a visitor."

Antonio stood up and walked to the door of his cell, which the jailer unlocked. He was led down the hall to a small visiting room, a twelve by sixteen foot space enclosed in glass. Along the far wall of the room were about a dozen telephones with a chair in front of each phone. On the outside of the glass room sat the visitors, who faced the inmate they came to visit and spoke on the telephone.

He had just entered the visiting room when he caught sight of Juanita. Juanita was wearing blue jeans and a grey, hooded sweatshirt. Antonio sat down on the chair opposite his wife and looked into her brown eyes. He noticed that her eyes, which usually sparkled with life, looked sad and tired. "She probably hasn't slept much more than me," Antonio thought to himself. Juanita tried to put on her brave face, but Antonio immediately saw through the affected composure. He leaned toward the glass as he picked up the phone.

"Nita......"

Words failed Antonio. Nothing he could say seemed adequate

for the immense tragedy that he had brought upon his family, not to mention the families of his victims.

Juanita nodded her head, signaling to her husband that she understood his thoughts. The absolute anguish he was experiencing was written all over his face. Juanita too found it difficult to speak. Neither of them knew what the future held for their family, but both were aware of the fact that it didn't look bright.

Juanita now leaned forward toward the glass to get as close to Antonio as she could without quite touching the glass that separated them. She whispered into the telephone:

"I love you Tony. I love you no matter what."

Antonio looked as though he were about to smile, but suddenly his chest heaved and he began sobbing, at first softly, but within seconds it was an emotional torrent, overwhelming Antonio and forcing out audible moans. It was as if his wife's tender, uplifting words were cast in stark relief against the devastation that he had set in motion when he picked up his first beer that fateful night.

Witnessing this surprising display of emotion from her normally stoic husband was too much for Juanita, who herself began to cry. She cried for her husband's dire predicament, for the uncertain future that the recent events threw before her, and most of all for their three young children, whose last days in the home with their father might well be behind them. If so, Juanita had thought about the fact that this man, who loved his children above all else, would be a stranger to them when he next breathed the air of freedom.

## 19

It was a cloudy Saturday afternoon in Chicago. A steady wind was blowing off the lake, putting a chill in the air. Earlier that morning it had rained, but now most of the rain had dried, except in the tall grass of some of the lawns in the city's neighborhoods. The windows on the west side of St. Michael's Church were opened, allowing fresh air into the strong, old, stone church with highly polished marble floors.

As he sat in the confessional, with fifteen minutes remaining in the regularly scheduled period for Saturday penance, Fr. Kearns could still detect the smell of rain in the air as the wind blew through the holes in the door of the confessional. This ancient sacrament had largely fallen into disuse, long before Fr. Kearns had been ordained to the priesthood. Still, the sign that had the mass schedule on it in front of the church had always said, "Penance: Saturdays from 2 to 4, and anytime by appointment." In the years that Fr. Kearns had been the pastor of the church, it never occurred to him to change the times of either the masses or of weekly penance.

Even on days like today when there was only a trickle of penitents availing themselves of the sacrament, Fr. Kearns thought the two hours went by quickly. He had adopted the practice of praying the rosary when the confessional was empty. He found this quiet time to be quite peaceful and conducive to personal prayer. Occasionally, the silence would be broken by the opening of one of the doors to the left or the right of the priest's entrance to the confessional and then the sliding of the window on the penitent's side of the curtain.

This succession of sounds was Fr. Kearns' cue to set down his rosary and turn toward the window to the confessional being opened. This time he heard the door to his right being opened and therefore slid open the window to that confessional. He then began the rite of penance with a short prayer, following which he sat quietly to allow the penitent to begin his part of the exchange.

"Bless me Father. It has been about twelve or thirteen years since my last confession."

As soon as the penitent began speaking, Fr. Kearns noticed that the voice did not seem to belong to one of his Saturday regulars. The speaker's second sentence confirmed this for the young priest, who allowed the penitent to collect his thoughts so he could continue to the recitation of sins.

"I have a terrible temper sometimes, Father. I say things that I don't mean. Lately, I think I've been snapping at my wife and children more than usual."

This voice was still unfamiliar to the priest, but St. Michael's was a large parish, and there were a number of faces in the pews with which the priest was unable to place a name. Although the identity of the penitent was irrelevant to the priest, he couldn't help but conjure an image to the faceless people speaking to him on the other side of the curtain. This sounded like a Caucasian man who Fr. Kearns guessed was in his thirties or forties.

"I have used the Lord's name in vain when I've lost my temper. I know that's really bad."

When the man realized that Fr. Kearns was not ready to reply, he continued.

"I don't have much patience with anyone anymore. I think it's because I've been so stressed at work. I've been really busy, and our company is not doing too well."

Fr. Kearns waited until the prolonged silence following the

man's confession signaled that he really was finished expressing his thoughts and wanted some sort of response.

"I am sure that our Father is happy that you are here today. You obviously want to be a disciple of His Son and are aware of the areas where you are falling a bit short. And you and I both know that in spite of your complete sincerity here today, you will sin again. Most likely, you will lose patience again at some point and snap at your wife or children. But you also know that our Father will forgive you again."

"I think our challenge is to try to extend the same degree of understanding to those who frustrate us as our Father extends to us. Don't expect more of other people than God expects of us. If we try to be more mindful of our Father's patience with us, it can help us become more patient with one another."

The man sat silently, taking in the priest's words. Fr. Kearns told the man that, for his penance, he would like him to say three "Our Fathers" and three "Hail Marys" with his family. He then gave the man absolution for his sins. When the man left the confessional, the priest picked up his rosary again and resumed his prayer. Though he had slept well the night before, the priest felt tired and low on energy. He closed his eyes and lowered his head as he held his own rosary in folded hands on his lap.

## 20

Tonight's AA meeting was the first Margaret attended without Fr. Kearns. Somehow the evening's discussion turned to obstacles to sobriety which then turned to obstacles to a Christian life. Margaret had engaged Fr. Kearns in a number of spiritual, if not exactly theological, conversations. She also had found herself reading her Bible regularly. The influence of these inspiring and inspired sources of faith were apparent as Margaret joined the discussion with her own testimonial.

"You know, money is said to be the root of all evil. I used to think that was a line that religious types spouted to poor people to make them accept their pitiful predicament. But I think it is really true."

The other group members listened politely with varying degrees of interest as Margaret continued.

"Money is probably the greatest obstacle to faith that there is."

A thirtyish man named, "Ed", who was a long-time but infrequent attendee of meetings at the Y interrupted Margaret.

"I think I could deal with having too much money."

Ed wasn't smiling so it wasn't clear if he was trying to be funny or was sincerely challenging Margaret. Margaret gave him the benefit of the doubt and continued her explanation.

"I have learned in the past year that my own ability to really pray to God in a way that I expect him to hear me depends on me approaching Him humbly. If I just start into my prayer during the day asking for something or trying to take something to Him, I tend to have trouble believing that he is hearing me. I often feel like I'm just talking to myself out of a sense of obligation to go through the exercise as a sort of spiritual insurance."

Margaret paused and observed that her self-disclosure had succeeded in captivating the attention of the entire group now.

"But when I force myself to think about the greatness of the God that I am addressing, it is easy to put myself, at least mentally, in a very humble posture as I pray. To help myself in doing this, I sometimes open with words that exalt God and that admit my own worthlessness. From that humble, lowly posture before God, I *know* that I am being heard."

"This gets to my point. In our world, money represents power and independence. When you have money, you tend to stop making requests of people. Instead, you make demands. People respond to your power by trying to please you, either because they want something from you or they fear what you can do to them if they displease you."

"With the habits of thought and action that come from the power of money, it becomes very foreign to be in a humble posture toward anyone. You think of yourself as "the boss" in your dealings with most everyone. And yet, if you have trouble achieving humility, which Scripture tells us is one of life's important virtues, then you probably cannot approach the Lord in the proper posture."

"We also know that we are told to act as servants to one another. If we aren't humble, we can't be servants. But I think that's the attitude we have to take on."

"How have you discovered this?" asked an impressed, older female from the group.

"Well, I guess from the Bible and .... ." Margaret's face reddened slightly as she hesitated. "And our friend Peter Kearns has demonstrated this since the day I met him."

Several heads in the room nodded slowly. All were well acquainted with Margaret's spiritual mentor. No one could dispute that Fr. Peter's very being was a case study in selfless service. Certainly not even the most committed among them would be devoting the time they were to the group if it weren't at least in part for their own therapeutic needs. But everyone knew that Fr. Peter wasn't a drinker. Nevertheless, he had been a consistent member since this group's inception.

It was also growing ever clearer to those around her that Margaret Millington was becoming a valuable contributor to the group. Tonight, she had become the unofficial spiritual leader of the group in Fr. Peter's absence. No one could be more surprised by this ascendancy than Margaret herself. And in all humility, she knew to whom she was indebted for her own awakening.

# 21

Juanita was awakened by the creaking of her bedroom door. As she listened further, she glanced at the alarm clock on her nightstand, which displayed "2:12 a.m." She looked down at the foot of her bed and saw little A.J. climbing in beside her. As he crawled up next to her, Juanita saw her son's face by the light that shone in from the hallway through the open bedroom door. A.J.s eyes were open as he lay with his head on his mother's pillow, staring up at the ceiling. She noticed that his eyes were red and wet, as though he had been crying.

"What's the matter, sweetheart?" Juanita asked tenderly as she kissed her young son's forehead.

"I had a bad dream and couldn't get back to sleep."

"Is that why you were crying, A.J.?"

The boy turned his head toward his mother now. Meeting her gaze, he answered.

"After I woke up I started thinking about Daddy. He helps me when I have bad dreams."

Juanita pulled her little boy to her side, squeezing him tightly against her. She considered and quickly rejected several alternative responses. Finally, Juanita simply whispered into her son's ear, "It's all right, honey." She kept her arm around A.J. and they both eventually fell asleep together.

The next morning, Juanita woke up early and took a quick shower. She dressed herself and then made breakfast for her children.

They ate breakfast together and Juanita drove the kids to the daycare and went to work.

One of Juanita's first chores upon her arrival at the Gas-N-Shop each morning was to start brewing the coffee and cappuccino. Juanita was lost in her thoughts as a customer entered the store, ringing the bell above the door. She was therefore startled when she realized that someone was standing immediately behind her.

Juanita looked up and there was Mark Slover, grinning at her. She wondered if it were her imagination or if Slover actually was gloating about something. Maybe he was now considering her to be his latest conquest rather than the challenge she once represented. Slover spoke first.

"Hey babe. I've been wondering about you." Slover was still smiling. Suddenly his expression changed and he took on the role of concerned friend.

"I heard about what happened the other night. I'm sure sorry. Is there anything I can do for you?"

Juanita found herself wondering what she possibly ever saw in this man. He suddenly appeared to her to be an awkward, gangling, superficial moron. Without a second thought, Juanita clipped off the response that came to her almost reflexively.

"I'm sure you'd like to do something for me, Mark, but I've got important things to deal with. Thanks anyway."

Juanita flipped the switch on the cappuccino machine, turned her back to Slover and started walking away from him toward the counter. No one else was in the store, but Juanita was still stunned at what came next. Slover quickly walked up to her and grabbed her around the waist with one arm and pulled her next to him. He then held her by the sides with both hands and started to kiss her.

Momentarily stunned, Juanita's reaction was delayed and before she said anything, Slover continued.

"Why the hard-to-get routine, Juanita?" Slover grunted, as he kissed her once on the lips and then started to nuzzle against her ear.

"If you get out of here right now, I might not have to call the police!" Juanita bellowed with anger.

Slover was now transformed as he snarled, "You're as crazy as any of them," and stormed out of the store.

Juanita felt her head boiling. She walked over and dropped herself into a hard, plastic chair outside the unisex restroom and leaned her head back against the wall, exhaling slowly through pursed lips. As the tension eased, Juanita's anger subsided and she began to actually feel a sense of relief. She was finished with the sneakiness, once and for all.

When the bell over the door signaled the entrance of another customer, Juanita stood up and walked toward the checkout area. It was a guy in his late teens or early twenties. Juanita stepped up to the cash register, inserted a key, and rang up his purchase of gasoline and cigarettes. As she thanked the young customer for his purchase, Juanita glanced out the window toward where Slover's van had been parked only minutes earlier. It was gone. She shook her head as if in disbelief at her own recent bout of immaturity, certain that the gravity of her current circumstances would help her avoid any similar indiscretions in the future. Her small children were without their father indefinitely. She knew that they now depended upon her more than ever.

**22**

Margaret had agreed that she would devote one afternoon a week to accompany Fr. Kearns on his visits to the sick and suffering that he saw on a daily basis. She wasn't sure if it was by design or mere coincidence, but on this cool, cloudy first day of Margaret's new work, Fr. Peter announced that he wanted to start out at St. Francis Hospital. He picked her up at home and they were now heading that way, ready or not.

The pair never wanted for topics of conversation. Margaret, who now had more experience with therapists than most, often thought Peter was more skillful than a typical therapist at gently guiding a person into matters that aren't generally discussed in modern, polite society. But he had once said that he figured if people could no longer discuss things as fundamental as heaven and hell and the alternative paths to each, mankind was surely doomed. Margaret found Peter's adroitness in steering a conversation seamlessly from something as mundane as the weather to the state of one's soul as energizing as it was impressive.

As they drove through Chicago toward the hospital, Margaret found herself telling Peter about her relationship with her sister, Ginger. Ginger was four years younger than Margaret and their personalities and interests were about as opposite as could be imagined of two girls born to the same parents. Margaret explained that, growing up, she was blessed with looks, while Ginger had the brains. Margaret was a risk taker, while Ginger, as a rule, played it safe. As a result, Margaret's abuse of alcohol and Ginger's solicitous response was nothing new to either.

Margaret knew that Ginger often envied her older sister's upscale lifestyle. Margaret was able to travel to exotic, foreign destinations and enjoyed social prominence even among Chicago's elite. But for her part, Margaret spent many years longing for the sort of marriage and simpler life that Ginger and Carl appeared to share.

"I think we both imagined the grass being greener on the other side of the fence," confessed Margaret.

"Imagine that," answered Peter with a smile.

Margaret began to feel nervous as they pulled into the parking lot at St. Francis Hospital. Margaret looked up at the windows on the east end of the 3rd floor. It was 1:15. Unless the schedule had been changed, Dr. Sekorski should be leading a group therapy session right now, Margaret thought silently. She wondered about the patients she had come to know during her time on Unit 5 and how they had been faring since her departure. As if he were reading her thoughts, Fr. Kearns broke the silence in the car.

"Would you like to stop in on the third floor while we're here today, Margaret?"

Margaret hesitated momentarily, sighed, and answered her friend with a grin. "Let's skip the frying pan thing and go right for the fire, Friar!"

Peter laughed. "Good. Why don't we stop there first then, okay?"

"That'd be fine."

The two visitors walked in through the hospital's main doors, maintaining their light spirits, and turned right toward the east wing of the hospital. Fr. Peter greeted everyone they passed in the hallway, and Margaret wondered how many of these people, most of whom returned his greeting, actually knew the priest and how many were simply responding to his friendly manner or to the dignity of his clerical dress. Occasional passersby would speak to Fr. Kearns by name, particularly those who appeared to be staffers at the hospital. He spoke to everyone they passed on their walk through the hospital's long, sterile corridors: young and old, men and women. No one was a stranger to Peter Kearns.

When they reached the elevator in the east wing of the hospital, Fr. Kearns excused himself as he reached past Margaret to push the "up" arrow on the electrical panel that was situated between the dual elevators. The bell rang over the elevator to their left and as the doors opened, the two unlikely ministers, who were now positioned in front of that elevator, stepped back to let the exiting riders pass out of the elevator. One of them looked up at Margaret and Fr. Kearns as she passed – an African-American woman about Margaret's age. Fr. Kearns said "Good afternoon" to the woman, who nodded slightly and offered a half smile in return. Margaret noticed that the woman was looking at her, and just after she broke the woman's gaze, a flash of recognition came to Margaret, and she turned half-way around to face the woman again.

"Hello, Patti. Remember me? I'm Margaret Millington."

"Oh yes, Margaret. How are you?"

It was a psych nurse from Unit 5. Margaret had not become well-acquainted with the nurse, who was generally strictly business as she tended to her patients.

"I'm fine. Just stopping in for a visit this time," Margaret said with a broad smile.

"That's good to hear. Take care, Ms. Millington. It's good to see you."

"You too."

Although the hospital was old, this elevator had only been installed a couple of years earlier, replacing an antiquated contraption that climbed and dropped too slowly for the expectations of its modern passengers. Margaret had started out dutifully staring at the lighted numbers above the elevator door, but surreptitiously stole a glance below and to her right to a young man who had his arm around a young pregnant woman, presumably his wife. Margaret remembered that on the fourth floor, immediately above Unit 5, was the hospital's maternity area.

As the young woman caught Margaret's glance, Margaret made polite inquiry of her.

"Are you due soon?" Margaret asked with a smile.

"My water broke at home about an hour ago, and my due date is in four days, so I guess this is it."

"Is this your first?" asked Fr. Kearns as the door to the third floor opened.

"Yes," replied the young woman with a nervous smile.

"Good luck to you then. To both of you," responded the priest as he looked back over to the father-to-be.

"Thanks Father," said the young man, whose apparent nervousness equaled and perhaps exceeded that of his wife.

As Margaret stopped at the desk to sign in and pick up a visitor's badge, she thought momentarily of how grateful she was to be entering this place in this new capacity.

"Hello, Jean," said Fr. Kearns to the desk attendant as the former continued his practice of speaking to all who passed. Peter stepped in closer to the counter to speak with the woman quietly, reaching across the narrow counter for her hand as he did so.

"How's your husband coming along?"

"Oh, he's doing better. The chemo isn't bothering him as much as it was for a while, so we can't complain."

"Well, I'll keep you both in my prayers," said Fr. Kearns, giving the woman's hand a gentle squeeze before disengaging.

Margaret looked up at the priest's chest as he pinned his own visitor's badge to his black coat. Instead of the ordinary plain, white visitor's badge with "Visitor" emblazoned in bold, black letters, Fr. Kearns' badge was silver with navy letters that said, "Fr. Peter Kearns."

"I don't remember you wearing that badge, or any badge come to think of it," stated Margaret questioningly.

"You're most observant, Margaret." Do you remember Sandy

Gordooze from the unit? She told me I needed a badge and made this one for me. She just gave it to me a couple of weeks ago. What do you think?" The priest proudly stuck out his chest to model the gift from Mrs. Gordooze.

"Most distinguished," Margaret replied sincerely.

As they walked down the main hall on Unit 5, they nearly bumped into Dr. Sankar, the psychiatrist, who seemed to be in a hurry as he exited a patient's room.

"Excuse me," offered the psychiatrist as he backed away from Margaret and lightly touched the top of her forearm. He then realized whom he was speaking to and took on a more friendly and casual manner.

"Ms. Millington, Fr. Peter. How are you both doing? It's good to see you, Margaret."

Margaret's initial thought was to defensively explain that she was continuing to do well and to offer that she was only there as a visitor, but then she quickly determined that the astute doctor had noted her conspicuous visitor's badge.

"I'm great, Doctor. Thank you. How has everything been around here lately?"

"Fine. Just fine." Then, more to Fr. Kearns, the doctor continued. "Fannie Williams was released to the jail last week. Her trial has been set for late September."

Ordinarily, doctors are not allowed to discuss their patients with anyone. Fannie, however, gave the doctors and nurses in Unit 5 permission to pass along her updates to everyone she knew. She even signed a release to back up her verbal consent. Margaret remembered with fondness the woman who had defended a weaker woman on the unit. Fannie had been waiting to be cleared by the psychiatrist so she could stand trial for beating her abusive boyfriend with a baseball bat. Evidently, her doctor now believed Fannie was competent to stand trial.

Margaret's understanding of the situation was that Fannie had suffered an anxiety attack related to the stress of her relationship with her former boyfriend. Fannie said her public defender informed her that her assault on her boyfriend "Maurice" did not qualify as self-defense. While Fannie had been beaten numerous times by the hot-headed parking lot attendant and could sense when Maurice was in one of his moods and about to erupt, her own taped statement to the police did not indicate that he had yet made any move against her immediately prior to the bludgeoning she administered. Fannie had resigned herself to the fact that she would ultimately trade in confinement at St. Francis for an even more restrictive confinement in a state prison. Although Fannie had never been incarcerated before, Margaret had been struck by the courage with which the woman faced her predicament and, in fact, sometimes drew strength from Fannie's display of equanimity under such adversity.

As Margaret and Fr. Kearns continued their visit to Unit 5, they met briefly with several patients and staff members. Few of the patients that were there when Margaret was a patient remained. After about an hour in the unit, the two visitors descended the elevator to the main floor so they could see some patients in other parts of the hospital.

Margaret watched Peter with interest as she observed which rooms he decided to enter and which ones to pass. She knew from her own experience with the priest that there was no discrimination made on the basis of religion, which had surprised her from the first. Between rooms they spoke little, the priest appearing to be thinking, maybe praying for the people he was seeing.

As they reached an end of a hallway on the oncology unit and had a bit more of an opportunity to talk, Margaret finally asked the priest flat-out what she was trying to figure out.

"Peter, how do you decide which rooms to stop in?"

The ever-considerate priest stopped walking momentarily and looked at the former patient thoughtfully. He then told her softly, but matter-of-factly: "I usually stop at the rooms of patients who don't seem to get many other visitors." He paused briefly and then continued, "Except that I try to stop at the room of any parishioner that I learn is here."

"And how in walking through the halls as we are right now do you come to know that?" Margaret pressed, somewhat intrigued by the priest's answer.

"Well, of course it is easy if a patient has visitors while I'm here. But I can also look for other clues."

"Such as?"

"Such as flowers or gifts in the room, cards on the door or on furniture in the room, and a telltale sign: when one of the visitor chairs from one-half of the room is left on the other half of the room for more than a day. I usually get here often enough to notice."

Margaret was dumbstruck. Seeing in her look that Margaret may be crediting him with being more magnanimous than he believed himself in truth to be, Fr. Peter continued.

"You know, Margaret. I think I can relate to the feelings of people like that better than to others."

She looked at him for a sign. Was he serious?

"Don't get me wrong, please. I love my sacramental calling. I find great fulfillment in my work. But the life of a celibate priest can be lonely. A priest really and truly is married to the Church. And some of the people we deal with are too caught up in the business of their own lives to have time to get close to their priest. So I spend most of my time visiting people who I find to be very much like myself. One key difference, in many cases, is that these people may not yet have received the gift of faith. And I know first-hand how that gift can transform a person's life. Nothing in the world gives me greater pleasure than sharing that gift with others, and in giving it, I feel that I too am blessed."

"Do you mind if we sit down for a minute, Margaret?"

"Of course." It looked to Margaret as though the priest was experiencing some sort of pain, as he allowed a wince to spread across his face.

"Are you alright?" Margaret asked with genuine concern.

"I think so," Peter answered, as a second wince flashed across his countenance.

"What's bothering you, Peter?"

"Oh, I don't know exactly. I've been having some pains the past few weeks. They show up in different parts of my body." Seeing the worry on Margaret's face, he offered reassurance. "I'm thinking about seeing my doctor when I get a chance."

"When you get a chance?"

"Okay. Soon." The pain subsided quickly and the priest smiled kindly at his friend.

"Is that better, mother?" the priest asked with good-natured sarcasm.

"That's more like it. You need somebody to stay after you to make you take care of yourself, don't you?"

After promising to make an appointment with the doctor, Fr. Peter felt another painful sensation run over his body. It occurred to the young priest that perhaps Margaret was right. Maybe he had been ignoring his own physical needs for too long. He made a mental note to call for an appointment on Monday morning.

## 23

The "chain gang" was the name given to criminal defendants brought over to the courthouse from the jail in handcuffs and joined together by a single large chain. A couple of armed jailers with two-way radios escorted the inmates through the corridors of the courthouse and up to the fourth floor, where they would each be called up to the judge's bench, one-at-a-time, for his own brief hearing. Today in this court, everyone who was scheduled for a nine o'clock hearing had been previously arraigned and had requested time to get an attorney. This was the hearing where they either showed up with their attorney, in which case they'd enter a plea, or showed up without an attorney and explained to the judge why they didn't have an attorney as planned.

Sometimes, a defendant would inform the court that he intended to hire his own attorney, only to discover later that the cost of a private attorney was far out of reach. In those circumstances the defendant would then typically show up and explain this difficulty to the judge, who would then conduct a brief inquiry to determine whether the defendant was "indigent" under the state guidelines and therefore eligible for the appointment of a public defender at taxpayer expense. The vast majority of criminal defendants in Cook County ultimately were represented by public defenders rather than by private attorneys.

Every once in a while a defendant would show up at this post-arraignment hearing and tell the judge that he had decided he didn't want an attorney after all. Usually this would occur when the defendant had simply decided to change his plea to "guilty" and didn't want to prolong the proceedings by getting an attorney involved.

The last of the eight defendants on the chain gang on this particular Tuesday morning was Antonio Montoya. Antonio had sat somberly as those before him variously plead guilty, scheduled a trial date or requested the appointment of a public defender. Attorneys for about half of the defendants had orally requested a reduction of the standard bond set at the time of arrest based upon the level of the crime. In two of these cases, the court did reduce the bond to amounts that apparently were going to allow the defendants to get out of jail as they awaited trial. Two of the defendants, both of whom faced more serious charges, had their requests for reduced bail denied.

Antonio presented no such issues for the judge to decide. When the bailiff called, "State of Illinois v. Antonio Montoya," Antonio was unshackled from his fellow inmates and approached the bench. Antonio appeared disheveled. His hair was mussed and his eyes were red. In fact, he hadn't slept more than a half hour each of the past two nights as he nervously awaited this hearing.

As Antonio stood before the judge, hands cuffed in front of him, one of the jailers kept his left hand on the upper part of Antonio's right, upper arm. Antonio's head remained bowed as the judge addressed him.

"Are you Antonio Montoya?" boomed the judge in a voice that echoed through the ornate courtroom.

"Yes sir," replied Antonio distinctly, but at a much lower volume.

"I don't see an attorney with you today. Have you hired a lawyer?"

"No sir," continued Antonio steadily.

"What's your pleasure then? Are you making any progress toward getting an attorney?"

"No sir. I've decided that I'm not going to need an attorney."

"You understand that if you can't afford an attorney, I can appoint one to represent you at no cost to yourself?"

"Yes sir, but that won't be necessary." Antonio was now looking up at the judge.

"Very well, Mr. Montoya. Then how do you plead to Count I, the reckless homicide of Vickie Bunch?" asked the judge with his gaze now fixed firmly on the prisoner before him.

"I am guilty, Your Honor," Antonio said firmly.

"And how do you plead then to Count II, the reckless homicide of Erica Benning?"

"Guilty."

"Has anyone threatened you or promised you anything to get you to plead guilty?" asked the judge.

"No sir."

"Are you under the influence of any medication or drugs at this time?" continued the judge.

"No sir," Anthony replied again.

"Are you under the care of any psychiatrist or psychologist, Mr. Montoya?"

"No I am not."

"And do you understand that you have certain rights that I read to you the other day that you are giving up by pleading guilty?"

"Yes sir."

"And you understand that among these rights is a right to trial by jury?" asked the judge.

"Yes sir, I do."

"Do you understand that you have the right to remain silent and cannot be compelled to testify?"

"Yes sir."

"And that the jury would be informed that it couldn't hold your silence against you?"

"Yes sir."

"Do you understand that if you went to trial that the State of

Illinois would have to prove that you committed this crime beyond a reasonable doubt?"

"I understand that, Your Honor."

"And do you understand that you would have the right to confront and cross-examine witnesses called by the State of Illinois to testify against you?"

"Yes sir."

"And that you have the right to have witnesses subpoenaed to come into court to testify on your behalf at no cost to you?"

"Yes sir."

"Do you understand that you would have the right to appeal any decision of the jury or of this court?"

"Yes sir, I understand."

"And knowing all these things you have chosen to give up all of these rights and plead guilty?"

"Yes, Your Honor."

The judge then turned to the Assistant State's Attorney - a slender young woman with dark hair pulled back, sporting a navy blue business suit. "Factual basis, please."

The young female prosecutor now spoke for the first time during the hearing.

"The facts are, Your Honor, with regard to Count I, that on the date set forth in the charging information, the Defendant, Antonio Montoya did then and there act in a reckless manner, performing acts likely to cause death or great bodily harm, in that after consuming alcoholic beverages beyond the point of intoxication, he operated a motor vehicle and struck a vehicle containing Vickie Bunch, thereby causing her death."

"Did you do that Mr. Montoya?" asked the judge.

"Yes sir," replied Antonio solemnly.

The assistant state's attorney then read Count II, which was identical except for the name of the victim, to which Antonio again verbally acknowledged his guilt.

"Very well. I find that the Defendant has made a knowing, intelligent and voluntary plea and hereby accept said plea."

The judge leaned over to a court clerk seated to his left and whispered something that was inaudible to Antonio. He then turned forward and faced Antonio again.

"I am going to order the probation department to prepare a long-form, pre-sentence report and deliver it to the court within fourteen days. I'll set this matter for sentencing on November 13."

"That's all on this case. Mr. Montoya is remanded to the custody of the Cook County Sheriff."

# 24

Jarrod Williams was a nineteen-year-old student in his second year at Elmworth Community College. He took a full course load of eighteen credit hours of his general education requirements, which he financed by a combination of grants, student loans and hard work. Williams worked forty hours per week in the kitchen at "Barney's," a greasy spoon diner frequented by college students and residents of the neighborhood, known by the college students as "townies".

Williams and his older sister, Veronica, two years his senior, were born out-of-wedlock and had never met their father, who their mother had said was a good man until he got addicted to crack cocaine when they were infants. Veronica remembered her father coming by their apartment a few times when she was very young, but Jarrod had no recollection of him at all. When Veronica was five and Jarrod was three, their father was shot to death in a drive-by shooting that police suspected to be drug related. His killer was never found.

Williams' mother had set the example for hard work that her son was now emulating. She dropped out of high school when she was sixteen and pregnant with Veronica. Throughout his childhood, Jarrod remembered his mother working two and even three jobs at a time - jobs that usually paid just above minimum wage. Amazingly, the Williams children never felt poor. In comparison with their friends' families, Jarrod and Veronica considered themselves relatively well-off.

On this Sunday evening, Jarrod had been studying for hours and looked up at the clock on his kitchen wall. It was 5:40 p.m. He had recently acquired the habit of going to visit his mother on Sunday evenings in a place that a few months earlier he would never have expected to find her. Jarrod got on the subway and took the thirty-minute ride into the city, reading from his history book along the way.

Fannie Williams looked forward to her son's weekly visits at the Cook County Jail. Although the visits were monitored and far too short, she loved to get updates on Jarrod's education, his work, his love-life, and anything else that was going on in her beloved son's life. For Jarrod, the challenge of these visits was to not cry. Seeing his mother in this predicament tore at the young man's heart, though he did his best to do as she had taught him and keep his chin up.

As a young boy, Jarrod was surrounded by people who were dealt a poor set of cards in life. He saw how many tended to use that as a ready excuse when things didn't go their way. But his mother pounded into Jarrod that his only limitations in life would be self-imposed, and that he had it in his power to do anything he set his mind to do.

Unfortunately, the one thing that Jarrod felt utterly powerless about was his mother's current circumstances. Whatever was going on in his mother's mind, her face did not reveal. He wondered if she ever broke down after his visits ended and he wasn't around. He found himself doing so regularly. It all seemed so unfair to Jarrod. Since Veronica had moved to the state of Washington, Jarrod felt he was all that his mother had.

Before getting locked up, Jarrod knew that his mother had a boyfriend that, much like Jarrod's own father, came and went over the past several years. Although he did not use illegal drugs, he had another habit that Fannie kept from her children: a penchant for drinking to excess and physically abusing Fannie. In the weeks leading up to the fateful incident, Fannie had finally become afraid of Maurice. She knew that she needed to get out of the relationship.

She had even gone to the courthouse once to find out how she might get a protective order against Maurice. Unfortunately, she had not followed through on it. Six days later, Maurice came home and had that familiar look in his eyes and that familiar tone in his voice. Fannie knew it well. She ended up beating him half-to-death before he could do something awful to her. Now she sat in an eight-by-eight cell and her own future looked exceedingly bleak.

Jarrod was buzzed into the visiting area, where he was immediately met by his smiling mother.

"How's my favorite man?" asked Fannie, bursting with joy at the sight of her son.

"I'm doing okay, Momma. How are you holding up?"

"I'll do fine as long as you keep them letters coming and don't forget me on Sundays."

"You know you don't have to worry about that." After a pause, the young man continued.

"Do you know which public defender is going to represent you at trial yet, Momma?"

"I don't think there's going to be no trial, Jarrod. It's too risky."

"Have they offered you anything better yet?"

Jarrod was referring to the plea negotiations between the Public Defender's Office and the District Attorney. So far, the best deal they had offered Fannie was six years. With credit for good time, she would probably serve about three and a half more years.

"I don't think it's going to get better. I do the six years or I go to trial. My lawyer thinks I'd get eight years if I take it to trial, 'cause he don't think we can win and the judge usually gives more time than what the D.A. offers."

"How about if we talk to somebody else; get a second opinion?"

"Honey, them opinions don't come cheap," Fannie replied soberly. "Private lawyers want $10,000 or more for something like this. If I had that kind of money, I woulda taken some time off a long time before they ever locked me up."

"Momma, I'm going to get somebody else to look at this for you.

You can't spend four years locked up!" Jarrod's emotions had flared quickly. The entire matter of Fannie pleading guilty had become a subject that she and her son had not been able to agree upon since Fannie's public defender first relayed the D.A.'s proposed deal to her.

Jarrod and his mother talked for another twenty-five minutes until his allotted visiting time was up, but Jarrod was distracted the entire time. All he could think of was how he could get his mother out of jail. He was determined to have someone help her, no matter the cost.

## 25

Peter Kearns had rarely seen a doctor in his adult life. He had always enjoyed good health and had made it his practice to "offer up" in prayer the sort of minor ailments that he would get from time to time. As he filled out the patient history form that the receptionist handed him, he sat back in his chair and rested his head against the wall, trying to recall how long he had been experiencing the symptoms of his present, unknown malady.

As he pondered the matter, it occurred to Fr. Kearns that he had probably been experiencing the occasional nausea for three or four months. The generalized achiness in the bones had been with him for maybe half that long. And the priest couldn't remember when he first started feeling fatigued, so he put a question mark next to that symptom.

In a short while, the nurse called Peter Kearns' name and he followed her back to a patient examination room. Just outside the examination room, she had him stand on the scales to be weighed.

"One hundred eighty-two pounds," announced the nurse as she wrote the priest's weight down on his chart.

She then opened the door and asked Fr. Kearns to have a seat next to a table along a far wall of the room.

"Remove your jacket, please," said the nurse, assuming control now that he was on her turf.

Fr. Kearns quickly slipped off his jacket and offered his right arm to the nurse, who was unwrapping the cuff to the sphygmomanometer in preparation to take her patient's blood pressure. The nurse cuffed the priest's arm and secured the Velcro wrap. She then placed the cold, metallic stethoscope against the inner part of his forearm, just below the elbow as she inflated the cuff. Within moments she again made an official pronouncement. "118 over 85."

As the nurse unwrapped the device from the priest's arm, she asked him what had been bothering him and he recited in further detail the symptoms he had outlined a few minutes earlier on the patient history form. The nurse listened intently, nodding her head thoughtfully as though she had already figured it all out.

About five minutes after the nurse left the room, Dr. Mark Tyler entered the room and introduced himself to his new patient. The young doctor, who appeared to be roughly Peter's own age, again reviewed Fr. Kearns' symptoms with him and then performed a general physical examination. When he was finished, the doctor jotted down a few notes on the chart and then turned away from the table to face his patient.

"I want to order a blood test for starters. If you'll take this slip down the hall and hand it to the young lady at the desk outside the lab, they'll take a little blood and we'll run a few standard tests on it."

"Let's go ahead and get a urine specimen too," added the doctor as if having an afterthought. "We'll call you in a couple of days to let you know if the lab work reveals anything. In the meantime, I'd suggest that you drink lots of liquids and get plenty of sleep. You may have some sort of virus and will need to conserve your energy to fight it."

The doctor smiled as he stood and offered his hand to the priest. "It's nice to meet you, Father. If you don't hear from us by the end of the week, you should call and ask for my nurse, Peggy."

"Okay, doctor. Thank you."

Fr. Peter left the doctor's office knowing no more than when he had entered an hour and a half earlier. But at least he could call Margaret and let her know that he just had a thorough check-up.

## 26

Juanita Montoya watched her husband being led from the courtroom with the other prisoners. He looked up at her as he walked toward the door, mouthing "I love you" as he crossed into the corridor outside the courtroom. Juanita lifted her hand and gave him a half-wave, immediately wishing that she had had an opportunity to tell her husband that she loved him too.

He had really done it. She knew that there was no changing Antonio's mind about his plea or about having an attorney appointed to represent him. He was as firm in this as she had ever seen him. He messed up horribly and was prepared to take his punishment. Juanita felt tinges of extreme sorrow, oddly mixed with pride. She hurried out of the courtroom and back to the elevator, where she located a courthouse directory on the wall between the elevators.

"Adult Probation - Room 424," Juanita read silently. She took the elevator up another floor and exited, looking for the offices of those who would be making recommendations concerning her husband's fate. Juanita found the offices of the Adult Probation Department and entered the outer door into the reception area.

"Hello," Juanita began somewhat meekly. "Uh, I'm Juanita Montoya and my husband just entered a guilty plea in court downstairs. I understand that this office is going to be preparing a pre-sentence report to give to the judge and that you might need some information from me to help prepare it."

The woman at the front desk appeared to be in her late fifties. She had gray hair and thick, black glasses. Juanita thought she appeared wrinkled beyond her years. The woman answered Juanita in a raspy voice.

"Please fill out this paperwork and bring it back within seven days. Someone will then call you to set up an appointment to get further information from you." The woman arched her eyebrows as if to say, "Any questions?" without the effort of an audible query.

Juanita politely thanked the receptionist and left. When she got home, she found her children as she had left them with Vada. Their father had just pled guilty to two counts of reckless homicide. It was now a virtual certainty that he would be gone for at least several years. Until Antonio was sentenced, Juanita decided there was really nothing more to say to the children about the matter. A.J.'s expressive young face conveyed clearly to his mother the pain that the subject caused him whenever it was brought up. And yet Juanita felt guilty to intentionally avoid mentioning Antonio's name to his own children. There was no good answer to this dilemma, and Juanita just had to go with her instincts on how best to handle it.

Vada pulled her sister aside, beyond earshot of the kids to get briefed on what had transpired at the courthouse. Vada hugged her sister upon receiving the news that Antonio had gone through with the guilty plea. "Oh God, sis… Oh God," Vada repeated with panic in her voice. She struggled to regain her composure to avoid further upsetting Juanita, but the reality of the situation was settling over the sisters, and the time for hoping for a better legal outcome was now officially past.

Juanita forced a smile and shrugged her shoulders - a silent confession that her family's future was now officially beyond her control.

## 27

During Margaret's extended stay at the hospital, she started out the loner, keeping to herself and trying to disclose as little about herself as she could get by with. Of course, by the time she left, everyone in the unit knew Margaret and Margaret knew everyone in the unit. When she had recently learned that Fannie Williams was now ready to stand trial, she wondered how Fannie was getting along. More specifically, she wondered about Fannie's legal situation and her emotional well-being.

No one, Margaret knew, was more affected by the suicide of Diane on Unit 5 than Fannie. It had seemed to Margaret that these two women had very little in common: where Diane was weak and timid, Fannie was strong and at least put up a façade of self-confidence. Although she didn't show it, Fannie actually had lost a great deal of her confidence as a cumulative result of the verbal and physical abuse that Maurice dished out. The "toughness" that remained was largely bravado.

But Margaret's impressions were shaped solely by appearances. It had appeared to her that Diane began clinging to Fannie for support and strength. Fannie looked out for the perpetually sad woman. Diane's death, Margaret knew from group sessions, struck Fannie especially hard, not merely because they had become daily companions during their overlapping stays at the hospital, but even more so because she felt she had failed in the job she assumed as Diane's protector.

Margaret was keenly aware of how much she herself was strengthened with the help of another. She decided she was going to be there for Fannie in any way she could. A few quick phone calls and Margaret was ringing the apartment of Jarrod Williams, Fannie's son whom she had never met.

She was pleased and greatly relieved to learn that Fannie's psychological health was very good. But within the first few minutes of their telephone conversation, Jarrod apprised his inquisitive caller about his mother's dire legal straits.

"The thing is, Ms. .... I'm sorry, what's your name again?"

"Millington. Please, call me 'Margaret.'"

"The thing is, Margaret, my momma really did what she had to do. She's not a violent lady. I've seen her pushed and pushed and pushed. She has the patience of Job."

Margaret smiled at the young man's biblical reference. She remembered that Fannie frequently quoted Scripture throughout her time in the unit, and in Margaret's first weeks in the hospital, the woman's "superstitions" as Margaret had initially viewed them, were rather amusing, if somewhat annoying to the agnostic that Margaret was at that time.

"So why can't her lawyer just show how she was acting in self-defense?" asked Margaret matter-of-factly.

"That's what I keep saying," Jarrod replied, revealing the frustration that this subject created in him. "Momma says the lawyer is convinced she can't prove it was self-defense since he hadn't done anything to her yet."

"Well, he may not have done anything to her that day, but it sounds like he had certainly established a pretty consistent pattern of mistreating your mother in similar situations. What was it if not self-defense?"

"Her lawyer says it's aggravated battery and that she's gotta agree to do six years or else she'll get hammered by the judge."

"Who is your mother's lawyer?" asked Margaret, who, between her divorce and commitment proceedings had spent much of the past year dealing with attorneys.

Jarrod gave Margaret the name and number of Fannie's public defender. After ending her conversation with Jarrod, she picked up the phone again and started pushing the numbers to the Cook County Public Defender's Office. She dialed about half of the numbers and then slowly put her finger on the receiver button and held it down for a couple of seconds, holding the index finger of her other hand to her pursed lips as though deep in thought. Margaret then dialed the number of Copeland, Rogerson and Zenhaus, the law firm that had helped her in her divorce proceedings.

Margaret asked to speak with Marvin Zenhaus. She knew that he was not a criminal lawyer, but wanted to find out from him who he considered the best criminal defense attorney in town. After a forty-five-second conversation with Mr. Zenhaus, Margaret was speaking to Robert L. Waite, one of Chicago's most well-known and highly regarded criminal defense attorneys, who was a partner of Zenhaus. Waite had taken on a number of high-profile criminal cases over the years, and Margaret was familiar with his name from the newspapers. She knew that he had successfully defended spectacular cases against common criminals, and not-so-spectacular cases against what had become an ever more elite and high-paying clientele.

Waite explained his fee requirements to Margaret and told her that he could do nothing for a client who is presently represented by another attorney, until that attorney has been discharged. Margaret thanked Mr. Waite for the information, and then quickly called Jarrod and instructed him to see to it that his mother immediately relieved her public defender. She then wrote out a check payable to Copeland, Rogerson & Zenhaus for Robert L. Waite's retainer fee. She couldn't remember when it ever felt so good to spend $30,000.

**28**

"Hello…. Fr. Kearns? This is Mark Tyler. Could you come to my office sometime today?"

Peter's mind raced. When had he ever had a doctor ask to see *him*? Peter was further concerned by the fact that the doctor himself was calling him rather than one of his nurses or receptionists.

"When can you see me?" asked the priest anxiously.

"Can you come in right now?"

That response did nothing to allay the priest's concerns. Father Kearns made a phone call to let one of the committees at his church know that he would not be able to make today's meeting. He then grabbed his overcoat and hurried out the door of the rectory.

When he walked into the waiting area at the doctor's office, the young woman at the front desk spotted the young priest with his black shirt and coat and his clerical collar and immediately greeted him by name.

"Hello Fr. Kearns. Dr. Tyler is expecting you."

The woman opened the door that separated the reception area from the hallway leading to the examination rooms and whisked her patient down to the far end of the hall, past the examination rooms to an office on the left. Dr. Tyler was seated at a large desk in the tastefully decorated office. As the doctor directed him to one of two leather chairs that sat facing the desk, Peter's eyes spied a number of family photos on a credenza behind the young physician's desk.

"Please, have a seat," the doctor intoned, as the priest was halfway down into the chair.

"How are you feeling today?" continued the doctor.

"Not bad." The priest paused momentarily and then added: "But I am rather anxious about my test results, given your call and all."

"Sure. Well, I'll get right to it then." Dr. Tyler walked around to the front of his desk and sat on the edge of the desk, now just three feet away from his patient. "I don't like the looks of your blood tests. Your white blood count is abnormally high. I'd like to run a couple of further tests if we could."

Peter nodded his head in silent assent to the doctor's request, waiting for more information about what the tests would be searching for.

"Do you think it's something serious, doctor?"

"It could be, but I'd rather defer judgment on that until we do these other tests. I'd like to get a chest series on you and then do a biopsy of your hip."

Now the priest was thoroughly perplexed. Surely none of his symptoms sounded like pneumonia, so why the chest x-rays? And although he had experienced some generalized achiness that he'd told the doctor about, he wasn't having any particular problem with his hips.

Seeing his patient's questioning look, the doctor continued.

"I want to rule out some blood disorders, and these tests are used to do that."

"Oh, he just wants to *rule out* something" the priest thought to himself, looking for something in the doctor's words from which to derive a measure of optimism from the doom that he had felt descending upon him with gathering force since the doctor's somewhat ominous phone call.

Dr. Tyler led the priest out of his office and down to a door that had "Radiology" emblazoned in red capital letters on it. He instructed the tech about what he wanted and told his patient that he would meet with him after he had reviewed the films.

"Then we'll schedule your biopsy for later this week at the hospital. We can do that on an out-patient basis."

The priest thanked the doctor and went into the radiology room where he was met by a short, burly man in a white uniform. The tech was wearing a small silver badge that identified him as "Gregory Gladding".

"Just stand here, please," directed the x-ray tech, who immediately disappeared behind a screen and out of sight. Peter heard a series of clicks and whirls and then the tech came back from behind his screen.

"Okay. That's it. If you'll follow me, the doctor will be with you shortly." The burly tech led the priest back down the hall and into a regular patient examination room and then left him with his thoughts.

Peter sat in the hard plastic chair with his back to the wall, between a small desk and an examination table. He didn't know much about the variety of blood disorders that a person could develop, but his mind ran the gamut as he awaited the doctor's return. As he sat pensively in the quiet room, he reached his left hand down into the outside pocket of his jacket and felt for his rosary. He pulled the rosary out of his pocket, brought it toward his bowed head and kissed the small, metal crucifix. Peter then made the sign of the cross and placed the rosary back into his jacket pocket, continuing to hold onto it by the first bead from the cross with his thumb and forefinger. The priest closed his eyes and began silently saying the familiar words of this ancient form of prayer.

When the priest was nearly finished with the fourth decade of the rosary and meditating on Jesus carrying his cross toward the place of his crucifixion, Dr. Tyler came back into the room.

"Your x-rays appear negative, though they will be looked at by a radiologist, just to see if he sees anything I don't see. Can you meet me at the hospital tomorrow morning at about 7:45?" asked the doctor.

"Sure. I'll be there."

"Please don't eat anything after midnight - clear fluids only, okay?"

"Alright, doctor."

The next morning, Peter was lying awake in bed from 4:15 on, looking at the time going slowly on his clock radio and wondering about the condition that he had so long ignored. Finally, at six, he got out of bed and began his morning ritual of shaving, showering and dressing. Peter then walked over to a kneeler just inside the living room in the rectory, where he knelt down in front of a statue of the Sacred Heart of Jesus and recited his morning prayers until it was time to leave for the hospital.

## 29

The front of the form was simple and straightforward enough. It contained basic biographical information, such as names, addresses, dates and places of birth of family members, educational attainment, etc. It was when they got to the backside of the form, where it asked for the desired sentence for the defendant, that Bob and Marianne Bunch began to struggle. Maybe it would be easier if it were in a "multiple-choice" format, but it wasn't. The State wanted the Bunches to tell them what they thought should happen to the man whose carelessness took the life of their teenage daughter. And while they were relieved that they didn't have to endure a trial for their daughter's killer, the issue of his fate was now being thrust upon them while the very fact of Vickie's recent death still wreaked havoc on their previously stable psyches.

All of the extended family and friends who had flown or driven in for the funeral had been back at work for weeks now. But for Bob and Marianne Bunch, the funeral seemed to continue. Vickie's bedroom was a memorial to their beloved daughter's life. Pictures of Vickie with her own friends adorned her room. She had a University of Illinois pennant in the corner of her mirror. She had been accepted into the School of Nursing just a week before she died.

"On one hand, Montoya seems to be a chronic drunk," began Bob Bunch, giving voice to his consideration of the matter. "On the other," he continued, "he has his own family that is suffering too."

Marianne Bunch had a different take on the issue. "He obviously didn't care about what he was doing to our family, so I frankly don't care about his. At least none of them are dead." The anger and hurt inside of Vickie's mother was bubbling to the surface.

"Well, do you think we should recommend something less than the maximum since he did admit to his crime?" offered Bob, attempting to gently push his wife to a softer position.

Marianne closed her eyes and began to sob. Bob scooted closer to her and put his arm around her shoulders, pulling her head to his chest. They sat together in this manner, consoling one another in their mutual grief, for several minutes. Bob finally broke the silence.

"I suppose the judge is probably going to give Montoya a sentence somewhere between what we ask for and what his lawyer requests anyway, so maybe you're right…."

Marianne cut him off. "No, Bob, *you're* right. I hate to be so … hateful. Let's recommend a couple of years off the standard sentence since he has at least admitted to what he did. He really did seem sincere when he spoke in court."

Bob Bunch smiled at his wife and hugged her again. They both felt a bit of relief about the decision they had made, painful as it was to get there.

**30**

"She did *what?*" shouted Fannie incredulously.

"You heard me right, Momma. You got yourself a top-notch lawyer now," Jarrod answered, as he faced his mother through the glass in the visiting room. Jarrod himself was beaming.

As though checking her own excitement to keep from getting carried away, Fannie added: "You know, he might tell us the same thing as the public defender."

"He might, Momma, but I don't think so," Jarrod replied, refusing to allow his unalloyed enthusiasm to be dampened just now.

"Well, the Lord must've heard our prayers, Jarrod. That's why we should never lose faith."

"I know, Momma. I know."

Fannie asked her son to phone the public defender's office to let them know that their services would no longer be needed. She was eager to meet her "real lawyer" and Jarrod assured her that he'd stop in to see her as soon as the lawyer's schedule permitted. Fannie knew that her ordeal was far from over, but it was great to be warmed by the sunshine of this good news, that had finally broken through the clouds of her despair. Fannie couldn't wait to personally thank her generous benefactor, whom she had known but little during her stay at St. Francis Hospital.

"You never know who the Lord is going to use to do His work," Fannie told her son in a voice filled with wonder. Jarrod listened to his mother's continuing expressions of gratitude throughout his visit, nodding his head repeatedly as he smiled broadly and patted his mother's hand.

# 31

It was two days since Peter Kearns' biopsy. The doctor had scheduled this appointment at his office at the same time that he scheduled the out-patient procedure at the hospital. He wanted to discuss the results of the biopsy with his patient, regardless of the outcome. As the young physician entered the room, he smiled at the priest, but the perceptive patient noticed that the smile appeared to be more forced than the smile he had seen on the doctor before. It seemed to evaporate quickly from the corners of the doctor's lips as he addressed his patient.

"I'm afraid the biopsy told us something we didn't want it to tell us, Father."

The young priest raised his eyebrows expectantly as the doctor continued.

"It looks as though you do have a serious blood disorder.... that appears to be a type of leukemia."

The priest nodded thoughtfully, saying nothing and maintaining a stoic countenance, as the doctor went on to explain the options that were available to treat the condition, periodically using phrases such as "chances for remission" and "life expectancy from the date of diagnosis".

When Dr. Tyler finished explaining the various courses of treatment available and offered the name of a cancer specialist he knew, Fr. Kearns responded simply and politely.

"That would be fine, doctor. I'll take your advice on this."

"Okay, good. I'll get you an appointment with Dr. Cappel right away. The quicker we act on this, the better your chances of recovery.

Later that day, Fr. Kearns went to the YMCA to meet with his regular AA group. Margaret hadn't seen her friend for a couple of weeks. She told him how she was helping Fannie Williams and caught him up on the more mundane things she had been doing since they were last together. Then she got to the subject that the priest had not discussed with anyone since his meeting earlier that day at the doctor's office.

"So what's the doctor telling you, Peter? Does he know what's causing your problems yet?"

The priest suggested that they discuss it after the meeting, and they agreed to meet afterward for dinner at a pizza place that they'd gone to several times before. When Margaret pulled up along the curb outside "Bruno's Pizzaria," she saw that Fr. Kearns' car was already parked across the street. Margaret walked inside the front door and found Peter standing in the foyer. Peter stepped toward Margaret and held the hand that she extended for him. The pair followed the hostess to the booth.

As they slid into opposite sides of the booth, Margaret teased her friend, playfully.

"I'm trying to start rumors, being seen in public with the parish priest."

"I feel like I'm living kind of dangerously every time you grace my presence, Margaret," Peter replied with a wink.

After a couple of minutes of small-talk, their conversation was briefly interrupted by the waitress, who took their drink order - two Diet Cokes - and then left them to get their drinks. The menus were left on the table as the two continued in conversation.

"I think our waitress used to go to our grade school," said Peter. "I want to say she was a volleyball player or something...some sort of athlete," he added, as he squinted his eyes as though to see back in time more clearly.

Within moments, the young waitress with shoulder-length, light-brown hair returned with the drinks on a tray. While she was writing down their orders, Peter's eyes suddenly widened and Margaret could almost see the proverbial light bulb illuminate above his head.

"Aren't you Millie Boatwright?" asked Peter triumphantly.

"Yes, Fr. Kearns," the waitress replied, surprising the priest with her own recall.

"What have you been up to for the past few years? I haven't seen you in ages."

A rather sheepish countenance came over the girl. She confessed to the priest that she had stopped going to church a couple of years ago.

"Well, Millie, you know you're more than welcome to come back any time."

"Thanks, Father, I might do that sometime," Millie replied unconvincingly.

After the waitress left the table, Margaret turned to her friend and asked him the question that had been on her mind throughout all the chit-chat since they had left the Y.

"What did Dr. Tyler have to say, Peter?" Margaret asked expectantly.

The priest pulled the straw from his Diet Coke and set it on the table before him. He then picked up the glass, lifted it to his open mouth and took a big swig of the drink, catching an ice cube between his teeth as he brought the glass back to level and then set it down on the table. The ice cube was tucked into Peter's cheek as he looked at Margaret and answered her.

"I guess I'm pretty sick, Margaret," Peter stated, causing his friend's mind to race with possibilities.

"What in the world does he think is wrong with you, Peter?" Margaret inquired, now less certain that she even wanted to know the answer.

Peter got up from the booth, walked around to Margaret's side, and slid in beside her. He grasped one of her hands between both of his and rested them on the table. He paused for a moment, and then calmly informed her that he had been diagnosed with leukemia.

Placing her free hand on top of the priest's soft, uncalloused hands, she parted her lips to respond, but then stopped herself by gently biting her top lip with her bottom row of teeth. Tears welled up in the older woman's eyes as she looked at the young man who had helped to bring her back from a spiritual and emotional abyss and had become such an important fixture in her life.

For a brief instant, Peter's eyes too appeared to glisten, but in a strong and steady voice he attempted to reassure Margaret.

"They've come a long way in recent years in treating leukemia and all kinds of cancers, Margaret. I'm young and strong. People a lot worse off than me have licked this thing, and the good Lord willing, so will I."

Although Peter was now smiling at her, Margaret was overwrought and embraced him in the booth.

Sobbing gently as she hugged him, Margaret did her best to emulate Peter's optimism.

"He *shall* will it… and so will I."

**32**

Fannie sat in her cell on the edge of her bed, knitting a decorative pillow cover as a small expression of her gratitude to Margaret Millington. Fannie'a aunt taught her to knit when she was around ten, but she hadn't tried her hand at the hobby for over twenty-five years until she was locked up. "It's kind of funny, the things that get pushed aside by the demands of daily living," reflected Fannie. Now she was finding that knitting helped pass time while she spent her days waiting for an opportunity to clear her name.

"Fannie Williams!" The jailer was outside of Fannie's cell block, unlocking the door to her block and then walking down the hall toward her cell.

"Step back!" boomed the jailer perfunctorily, without really looking up to notice whether Fannie was standing by the door to her cell or not.

The jailer was older and tired-looking. As he swung open the door to her cell and then led her back down the hall toward one of the attorney conference rooms, Fannie observed that the jailer's skin appeared a whitish-gray, as though he himself no longer ventured outside the walls of the jail, but had become just another fixture in the gloomy, old chambers.

As soon as the jailer opened the door to the conference room, Fannie saw him. Robert L. Waite didn't even look like the public defenders she had spoken with before. Tall and slim with a full head of silver hair that contrasted with his stylish, black-framed glasses, the man exuded a confident professionalism. Fannie had a good feeling about him immediately. Extending a hand to his new client, Waite introduced himself.

"Ms. Williams? Bob Waite. It's nice to meet you."

The words rolled off the barrister's tongue with the mellifluence of a professional golf broadcaster. Waite had a firm handshake. Fannie noticed that he also had piercing grey eyes - the type that made you feel that by looking into them you might be exposing your innermost thoughts to his penetrating review.

"It's nice to meet you," Fannie replied, barely managing to conceal her nearly childlike glee.

The client and attorney sat down at a small metal table, which Fannie imagined had been witness to countless similar meetings between the accused and their defenders over the years. Waite laid his thin leather briefcase on the table, sprung it open, retrieved a traditional eight and one-half by fourteen inch yellow legal pad and set it in front of him on the table. Primed to begin talking about the circumstances leading to the battery of her former boyfriend, Fannie was caught off guard as the attorney instead began the interview by asking Fannie about her early childhood and slowly worked forward in time.

An hour and a half into the biographical portrait of his new client that he was composing, Waite finally started talking to Fannie about her relationship with Maurice. At about the time that Fannie was explaining to Waite how they had met, the jailer returned to the conference room and, after knocking on the door, unlocked it and announced that dinner was being served to the inmates. The jailer offered to allow Waite to wait for Fannie in the conference room, and, to Fannie's surprise, he accepted.

"That would be fine, thank you." And looking now to Fannie: "That will give me a chance to review my notes."

"Alright then. She'll be back in about 30 minutes." The jailer led

Fannie out of the room and back down the hall, as her attorney sat back down at the table.

Twenty-five minutes later, Fannie was returned to the conference room, now by a jailer from the evening shift. Fannie resumed her seat next to Waite and they began talking about her life with Maurice Thompson. Waite wanted to know everything about Thompson there was to know. He asked Fannie about Thompson's own family, his marriages and relationships, and his criminal history. Fannie answered all of these questions to the best of her ability, but with varying amounts of available information. At each point where Fannie's knowledge was limited, Waite explored with her the most likely sources where the information might be obtained. Unbeknownst to Fannie, Waite had an investigator and a bevy of staffers from the law firm that he would set to work filling in the blanks later.

At 7:45 p.m., nearly three hours after his arrival, Robert Waite stood up and stretched. He pushed a button by the door that summoned the jailer. He thanked Fannie for bearing with him under his extensive questioning. As Waite reached out to shake her hand, it was Fannie's turn to surprise Waite. She ignored his hand and walked up and hugged him.

"Thank you for taking my case, Mr. Waite, and God bless you." Waite broke into a broad smile and promised Fannie that he would give her case his best efforts. After spending the afternoon with the man, that's all Fannie needed to hear.

**33**

In the men's section of the same jail, Antonio Montoya was sitting in his cell looking at an issue of Time magazine from eight months earlier, which had been donated by a local philanthropic organization that sought to broaden the horizons of the county's boarders as they pined away their days in this short-term holding facility. The inmates in the Cook County Jail were either being detained awaiting trial, or were serving time for sentences of less than six months, generally for a misdemeanor or low-grade felony crime. Once an inmate was sentenced for any offense for a term of six months or longer, he was shipped out to one of Illinois' many state correctional facilities.

The next day, Antonio was going to be sentenced for the deaths of the girls he had killed in his drunken ignorance. As a result, he found himself staring at the pages of the Time magazine and realized that his mind was a million miles away from the articles that his eyes had been scanning. Finally, he put the magazine down on the end of his bed and stood up in his cell. Antonio walked over to the door of his cell and looked across the hall to the cell of Arenzo Blackmun, a nineteen-year-old who was also going to be sentenced the next day. Blackmun had been convicted of dealing crack cocaine in his neighborhood on the city's south side. Blackmun was sitting on the floor of his cell, with his back against the door, his long braids hanging out of the door.

"Hey Blackmun," Antonio called, just loud enough to get the attention of the young convict.

Blackmun turned and looked at Antonio, not yet giving any audible response to his greeter. Blackmun's expression was one of nothing more than mild curiosity, presumably wondering why his normally silent blockmate was addressing him now. Antonio continued.

"You going to court tomorrow, aren't you?" Antonio asked.

"Yeah, man, finally. You?"

"Yeah. Do you have a deal?" Antonio wondered if the young man had any more of an idea about what his sentence was going to be than Antonio himself had.

"No. I had a P.D.," Blackmun answered, referring unflatteringly to his public defender.

Antonio laughed. "Man, I thought *you* had the rocks, not your lawyer."

"You been down before?" Antonio had quickly picked up the lexicon of the jail house.

"Yeah. I been in a couple times."

"Where'd you go before?" Antonio pressed inquisitively.

"I did eight months in Peoria when I was sixteen and got two years last year, but only had to do a year."

"Where did you go that time?"

"Downstate in the sticks."

Antonio, the senior in age if not in criminal exploits, was clearly seeking to learn what to expect the next day and knew Blackmun had more experience in these matters.

"So where do they send dudes like me?" Antonio asked.

"Man, I don't know. You got bigger problems than I've had," Blackmun taunted mildly. "You'll probably go someplace with more bars than I've seen, since ..." Blackmun's words trailed off as he made eye contact with Antonio and saw in Antonio's steady gaze that he found no humor in this subject.

He quickly ditched the smirk and decided to drop the pretense of knowing more about the local criminal justice scene than he really did. In this case it could only get him into trouble

"Hey, just ask your lawyer, man," Blackmun suggested cautiously.

"I don't have a lawyer. I hoped maybe you were the next best thing."

Now Antonio's mouth showed the slightest hint of a smile, but Blackmun just shrugged his shoulders and faced forward in his cell once again, allowing his head to rest against the door of his cell. Antonio realized that the conversation, and Blackmun's well of useful information, had run dry, so he walked slowly back to the far side of his cell, away from the door.

Just as Antonio had returned to his previous position on the edge of his bed and had picked up the magazine again, he heard the booming voice of Carl, the 330-pound black jailer who worked the hoot-owl shift and had been one of the kinder jailers since Antonio had been locked up.

"Montoya. You've got a visitor."

Antonio was surprised by Carl's announcement. He knew that it wasn't visiting hour, or visiting day for that matter. The only exception to the regularly scheduled visiting hours of which he was aware was for lawyers, and, of course, Antonio didn't have a lawyer.

Nevertheless, Antonio wasn't kept in the dark for long, because just a few paces behind Carl walked Antonio's visitor. As soon as he appeared from the shadows of the hall outside Antonio's door, Antonio recognized the familiar visage of his parish priest, the ubiquitous Fr. Peter Kearns.

Although it was good to see a familiar face, especially one as friendly as Fr. Kearns', Antonio felt ashamed to be seen by his parish priest in this place. And he really didn't feel much like entertaining company in any case.

"How are you doing, Antonio?" the priest asked as he offered the inmate his hand.

Montoya shook his pastor's hand, but kept his head down and made little effort at direct eye contact with his visitor.

"Okay, Father. Thanks for coming."

The response was painfully obligatory in its tone and delivery, and Antonio didn't really care. He had a great deal of respect for Fr. Kearns, but he was so filled with self-loathing and shame that he didn't feel worthy of a visitor like this. Antonio put his hands in his pockets and when he finally made eye contact with the priest, Antonio gave a shrug of the shoulders as if to ask his visitor what brought him to this unholy site.

Fr. Kearns was saddened to see the resigned and defeated look on Antonio's face. Whenever he had been around him before, Antonio had seemed possessed of a confident air that had evidently been sucked away by his recent experiences.

Without being invited to do so, Peter sat down on the edge of Antonio's bed and scooted down to one end. "Sit down and talk to me," said the priest, patting the far end of the hard, narrow form of lightly cushioned steel. Antonio complied, albeit with visible reluctance.

"How's the food?" Peter asked, still trying to break the ice.

"It's fine," lied Antonio. He had barely tasted the food since his incarceration, not so much because it was poor but because he had lost his appetite.

"Well, your face looks thinner, so I just wondered."

Antonio unconsciously reached up to his unshaven face as though to verify the accuracy of the priest's observation. He slowly stroked his whiskers and gazed vacantly across the cell.

With the formalities out of the way, the young priest addressed the inmate more substantively. "Is there anything I can do for you, Antonio?" asked Peter in a fatherly tone.

"Pray for Juanita and the kids," replied Antonio with a rapidity indicating that his family's well-being was always uppermost in his mind.

"I do, Antonio. ...And for you too. Is there anything else?"

Antonio sat quietly, considering the priest's question. After several seconds, Antonio answered.

126

"Yes, Father. Could you tell the Bennings and the Bunches that I am …. ." His words choked off as he was suddenly overtaken with emotion. No longer able to sit still, Antonio sprang from his bed and began pacing wildly, back and forth across his cell, grabbing his hair with both hands. Obviously overwrought, Antonio spun back facing his visitor, and, trying to regain some semblance of composure, began again.

"Tell the girls' families that I am so sorry. I am so terribly sorry."

The larger man's shoulders began shaking uncontrollably and tears began to stream down his face. Weeks of pent-up sorrow burst forth in torrents of tears and unrestrained emotion. Fr. Kearns gave him space, not wanting to intrude on this psychological milestone that he knew had to run its course before Antonio would be ready to move forward.

After several minutes, the audible sobbing subsided and Peter Kearns walked over to Antonio and put his hand on the man's shoulder from behind. Antonio wiped his eyes with the back of his hand and turned towards the priest. Peter kept his hand on the shoulder of the sorrowful prisoner who stood before him. Antonio turned and faced the priest who then spoke to him.

"The Bunches and the Bennings probably suspect that you're sorry, but it wouldn't hurt for you to send them each a letter telling them so. I would be happy to deliver them for you," offered the priest. "But it is equally important for you to forgive yourself," he continued.

"I don't deserve to be forgiven, Father," Antonio replied with absolute conviction.

As the inmate lowered his head in shame, the priest addressed him in a voice just above a whisper. "Look at me, please, Antonio."

Antonio lifted his head, revealing tear-filled eyes and a reddened face, contorted by intense emotion.

"You yourself are a child, Antonio - a child of God our Father. You were made in his image and he loves you to a degree greater than you even have the capacity to comprehend in this lifetime. So you *do* deserve to be forgiven, if for no other reason than your importance to your heavenly Father."

Antonio remained silent as Peter continued.

The young priest became more animated now and spoke forcefully. "Our Savior's entire life on earth was about the redemptive power of forgiveness and the love that motivates it. If you will forgive yourself and muster the courage to ask Christ for forgiveness, Jesus not only is *capable* of forgiving you; he will have already forgiven you and put your sin out of His mind forever by the time your own apology passes your lips."

Antonio felt the priest's grip on his shoulder tighten as he spoke. The light of faith emanating from Peter Kearns' expression was nearly palpable, so radiantly was it shining at this moment.

Not knowing what else to say in response to his visitor's powerful statement, Antonio promised him that he would follow his advice.

"Good. Can I pick up your letters tomorrow?" Peter asked.

"Sure, Father. I'll write them this evening and give them to you tomorrow."

The jailer was summoned and promptly returned to the cell to escort the priest out of the cell block. As Peter Kearns walked out of the jail, he noticed that the air outside was fresher and easier to breathe than the dank, musty air in the depths of the jail. What he could not fully appreciate was the extent to which he had breathed life back into the soul of Antonio Montoya.

## 34

Back at home, Margaret finished dinner at the breakfast bar in her kitchen alone and in silence. She didn't know whether it was the stress of Peter's health news or simply a new phase in her alcohol addiction, but Margaret's thoughts about her young friend were persistently being interrupted by and interspersed with fantasies of sitting on her living room couch and indulging in a bottomless cocktail. To distract herself from these distractions, Margaret picked up the remote control to her kitchen television and flipped it on. A romantic film from the '90s filled the screen of the L.E.D. television and Margaret tried to get into the movie, which appeared to be to a fairly advanced stage, by what she could gather. About ten minutes into her viewing of the show, the main couple of the show ended up in a scene in a bar, sipping martinis.

Margaret cursed under her breath and flicked off the TV, rising from her chair and retrieving her phone from her purse. For the first of several times in the coming weeks, Margaret called Jasmine, a woman half her age with nearly five years of sobriety who had agreed to serve as her sponsor. In the struggles with addiction, some days were certainly easier than others.

**35**

It was a cool, cloudy Monday in downtown Chicago. The Willis Tower and a few of the other tall buildings in the city's skyline extended up through the clouds. An occasional sprinkle could be felt by the teeming pedestrians milling below, all on their way to somewhere, but for the most part, oblivious to one another as they each headed for their own destinations.

At a point nearly equidistant between the ceiling created by the clouds and the people below stood the Windy City Commercial Center. A monument to modern architecture, dropped amidst buildings that had stood for over a century, the Windy City Commercial Center stood 28 stories tall. Halfway up this structure that was home to a bank, a commercial real estate agency and a handful of miscellaneous offices and shops was the law firm of Copeland, Rogerson & Zenhaus.

The law firm was presently comprised of forty-two partners and seventy-five associate attorneys, along with several dozen paralegals and secretaries. Like many 21$^{st}$ century law firms, Copeland, Rogerson and Zenhaus was somewhat of an amalgamation of disparate law "sections" that had evolved over the years.

Steven Copeland, a corporate attorney who died in 1970, was a founding member of the firm. William Rogerson, a tax law specialist, had headed up the firm's tax section. Although he died in 1984, his son, William Rogerson II, had followed in his father's footsteps and currently headed the firm's tax section. Marvin Zenhaus, a civil litigator, had come over to Copeland & Rogerson twenty years ago from a competitor, which happened to be Chicago's largest law firm. He was now the firm's senior partner, and at seventy-two years of age, Zenhaus continued to bill fifty hours a week.

Down the hall from Zenhaus's corner office was the office of Robert L. Waite. Waite was supported in the criminal section of the firm by four partners and ten associates, all of whom, except for the three newest associates, were together at an independent criminal firm until joining Copeland, Rogerson and Zenhaus about ten years ago. They were brought aboard as part of the firm's effort to become a full-service law firm. Waite himself was an indefatigable leader, for whom the law was both his vocation and avocation. Waite was known among his subordinates as a perfectionist; however, the standards he set for himself were the strictest of all.

On this particular Monday morning, Waite had put three associates, with a paralegal to assist each, on the Fannie Williams case. He authorized his team to retain an investigator, if necessary, in order to uncover every fact that supported his client's defense. And Waite had scheduled daily meetings at five in the evening so that he could stay abreast of all developments and maintain control over the direction of the effort.

The associates assigned to the Williams case included one man and two women. The man was thirty-two-year-old Paul Erikson, a Yale-educated bachelor whose work habits closely paralleled those of his boss. As a result, it appeared that this associate was well on his way to becoming a partner in the firm. Erikson, though not the oldest, was the senior member of the team of associates working on Fannie's case in terms of his status in the law firm.

The two female associates on the case were Karen Grigsby, a thirty-year-old attorney from Atlanta. She was married and the mother of two elementary-school-age daughters. Grigsby was especially skilled at using the computer to dig up useful information on cases, and was asked by Waite to direct the research on this case.

The final member of the criminal defense team was Eleanor Rubin, a divorced associate attorney, thirty-seven years old, with vast litigation experience in the Cook County Public Defender's Office. Rubin had developed a specialty in domestic abuse cases. She also had strong working relationships with the staffs in all of Chicago's criminal courts and was considered by Waite to be a valuable addition to his section of the firm.

Although all of the lawyers on the Williams case had a number of different cases they were working on, both for Waite and for the other partners in the section, Waite made it clear that he wanted this case to be given priority status. No other case that any of these associates were assigned involved the degree of daily oversight that Waite was instituting in this case.

At the end of the day, the team assembled in the conference room shared between the criminal section and the workers compensation section, whose offices adjoined those of the criminal defense lawyers. Waite took his place at the head of the table and, after a few opening comments, asked for reports from each of the attorneys who had begun work on the case. Waite's personal secretary, Monique Duvall, took shorthand notes of each report for her boss.

Since they had just begun work on the Williams' case, each attorney at this first daily conference presented outlines of the case strategies they had developed to accomplish their assigned duties within the time allotted by Waite. Waite asked Grigsby to give her report first.

The tall, attractive woman with brown skin, whose hair was neatly braided to her head, rose to address the team. She explained the precise state of the law on the particular type of self-defense that was going to be advanced on Fannie's behalf. Because there was no immediate threat of violence by the victim of Fannie's battery, it was going to be necessary to establish the specific pattern of conduct her boyfriend had engaged in during the term of their relationship, in order to establish that it was reasonable for Fannie to fear him at the time of her attack. Grigsby provided the names and citations of appellate cases within the jurisdiction that dealt with this issue and summarized each of these cases for the team.

The next attorney to address the team was Eleanor Rubin. Barely five feet tall, this exceedingly well-spoken woman quickly dispelled any doubts created by her diminutive stature that she was indeed a force to be reckoned with. Rubin was going to be handling the interviewing of witnesses and helping Waite to prepare for the discovery depositions of all of the witnesses who were expected to testify in the case. Because the list of witnesses would necessarily grow as the discovery process unfolded, Rubin's statement on this opening day of case preparation was very brief.

The architect of the team's discovery plan was Paul Erikson, who was the final attorney to address the group. Erikson reviewed the discovery plan that he had begun to develop, calling for interrogatories, requests for production of documents and depositions. The goal of this discovery was to obtain as much evidence as possible to support the defense's theory of the case. Erikson drew charts on the presentation board in the conference room to list the areas of his intended focus and to explain the sequence of the specific discovery tools he intended to employ to find what he needed to build the case.

Immediately before the meeting began, the associates murmured among themselves about what appeared to them to be an unusual use of the "team approach" to a legal defense. Most of the time, if more than two attorneys worked together on a case it was due to the complexity of the subject matter. Here there were four attorneys on a relatively straight-forward battery case. Erikson himself opined that it seemed a bit of an overkill. What none of the three associates assigned to the case yet realized, however, was that Marvin Zenhaus had made it clear to Waite that a very important client of the firm was providing this defense for Fannie Williams. Waite had no intention of letting his senior partner, or Margaret Millington, down. And it didn't take long for Fannie's winsome personality to give Waite added incentive to do his best. If this defense ultimately proved unsuccessful, it was certainly not going to be for a lack of preparation.

**36**

Dr. Amelia Cappel was a highly regarded oncologist with a national reputation. Dr. Tyler had been referring his cancer patients to her since she moved her offices from Kansas City to Chicago nine years earlier. Dr. Cappel was sixty-six years old. A Swiss emigrant, she possessed a confident air and retained just a trace of an accent. While Dr. Cappel treated a variety of cancers, she had developed somewhat of a subspecialty in the treatment of blood disorders such as leukemia.

Fr. Kearns had been sitting in the patient waiting room for approximately ten minutes when Dr. Cappel, taller than the priest by a couple of inches, entered the room, trailed by a female nurse who appeared to be carrying Fr. Kearns' medical records. After quick introductions, the physician performed a routine physical examination of her new patient and then began to answer the range of questions which, as with most patients, filled Fr. Kearns' head. Finally, she addressed *the* question that predominated in the priest's mind: how was this disease to be treated?

"I would like to schedule you for a bone marrow transplant. But first, we need to treat the cancerous cells with an aggressive regimen of chemotherapy and then do a transplant to eventually get you producing healthy blood cells again."

Fr. Kearns nodded his understanding. He knew little about leukemia at this point, but he was aware that transplanting bone marrow was a part of the treatment for the disease. And Dr. Cappel continued.

"Medicine has achieved dramatic gains in the treatment of leukemias and really all cancers. However, you have a very rare type of an acute leukemia that is unusually aggressive and will ultimately require a bone marrow transplant from a blood relative donor. I would suggest that you talk to your family members about this right away."

The priest shifted in his seat and cleared his throat before responding.

"How important is it to have a family member donate the bone marrow?" he asked.

"Well, as I said, we have advanced in our treatment of most leukemias where there are other treatments available, including stem cell transplants, autologous transplants, various chemotherapies and many other treatment modalities. Unfortunately, for this particular form of cancer, which I have never personally seen before but am familiar with from the literature, a bone marrow transplant from a blood relative is the only treatment that has been found to be effective. Chemotherapy is used to kill the diseased blood cells prior to the transplant, but eventually the transplant is imperative." The doctor, sensing that this seemed to be causing some unease for her patient asked him directly: "Do you have any promising prospects?" asked Dr. Cappel.

"Not immediately, doctor. To tell you the truth, I was raised in foster homes and do not know any of my biological family. My foster parents didn't know my biological parents. I don't even know if I have any blood relatives living and wouldn't know where to begin looking."

Peter queried Dr. Cappel further about the other treatments for leukemia, asking her specifically about the autologous transplants. Dr. Cappel then explained in layman's terms how this particular treatment uses the patient's own blood and is highly effective with a number of leukemias and other cancers. Unfortunately, this form of treatment was completely ineffective for Peter's condition. She then went into considerable detail explaining how she would proceed with his treatment over the coming weeks and months. But the doctor said she was extremely reluctant to begin the process until a donor was located unless his worsening condition left them no choice.

"And if no donor is *ever* found doctor?" Peter asked.

Dr. Cappel put her finger to her lip in a pose of deep contemplation. "Let's see what you can come up with Father, and we'll be ready to schedule your chemo as soon as something works out."

The doctor and her patient spoke for a few minutes longer and then Dr. Cappel ordered an extensive series of blood samples. She told Fr. Kearns that his information would be entered into a database so that she could determine the ideal criteria for the relative donor. Depending upon the speed with which an appropriate donor could be identified, the transplant could be performed within weeks. In the meantime, Fr. Kearns was put on three different medications to begin readying his body for the procedures that awaited him.

## 37

"Let's go, Montoya," boomed the familiar bass voice of Carl the jailer. Although his eyes had been closed when Carl arrived outside his cell, Antonio hadn't slept the entire night. While he remained at peace with his decision to plead guilty to the charges against him, Antonio couldn't help but consider his fate.

"We're showering today, Montoya. Got to look good for the judge," Carl said with a wink. Carl was well aware of how anxious Antonio was to put the sentencing behind him. In truth, Antonio was prepared for the worst, and didn't hold out great hopes that his sentence would be much shorter than the maximum.

"If you're the judge," Antonio said, looking at the jailer, "you give me the max and satisfy the girls' families. The only one you risk upsetting is the con. But if you give a break to the con, you got the families and the whole D.A.'s office to deal with, not to mention the press. You see any other way of looking at it, Carl?"

"I don't get involved in any of that," answered the jailer, gesturing as though waving Antonio off and turning away from him, but smiling all the while.

Antonio was led out of his cell to the showers. "Two minutes," Carl reminded his prisoner, no longer smiling but reassuming the mantle of authority over his charge.

Exactly two minutes later Antonio was dripping back toward his cell with his towel draped over his shoulders. Carl was now holding a suit that was neatly folded. He extended the bundle to Antonio, who appeared to be caught off guard.

"Your wife brought these for you. Don't get too comfortable in them though," kidded the jailer, as Antonio began looking through the clothes that he had just been handed. It was his one and only suit, a navy-blue one that he had bought for a wedding about five or six years earlier and had worn only two or three times since. He also had a neatly pressed white dress shirt, which Antonio immediately realized was new, along with a red and white print tie.

Seeing these civilian clothes was surprisingly painful for Antonio, who was reminded by the clothes of how different he felt the last time he wore the suit. "It's funny how we take freedom for granted," Antonio thought to himself philosophically.

A few minutes later, Antonio was adjusting his tie in the mirror and was then handcuffed for the trip to the courthouse.

For the first time, Antonio was led by a pair of sheriff's deputies into the courtroom unaccompanied by the chain gang. The deputies instructed Antonio to sit in one of the pews in the visitors' gallery, while they waited for his case to be called. Antonio looked around the half-filled courtroom. Behind him he saw a group of people whom he recognized as the Bennings and the Bunches, along with some of their friends who were providing moral support. He made only fleeting eye contact with one of the girls' mothers - he wasn't sure which - and saw only sorrow. He remembered those very same eyes at his initial hearing, when he learned what it meant to have daggers metaphorically shot at him from another person's stare.

Antonio quickly cast his eyes down to avoid further eye contact. He then looked up cautiously to the other side of the courtroom and quickly found Juanita sitting in the front row, behind the defense table. She too was dressed up and had her long, brown hair down, allowing it to flow over her shoulders. Juanita's eyes met his and she smiled. Antonio, fully conscious of the eyes upon him, would not allow himself to smile back. But he nodded to Juanita as he maintained eye contact with her for several seconds.

"All rise," intoned the nasal voice of the bailiff, as mechanically as though it were the only phrased he'd ever uttered. "Cook County Superior Court is now in session, the Honorable Javitt Grant presiding."

The sentencing judge had not been present at the earlier stages of the proceedings. Judge Grant appeared to be racially mixed - maybe black and white, maybe some American-Indian. He was very tall, probably six-five, Antonio guessed, and very thin. He appeared to be in his late fifties or early sixties.

"The first case …The People of Illinois v. Antonio Montoya."

Antonio stood and was quickly brought to the defense table. Across from him at the other table was the female assistant D.A. whom he recognized from previous hearings. The judge advised all present that he had received a copy of the probation department's pre-sentence report, and told the bailiff to provide a copy to the defendant. The bailiff walked over to the defense table and handed Antonio his copy. No longer handcuffed, Antonio reached out and thanked the bailiff. The judge then asked the district attorney to begin the proceedings by calling the State's first witness.

"The People calls Marianne Bunch," said Janet Houser, the deputy district attorney, in what sounded like a stage voice.

Marianne Bunch was seated in the second row of the spectators' gallery, next to her husband. When she heard her name announced, Marianne Bunch released the grip she had on her husband's hand and stood to approach the witness stand.

Judge Grant nodded a somber greeting to the witness, whose identity he must have either known or guessed. As she came to the witness chair, the judge raised his own hand as a signal to the witness.

"Do you swear or affirm under the penalties for perjury that the testimony you are about to give will be the truth, the whole truth and nothing but the truth?"

"I do," answered the woman in a surprisingly strong voice.

"You may ask," directed the judge, now looking at the deputy district attorney.

Janet Houser appeared to be in her mid-thirties. Today, she was wearing a navy blue suit and had her frosted hair pulled up and pinned on top of her head. She was slender and had a long, narrow face with high cheek bones. She had a deep tan and an athletic look to her. As she stood at the prosecution table to address the witness, Marianne Bunch turned in her chair to face her questioner.

"Please state your name for the court."

"My name is Marianne Bunch."

"And where do you reside?"

"I live at 4236 West Walnut Creek Drive, Evergreen Park, Illinois," answered Mrs. Bunch.

"What is your relationship to Vickie Bunch, one of the two victims in this case?" continued the D.A.

"I am her mother," responded Mrs. Bunch, unable to avoid having her inflection altered slightly with emotion.

"And you have prepared a victim's statement for the court today, have you not?" asked Houser.

"Yes. Yes I have."

"May I approach the witness, Your Honor," asked the attorney, respectfully facing the judge's bench with her hands folded neatly behind her back.

"You may," responded the judge, as he motioned with his hand for the prosecutor to step forward.

"Mrs. Bunch, I am going to hand you what has been marked for identification as "People's Exhibit A" and ask if you can identify this document for the court.

The witness reached up and received the exhibit from the prosecutor. It appeared to be two or three pages long.

"Yes. This is the victim's impact statement that my husband, Bob, and I prepared.

"And does this statement accurately address how the Defendant's criminal act has affected your family?"

"Yes. I think it does," answered the witness sorrowfully.

As Marianne Bunch was looking at her statement and answering, Houser was handing a photocopy of the exhibit to Antonio, who left it lying on the table in front of him as he kept his attention riveted on the witness.

"I'd like to offer People's Exhibit A, Your Honor," announced the D.A. as she again faced the judge.

The judge looked at Antonio and said to him: "Mr. Montoya. Do you want to read this statement and let me know if you have any objection to it being taken into evidence and considered by me in making my decision today?"

Antonio picked up a corner of the document, looked down at it for just an instant, and then glanced quickly over at the witness and then back to Judge Grant.

"No. That's okay, Your Honor. I don't have any problem with that."

"There being no objection from the Defendant, People's A is admitted," intoned the judge, taking on a more authoritative tone.

"And, please, tell the court," continued the prosecutor, "in your own words, how this has affected your family, Mrs. Bunch."

The witness looked at Antonio and then looked up, as if to heaven, and exhaled long and slowly before speaking.

"Our lives have been changed forever," she began. "Since Vickie was a baby, our dreams for ourselves gradually gave way to our dreams for her." Tears were now visibly welling up in the witness' eyes.

"Vickie was the center of our lives…. We looked forward to our only child giving us grandchildren in the next few years and coming to see us with her children as we grew old together…." The witness was now softly sobbing on the witness stand, and half of the people in the gallery were becoming misty-eyed too. After what started out as a hesitation - a break to regain her composure - it was clear that the witness was through with her testimony. Ms. Houser walked over to her witness and offered her a box of tissues. The witness reached for one and nodded her appreciation. As she walked back toward the prosecution table, Houser announced to the court that she had no further questions.

Judge Grant then asked Antonio if he had any questions for Mrs. Bunch. Antonio simply shook his bowed head, directing his gaze to the table in front of him.

The judge then instructed the State to call its next witness.

"The People call Robert Bradford," said the deputy D.A. with noticeably less drama.

Bradford was a white-haired probation officer, whose full-figured form poured out of the sides of the witness chair as he seated himself before the judge after being sworn.

"Please state your name and occupation for the court," resumed the prosecutor with her new witness.

"I am Robert Bradford, Cook County Probation Officer."

"And how long have you worked in this county in that capacity?" Houser continued.

"I have been an adult probation officer for thirty-two years," replied Bradford.

"And have you been assigned the task of preparing the pre-sentence report for the court in the case of People vs. Antonio Montoya?"

"I have."

"And have you, in fact, submitted your report to the court," continued the D.A.

"Yes, I have."

"I've read the pre-sentence report," stated Judge Grant from his perch behind the bench. The judge then briefly interrupted the questioning by directing another question to Antonio.

"Mr. Montoya, I understand that you have been provided with a copy of the pre-sentence report, is that correct?" asked the judge.

"Yes, Your Honor. I read it yesterday."

"Do you have any corrections to the factual information contained in that report?" asked the Judge.

"No sir. I believe it's all accurate," responded the Defendant.

The judge then turned back to the prosecutor. "You may continue, Ms. Houser."

The deputy D.A. then took the witness through Antonio's family and work history and then finally got to the heart of the hearing.

"What sentence do you recommend to the court, Mr. Bradford?" asked Houser, looking over to the Defendant as though to gauge his reaction to the witness' testimony.

"We would recommend that the Defendant serve a term of four years, executed, Your Honor."

Judge Grant then put a question to the deputy D.A. herself. "Do you concur in that recommendation, Ms. Houser?"

"Yes, Your Honor."

"Very well," continued the judge. "Mr. Montoya, you also have a right to ask any questions you wish of the probation officer."

"Thank you, Your Honor. I don't have anything to ask." Antonio kept whatever emotions he had at this moment to himself. It appeared that the recommendation may have been about what Antonio had expected.

"The People would rest," concluded Ms. Houser.

"Mr. Montoya … You have a right to make a statement at this time."

Throughout the hearing, Antonio sat passively, passing on any chance to make objections or to question the witnesses. As a result, nearly everyone in the courtroom was surprised when Antonio stood in response to the judge's invitation to make a statement.

He looked out at the people seated in the courtroom. Bob and Marianne Bunch and Erica Bennings' parents, who were divorced, were all seated together in the second row of pews in the gallery. Turning his back to the judge, the court reporter, the bailiff and the district attorney, Antonio squarely faced the victims' families. Juanita looked on nervously from her seat on the other side of the courtroom.

"I have nothing to say about my sentence. I will serve whatever time you think I should," Antonio said. The courtroom grew still as everyone's attention fell on the defendant, who had a jailer not more than two steps behind him on his left. Dressed in civilian clothes, Antonio no longer looked the part of a criminal.

"I want to tell the families of Erica Benning and Vickie Bunch that I have no words to express the sorrow in my heart. I know that my poor words can do nothing to ease your pain. I don't have anything more to say than what I said in my letter to you."

Marianne Bunch nodded slightly, indicating that she had read his letter.

"Still …" Antonio struggled momentarily for his words, "I want you to know that I am sorry." At this point, Antonio hesitated, pursing his lips. "I have children myself," the Defendant continued, "and if someone did to either of my children what I did to yours….."

It looked for a moment as though Antonio was going to be silenced by his emotion as Marianne Bunch had been earlier, but he then quickly continued.

"… I know that I would want him to die. But I am truly sorry. Sorrier than I ever knew I could be."

Antonio sat back down, at first looking at the table in front of him, but then pulling himself up straight in his chair and facing the judge, in anticipation of the sentence to be handed down.

"Thank you Mr. Montoya. Do you have anything else to present?"

Antonio shook his head.

"Alright," continued the judge, "I will adopt the State's recommendation and sentence the Defendant, Antonio Montoya, to four years in prison, and assess the court costs against the Defendant. Following your release from prison, Mr. Montoya, I will place you on formal probation for a term of two additional years. Do you have any questions?"

"No, Your Honor."

"Very well. This hearing is concluded."

"All rise!" bellowed the bailiff.

A teary-eyed Juanita Montoya found her way to her feet and walked forward to the bar that separated the gallery from the front of the courtroom. As Antonio was led by the jailers back toward the side door to the courtroom, he looked up and spotted Juanita, who was clutching the rail with both hands. "I love you, Tony," she said softly. Antonio was unable to hear her over the din of the crowd, but her expression told Antonio how his wife felt. He nodded to her sadly as he was led out of the courtroom and back to the jail. Although his sentence was far less than what he might have received, both of the Montoyas knew that their children would be growing up without a father for what was still going to be a very long time.

**38**

Jamika Smith looked older than her fifty-one years as she mopped the hallway in the Booker T. Washington Junior High School after hours. The school was quiet now; the students had been gone for over an hour. The woman stopped to wipe sweat from her brow and stretch her back, when she realized someone was walking up behind her. She turned and was somewhat surprised to see a well-dressed, white woman whom she had never seen before approaching her in the hallway.

"Hello," came the greeting from the stranger. "Are you Jamika Smith?"

"Maybe. Who wants to know?" answered the custodian suspiciously.

"I'm sorry. I know you don't know me. My name's Eleanor Rubin. I'm an attorney. Do you mind if we talk for just a few minutes?"

"What about?"

"I just have a few questions about a case I'm working on involving someone I think you know."

"I guess so," Smith replied, still somewhat warily.

"Is there somewhere we could go and talk?"

"Well, I was thinking 'bout takin' a little break anyway, so we can sit down a spell in the cafeteria."

The attorney stepped back as the custodian walked past her to lead the way down the hall toward the cafeteria. Rubin walked a step behind her. Just outside the cafeteria, Rubin looked up at the wall where there was a large mural, depicting a number of heroes from American history in action in the various fields in which they'd made their marks. Rubin was admiring the mural when Ms. Smith found a spot to chat.

"We can sit right over here," she said, pointing to the first table inside the cafeteria.

"Fine, thank you," replied the attorney, as she pulled out a chair from the table and descended into the hard, plastic, school-issue lunch seat.

"So what can I do for you, Ms. ...."

"Rubin."

"Yes. Ms. Rubin. What do you want to know?"

"I understand you were once married to Maurice Thompson?"

**39**

Juanita flipped on the gas pumps moments after arriving at the Gas-N-Shop. One of her co-workers, Kim, who had gone out with Nita and some of the other female employees of the Gas-N-Shop after work on occasion, hadn't worked a shift with Juanita since Antonio's sentencing. She had been in the stockroom when Nita entered the store and came out to join her behind the counter. Affecting a closer friendship than the two women actually enjoyed, Kim hugged Juanita, unexpectedly. Juanita smiled appreciatively at her co-worker's effort to comfort her.

"So how're you doing, Nita?" Kim asked consolingly.

"About the same, Kimmie. Thanks."

A bell in the store rang, signaling the arrival of a customer at the pumps. Nita glanced out the picture window behind the register and spotted a car that she recognized. The driver emerged from the red BMW - a tall, dark-haired man with a slender build. He snapped open the door to his gas tank and inserted the nozzle, looking up at the window to the store as he did so. Nita made brief eye contact and, slightly embarrassed, quickly looked out toward the street and then turned her back to the window and busied herself behind the counter.

A few minutes later, the customer entered the store to pay for his gas. As he approached the counter, Kim elbowed Juanita knowingly.

Juanita ignored this mild ribbing and greeted the man with her most studied expression of nonchalance.

Gary Blanning handed his credit card to Juanita. Even though the pumps accepted credit cards outside, some customers who bought nothing else once inside the store still opted for the more traditional method of payment at the cash register. Juanita rang up the purchase and tore the credit card slip from the top of the credit card machine and slapped it down on the counter, looking everywhere but at her customer as he scribbled his illegible signature on the slip. He started to back away from the counter and then, as though struck with an after-thought, he pivoted back toward the counter and picked up a pack of breath mints and tossed them back up on the counter.

Juanita sighed, as though bored, and rung up Blanning's second purchase.

"Do you want a sack?" Juanita asked without smiling.

"Do I want to *what*?" Blanning replied, feigning not to understand Juanita in an effort to engage her in a friendlier level of conversation.

"A bag for the mints," Juanita answered curtly.

"Oh, yeah. I'd like a sack." Blanning flashed a set of perfect teeth at Juanita as he gave her a playful smile.

"Here you go," Juanita replied, handing the empty bag to the man, without either opening it or offering to put the mints inside.

Rebuffed, Blanning bid the women behind the counter a good day and exited the store.

"Are you kidding me, Nita?!" Kim yelped, as soon as the front door closed.

"What's the matter with you?" Nita asked innocently.

"Don't give me that," Kim retorted. "Look, I know you're walking the straight and narrow and everything, and I think that's great, but give me a break! That guy is the hottest man we *ever* get in this place and you pretty much just told him to get lost. What's the deal?"

Juanita shrugged her shoulders and acted for a minute as though she expected that response to end the conversation, but Kim was having none of it.

"Come on, Nita, my goodness. Are you some kind of a nun now all of a sudden, or have you just kind of gone crazy on me?" The disbelief in Kim's voice had not subsided.

"I'm just through flirting with customers… and men in general, if you must know the truth. It does nothing but cause trouble."

"Well, if you aren't gonna do that anymore, you'd better ask for a raise to make this place bearable," Kim teased.

"I could use a raise," Juanita muttered, almost under her breath. The bell rang twice in rapid succession as the morning's business at the Gas-N-Shop began to pick up.

**40**

Most parish priests feel that they are spread too thin in the best of circumstances. Fr. Kearns truly did double duty with his ministry to the aged, infirm and otherwise afflicted in addition to his regular pastoral duties at St. Michael's Parish. As a result, he was thrilled to have Margaret Millington becoming increasingly involved in this ministry with him and occasionally in his stead. From time to time, however, Margaret would run into a situation that she did not know how to properly handle, in which case she would usually discuss the matter with Fr. Peter. He would then either advise Margaret on how to deal with it, or, not infrequently, would step into the situation himself, regardless of whether he was acquainted with the individual to whom Margaret was ministering or not.

One particular individual who was not previously known to Fr. Kearns was a man in his mid-sixties whom Margaret had met at the Whispering Willows Convalescent Center by the name of Walter Midland. Another resident of the center that Margaret had become acquainted with through Fr. Kearns had suggested to Margaret that she stop in and see the man, who, according to the resident, always appeared to be depressed. Margaret had thought that her own struggles with depression might allow her to relate to this patient, as it had with others suffering from that affliction. But after meeting with Mr. Midland on two separate occasions, Margaret felt that she was unable to move the man from his deep despondency. He had, by his own account, given up on life as the result of his medical condition. He had terminal pancreatic cancer that had ravaged his once-robust constitution, leaving him but a mere shell of his former self.

As Walter Midland faced death in a depressed state of mind, he was at the same time terrified of death, thereby creating within himself an insoluble emotional dilemma. Margaret's best insights about depression, which she shared with the man, had no apparent effect on him. He would speak to Margaret politely and thank her for visiting, but he maintained a deadpan expression, and Margaret could clearly see the inefficacy of her efforts. During a conversation with Fr. Kearns one morning, Margaret briefed the priest on Mr. Midland's situation. The next day, Fr. Kearns skipped lunch in order to free himself from his obligations long enough to meet with this rather hopeless individual.

The day that Fr. Kearns stopped in to Whispering Willows was not one of his regularly scheduled visits to the home. Because he did not have time to make his rounds in the home, he walked briskly through the halls, keeping his eyes straight ahead of him, until he reached room 132 - the room that Margaret said was Walter Midland's.

Fr. Kearns, as was his custom during such visits, looked at the outside of the door and glanced around the small room for signs of gifts or mementos from family or friends. Often, the priest would, by a few furtive glances around the room, gain useful information about a person by such artifacts, such as whether he was married or had children or received mail from anyone concerned about the resident's well-being. Noticing the walls and desk to be fairly unadorned, Fr. Kearns rapped lightly on the half-open door. As he did so, he saw that the man in the room was lying in bed, with the bed raised at about a 45-degree angle from the floor. He had the television turned on, but didn't appear to be watching when his visitor appeared in the doorway.

"Mr. Midland?" the priest asked, to assure himself that he was in the right room.

The man turned his head to the right to face the unknown cleric who was standing in his doorway.

"Yeah. May I help you?"

"I hope I'm not interrupting anything. My name is Peter Kearns. I'm a friend of Margaret Millington."

The man's initial hesitation in greeting the priest was reminiscent of his first visit to the woman whose name he had just spoken. The man reached down to the side of his bed and pushed a button. As he did so, the back of his bed was raised until he was more sitting than lying down and he turned toward the visitor.

"Please. Come on in. Have a seat," offered the man, pointing to a wooden chair at the foot of the bed. The words of the reluctant greeting were warmer than the multitude of non-verbal cues that accompanied them. Fr. Kearns pulled the chair around the side of the bed and sat it next to the moderately upholstered chair that was directly beside the bed, but had not been offered to him.

"I hear that you are quite a Cubs fan," the priest began, in an effort to break the ice.

"Yeah. I've been a fan for fifty years. Undying loyalty, I guess," said Midland with the first hint of a smile. "Are you a baseball fan?"

"Oh, I actually loved the Cubs as a boy. I'm afraid I haven't followed the game much in the past ten years or so. I have caught a few Cubs and Sox games with parishioners over the years, though. I have to admit, it isn't the same when you don't know the players."

Midland made no reply. Since it seemed that this topic had pretty much run its course, Fr. Kearns shifted gears.

"How long have you been living here?"

"Chicago?"

"Well, I was actually referring to Whispering Willows," replied the priest.

"Oh. I've been here for about two months."

There was an awkward, momentary silence, broken by Mr. Midland.

"What can I do for you, Father?" asked the man in a tone that conveyed that he had exhausted the limits of his hospitality.

"I hear that you're having a rough time dealing with your disease," answered the priest, now mirroring Midland's directness.

"Well, Father, I have to admit that I'm not real crazy about the idea of dying just yet."

"I can't blame you there, Mr. Midland. Are you a member of any church?"

"No. I'm afraid I'm not much of a church goer," Midland replied.

"Has that always been the case?" continued the priest.

"Well, as a matter-of-fact Father, I was raised a Catholic. But me and the Church haven't seen eye-to-eye on a few things, and, well …. I guess I just didn't see much point in continuing to go through the motions."

"How long has it been since you've gone to mass?" asked Fr. Kearns.

"If you don't count two or three weddings that I attended, I guess it's been better than 20 years now." Midland squinted his eyes and stuck his chin forward as he gave his unexpected visitor an almost challenging stare as he spoke. Fr. Kearns pressed the issue further.

"Do you believe in God?"

"Yeah, I'm sure I do. I mean, I don't have any doubt that somebody had to start all this." Midland made an arc with his arm, as though encompassing all of his surroundings.

"Do you believe that God sent his son, Jesus, to earth to redeem us of our sins?"

"Yeah. I still believe in Jesus. I also think he's the Son of God."

"Do you believe that the Holy Spirit is from the Father and the Son, and that he continues to love you and me and is concerned for us?"

"Well, to tell you the truth, now you're starting to hit on some things I'm not so sure about. See, if God, or whoever, cares about us, why does Hew let terrible things happen to us? I mean, take me for instance. I'm not such a bad guy. I haven't been the most religious guy around, but I treat people fair and mind my own business. I realize that I've lived longer than a lot of people get to live, but why should I die now? Why should any of us have to suffer?"

The priest sat back in his chair, considering the questions carefully. After a few seconds, Fr. Kearns leaned forward and attempted to address this commonly held stumbling block to faith.

"A lot of deeply spiritual men and women over the centuries have discussed the question of human suffering. My own view is that our Lord allows us to experience hardship for two reasons: to test our fidelity to Him, and so that we can more fully appreciate the beautiful gift of his grace."

Mr. Midland gazed down at the foot of his bed in silence. Fr. Kearns explained what he meant.

"We know that our Father created us in His image. People spend their lives restlessly searching for happiness. Many roads that people take in their search for happiness end up being dead-ends: money, sex, drugs, alcohol, power, fame. But I believe that that natural restlessness is our deep-seated desire for God our Creator. One of the Church's early great thinkers was St. Augustine. He wrote, 'You have made us for yourself, O Lord, and our heart is restless until it rests in you.'

I guess the idea is that only when we find Him do we find peace. That peace then becomes perfect in Heaven when we are reunited with Him. Maybe if we didn't have suffering in this life, we'd have nothing to impel us to search for our God. And we might be less likely to learn to rely upon Him, which he wants us to do, as we know from Scripture."

Walter Midland looked back up at his visitor and put another question to him.

"Have you ever suffered, Father? I mean *really* suffered?"

The young priest shook his head. "No. Not yet."

Deciding that they he had engaged his suffering host in enough spiritual talk for his first visit, Fr. Kearns rose from his chair and reached for the older man's right hand. The priest took the man's hand between both of his own and told him he'd be back to visit him again soon. Although he wasn't sure if he was having any more success getting through to the man than Margaret did, he was pleased about the fact that he had the man at least talking about the way he felt.

**41**

It had been over a month since Fr. Kearns had been to see Dr. Cappel. He had been stopping in and giving blood samples weekly since his last appointment with her, but today he was going to find out where he stood with the bone marrow transplant surgery. He had checked in with the receptionist and had just sat down when his name was called.

"Peter Kearns?" bellowed Dr. Cappel's male nurse.

Fr. Kearns stood up and walked toward the nurse.

"How are you today, Reverend Kearns?"

"I'm fine. How are you?"

The nurse escorted his patient back to an examination room, where, for a change, Dr. Cappel was already waiting.

"Hello, Fr. Kearns," the doctor said as the pair approached.

"Have you checked his weight yet?" asked the physician, looking at his nurse.

"No, not yet."

"Okay Father, let's step up here on the scales then," directed the doctor, motioning to the scales that were just outside the exam room. The doctor slid the weights across the top of the cross bar on the scales and tapped it gently a couple of times until the arrow reached a state of equipoise. "One hundred sixty-two pounds," announced the doctor in an official manner, as though weighing in a boxer before a championship bout. The nurse made a quick note in the priest's medical chart as the doctor led Fr. Kearns into the exam room.

Fr. Kearns had maintained a fairly steady weight of 190 pounds before his illness. He had weighed 174 pounds a month earlier at his visit to Dr. Cappel. Again following his doctor's instructions, the priest sat on the edge of the examination table and held out his arm so that the nurse could take his blood pressure. While this was being done, the doctor put her hands on the side of her patient's neck and palpated the area of his throat and back up under his ears.

"How are you feeling?" Dr. Cappel asked.

"One twenty-one over eighty-five," interrupted the nurse as she removed the cuff from the priest's left arm.

"I'm not feeling too bad," replied the priest, who had actually been feeling increasingly more fatigued of late, but had trained himself not to dwell on his condition.

"I think we need to talk about your condition, Father," Dr. Cappel said flatly as the nurse left the room. The doctor wore reading glasses, attached by a chain around her neck, as she flipped through her patient's chart and sighed. Dr. Cappel laid the chart on the examination table next to her seated patient and removed her reading glasses with the other hand.

"Let's talk then, please, doctor," replied the young priest, anxious about the status of his leukemia before reading the obvious look of concern on his physician's face.

"You are not doing well, Fr. Kearns. In fact, I'm surprised you're still functioning as well as you say you are. It cannot go on like this much longer, I'm afraid. Any news on the donor situation?" asked the doctor.

"Well, that's still a problem. We're doing all we can to try to find my family of origin."

Dr. Cappel frowned. "I'm becoming concerned about your body's ability to hold out until a suitable donor can be found. Once we have a donor, the chemotherapy will be increased dramatically." The doctor pursed her lips and continued. "I want to make sure you can withstand the impact of the chemotherapy and then the bone marrow transplant procedure."

The oncologist began a complicated discussion of how a patient can sometimes serve as his own bone marrow donor for a transplant. She explained that this procedure was routinely utilized in the treatment of more common blood disorders other than his variety of leukemia. However, in the case of his particular diagnosis, the bone marrow itself is compromised and cannot be utilized. Studies have definitively demonstrated that only bone marrow transplants from a third-party, sharing genetic similarities only found in blood relatives, are effective.

"So, how long do you think I can wait before I have a transplant, Doctor?"

"I think we need to do this within the next few weeks if it's going to be done."

Peter Kearns remained seated on the examination table and suddenly felt warm and slightly dizzy as he absorbed the impact of this pronouncement. Dr. Cappel spoke to her patient for a few minutes longer about cross-referencing databases and some other jargon that he only partially heard as he contemplated the life-and-death urgency of his situation.

**42**

Paul Erickson had scheduled depositions of all of the witnesses that the District Attorney had listed on the State's "Pretrial List of Witnesses and Exhibits". At the same time, Fannie's defense team was compiling its own list of witnesses for her case. Today was the deposition of the person that found Maurice Thompson lying in a pool of his own blood on that fateful evening nearly fourteen months earlier.

The deposition was being taken in one of the conference rooms in the criminal section of Rogerson, Copeland & Zenhaus in the Windy City Commercial Center. Present in the room were Garrison Blaze, the Assistant State's Attorney who was prosecuting Fannie; a court reporter introduced only as "Annie," who appeared to be sixty-five to seventy years old; Paul Erickson from Fannie's defense team; and the witness - a young black woman who was seated in the middle of the long, mahogany table. Microphones had been placed on the table in front of the witness and both attorneys. The young black woman was seated beside the Assistant State's Attorney. Paul Erickson sat directly across from the witness, leaving a chair between himself and the court reporter. The small assemblage of persons who had gathered around the center of the table occupied only a fraction of the chairs in the spacious conference room.

"Would you please state your name," Erickson began after the witness was sworn by the court reporter.

"Yes. My name is Chanelle Riggy," replied the witness softly.

"As you know from our earlier introductions, my name is Paul Erickson. I represent Fannie Williams in the case entitled, 'People of the State of Illinois vs. Fannie Williams.' Now I'm going to be asking you a series of questions here this morning, and all my questions and all of your answers are being recorded by the court reporter. Later, she'll have the recording transcribed and printed out in booklet form. So it's very important that you let me finish each question before you attempt to answer it. Otherwise, if we're both talking at the same time, she's not going to be able to tell what we're saying when it comes time for her to type this up, okay?"

The young woman nodded her understanding.

"And because this is being recorded," the defense attorney continued, "it's really important that all of your responses be verbalized. In other words, no shaking or nodding of the head, since the court reporter can't pick that up. Fair enough?"

"Yes," voiced the witness, signaling that she had indeed been listening to the attorney's instructions.

"And finally," continued Erickson, "please remember that even though we're not in court here today, this deposition is being given under oath. You've sworn to tell the truth and it's critically important that you be as truthful in here as if you were in a court of law. Do you understand that?"

"I understand," Ms. Riggy replied confidently.

"Okay. Please tell me your date of birth."

"July 15, 1983."

"And where were you born?"

"Gary, Indiana."

"And can you please tell me your parents' names?"

For the next twenty minutes, the attorney continued to flesh out the biography of this young woman, including her education and employment history as well as her important social relationships. After establishing that the witness was a niece of Maurice Thompson,

Erickson began to probe the area of her anticipated testimony for the State.

"Do you have any recollection of where you were on August twenty-fourth of last year?" asked the attorney with a practiced lack of drama in his voice.

"The day I found Maurice?"

"Why don't you tell me? Did you find your uncle Maurice somewhere on that date?"

"Yes. I think that was the day. We was doing a garage sale at my momma house the next day.

Erickson interjected: "When you say 'we,' you are referring to yourself and who else?"

"Me and my momma. Anyways, uh, we was doin a garage sale and we was gonna use Maurice's, see, Maurice had some tables, like some old, fold-up card tables and we was gon' use them to put the clothes out on."

"When had your mother spoken with Maurice about this?"

The young witness paused for a moment and then answered. "I think my momma talked to Maurice earlier that day. I ain't no idea what time."

"So would I be correct in assuming that your mother had just asked you to go by and get the tables shortly before you went over there?"

"Yes."

"And had you personally had any conversation with Maurice that day before you went to his house?"

"No. I hadn't talked to Maurice for a minute."

"A minute?" Erickson asked.

"Well, a long time. Months."

"Where was Maurice living at the time?"

"He was living with Ms. Williams. I think she rented the home on Stallings Avenue."

"And was it your understanding that Maurice was actually living there at the time?"

"Yes. They lived together off and on for a while. Maurice might have left there for a couple of days here and there, but that was pretty much his place too I think... ."

"And what time did you arrive at your uncle's home?"

"It had to be right about 8:15 in the evening."

"How do you know that?" asked the lawyer.

"Because I ate dinner with Momma. We cleaned up the kitchen and was goin through some of the boxes of things we was goin to sell and I know Momma axed me to go while she finished gettin' things together. It was a few minutes before eight when I left."

"How long does it take to drive from your home to Maurice's?"

"It usually took about fifteen to twenty minutes if the traffic wasn't too bad."

"And what, if anything, do you remember about the traffic that night?" asked Erickson.

"Pretty normal. Not real backed up or real fast, you know what I'm saying?"

"Did you have any other business before going to Maurice's, or did you drive directly to his house?"

"Straight to they house."

"Okay, Chanelle. Now tell me what you remember that evening, starting from when you first went up to the house."

"Well, I walked up the walk to the front door. They had a screened-in front porch, and I opened the door to the porch and walked up to the front door."

"Do you recall on this August evening whether the front door was opened or closed?"

"I think the door was closed. I am pretty sure I rang the doorbell."

"Okay. What happened after you rang the doorbell?"

"Well, nobody answered, so I rang it a few more times."

"And...."

"I finally just opened the door and walked in."

"What did you see upon entering the home?"

"I saw that the front room was a mess. I know they usually had a pretty neat and clean house, so things didn't look right. It was kinda messed up. Then I walked in a little farther into the house and I could see a leg sticking out from the couch where I was standing."

"What happened next?" continued the lawyer, appearing to be engrossed in the gory scene that was being painted by the witness.

"I walked into the middle of the front room and stood where I could see who was down there."

At this point in her testimony, Chanelle became emotional. Tears suddenly appeared in her eyes. Erickson swallowed as the witness continued.

"It was Maurice. He was lying on the floor." The witness was holding her hands up, touching her cheeks with both hands as she struggled to get through this obviously painful testimony. "I thought he was dead!" she blurted as she began to cry audibly.

"Would you like to take a break?" offered Erickson gently.

"No, I'm okay," Chanelle assured.

"Okay. How did you determine whether your uncle was alive?" Erickson continued.

"I think when I walked over by him, I kind of woke him up or something. He sort of moved his head like he was trying to see where my footsteps was coming from. I screamed and he like jerked or something and then passed out again. I called an ambulance from inside the house."

"Let me hand you some photographs of the inside of the house as the police found it and ask you some questions about these. All right?"

"That's fine."

The lawyer then methodically went through about a dozen photographs of the interior of the home from the police file, asking the witness to first identify the scene depicted and then asking several follow-up questions about each photo. Finally, Erickson came to a photograph which he had the court reporter mark as "Defendant's Deposition Exhibit #11.

"Can you tell me what this is?" asked the lawyer, handing the picture to the witness.

"Yes."

"What is that, please?"

"That's the baseball bat."

"And where was that when you first saw it?"

"Right there like you see it, lying upside my Uncle Maurice's head."

**43**

Juanita had been off work since ten that night. She had picked up her kids from "Maggie's Kids Evening Care," a few blocks from her home, as she did whenever she worked the evening shift. Johnnie was already asleep when she picked them up and slept through the ride home and from the short trip from his car seat to his bed. A.J. was exhausted, but tried to fight sleep until about 10:30, when a short bedtime story from his mother worked its usual magic. The baby, Inez, was another story altogether.

Inez had been sleeping when Juanita picked her up from the sitter. Now she was wide awake, and Juanita had to go back in at eight o'clock the next morning. After leaving Inez in her baby bed screaming while she tended to A.J., Juanita went into the nursery and retrieved her near-hysterical, fifteen-month-old daughter.

The overhead light in the child's room was turned off, but a warm glow from a lamp that doubled as a nightlight with a second turn of the switch illuminated the room. The lamp was in the shape of a balloon. In fact, it was the balloon from "The Wizard of Oz" that was supposed to take Dorothy back to Kansas. It provided sufficient light for Juanita to perform an occasional late-night diaper change without disturbing the child in her more restful moments.

As Juanita entered the nursery, Inez was standing in the baby bed that had been used previously in succession by the Montoya's two sons, each relinquishing it and graduating by necessity to a regular bed upon the birth of a younger sibling. The seemingly life-threatening cause of Inez' present meltdown dissipated immediately upon the appearance of her mother. By the time that Juanita reached out to pick up her baby girl, Inez was jumping up and down with excitement as she gripped the top rail of the baby bed.

"There, there…. shhhhh," Juanita lovingly implored, holding the baby against her with one hand under the child's bottom and the other hand behind its small head, pressing it into the sanctuary of her mother's bosom. Juanita paced the room with the baby placed in this position for the next ten minutes. The child continued babbling happily, oblivious to her mother's desperation to get both of them some much-needed sleep.

As the baby's babbling decreased, first in frequency and then in volume, Juanita eased herself into the rocking chair in the far corner of the nursery and rocked Inez gently, until the baby's primitive attempts at speaking were replaced by a deep and steady breathing, indicating to her grateful mother that Inez was peacefully drifting off to Oz.

After laying the baby in her crib and tip-toeing out of the nursery, Juanita paused in the hall and slowly and quietly closed the door. On her way back to her own bedroom, Juanita passed the kitchen table where the day's mail had been tossed earlier, unopened. She reached down to the small stack of mail and flipped through the envelopes, scanning the return addresses to see who the letters were from.

"More bills," Juanita thought to herself. The Montoyas' bills were outpacing Juanita's modest weekly paychecks from the Gas-N-Shop. As she walked back to her bedroom to undress and get into bed, Juanita regretted having looked at her mail, adding as it did to the stress that she knew would delay her sleep. As she lay in her bed trying to force the worries from her mind, Juanita's thoughts turned to her husband. She considered how much worse Antonio's situation was than her own; she at least had her freedom and got to be with their children. Unfortunately, these thoughts did little to help Juanita relax, yet in the late-night struggle between her racing mind and her fatigued body, the fatigue eventually won out.

**44**

During Margaret's last conversation with Fr. Kearns before his visit to his oncologist, she made him promise that he would call her with an update on his condition as soon as he returned from the doctor's office. As it was, Margaret was at home alone, rinsing out the bowl she had just used to eat a Caesar salad at lunch, when she got the call.

"Hello, Peter. How did it go today?" Margaret asked hopefully. But Margaret's heart sank quickly as her friend related the dire situation that Dr. Cappel had confronted him with.

After listening silently to all that Dr. Cappel had told him, Margaret repeated the sentence that produced the greatest anxiety in all that she had heard: "You need a blood relative for your bone marrow transplant?" Margaret hesitated, and then asked the question that was pounding in her head. "How does someone who grew up in foster homes and has no idea about his birth family find a blood relative?" When Fr. Kearns remained silent on the other end of the line, the full import of the doctor's prognosis hit Margaret like a ton of bricks. Dr. Cappel was essentially telling her dear friend that he was going to die.

Summoning her courage, Margaret said that they would simply have to find Fr. Peter's biological family. She offered a few weak words of encouragement, and at the end of the conversation, Margaret set down the receiver and stared. A few seconds later, she picked the phone back up out of its cradle and began to dial.

The phone rang on the other end into a small office in a one-story building near Wrigley Field. "Hello, Dombrowski Detective Agency," came the answer by a sixtyish, female receptionist with a raspy smoker's voice. "May I help you?"

"Yes," replied Margaret. "I need to speak with Mr. Dombrowski, please. Tell him it's Margaret Millington."

Seconds later, a bald man in his mid-fifties with broad shoulders, a large chest, and a gut that was gaining on it was on the line. "Margaret! What a surprise to hear from you. To what do I owe this privilege?"

Len Dombrowski had helped Margaret and her attorney uncover a large amount of hidden assets in her recently-concluded divorce proceedings. He had given Margaret his card, but didn't get much repeat business in his line of work, apart from attorneys and insurance adjustors. Dombrowski had the appearance of a retired pro football lineman, but he had impressed Margaret with his ability to link together seemingly unconnected items and to unearth cleverly disguised corporate subsidiaries and hidden accounts.

"Len, I'm going to need your help." Dombrowski noticed that Margaret's voice did not betray desperation, but a calm determination that he had not seen demonstrated in his earlier dealings with her. As he would learn over the course of the next several weeks, the woman on the other end of the line was no longer the Margaret Millington he had dealt with before. She scheduled an appointment to meet with the detective the following afternoon.

As Margaret approached Wrigley Field on her right on Waveland, she came to the corner of North Seminary Avenue and turned left at the fire station. Margaret then pulled into the parking lot outside of the Dombrowski Detective Agency. Although Mr. Dombrowski's services had been useful to Margaret in the past, she had never been to Dombrowski's office, and most of their prior engagement had been handled by Margaret's lawyer. Margaret's initial thought as she climbed out of her car and approached the front door of the business was that Len Dombrowski should charge clients a contingency fee when he is searching for assets in high-dollar divorce cases, because if he had, she figured he'd be ready for an upgrade in his professional accommodations. Her attorneys, on the other hand, had no difficulty in maximizing their return for man hours devoted to her case, as she was reminded with each monthly statement that she received as her divorce was wending its way through the process.

Margaret entered the small reception area and was greeted by the same raspy-voiced woman who had answered the phone a day earlier. Claudia, the receptionist, looked up from her computer as Margaret approached her window and told Margaret that Mr. Dombrowski was ready. She rose and opened the door to a short hallway that led to Len Dombrowski's office. Dombrowski led Margaret to an ancient, black, leather chair – one of two that sat opposite the detective's large and highly cluttered desk.

After a brief exchange of pleasantries, Margaret got down to business. "Mr. Dombrowski…"

"Please Ms. Millington. Call me Len," interrupted the large man seated across the desk.

"OK, Len. I hope you are as good at finding people as you are at finding money." With that, Margaret launched into the sad story of her young priest friend's critical medical situation and emphasized that she would spare no expense in tracking down the priest's biological family, if any existed.

The detective had Margaret relate to him all that she knew of Fr. Peter's life story. At the end of the meeting, the detective said he would like to meet personally with Peter himself to see if any other clues about his family of origin could be unearthed. Margaret promised she would get Fr. Kearns into his office immediately in case he had any other useful information that he had not shared with Margaret. Her concern was that Peter had always indicated that his early childhood was shrouded in mystery, including the serious burns that he had received at some point in his young life. Margaret's hope was that some tidbits of information that Peter had considered innocuous might prove useful in the hands of an experienced investigator.

**45**

Fr. Kearns invited Len Dombrowski into the living room of the rectory of St. Michael's Parish. The priest sat on the near end of the couch and offered his guest a deep, well-cushioned suede easy chair to his right, at the end of the coffee table. Dombrowski glanced around the living room, did a quick scan of the photos and religious artifacts and knick-knacks positioned throughout the room, on the walls, tables and shelves. Fr. Kearns caught his inquisitive guest's eye and asked the detective if he had always lived in Chicago. Dombrowski said that he had. He then mentioned, almost as a confession, that he was brought up Catholic, but hadn't attended mass since he moved out of his parents' house at nineteen. Suppressing the well-trained urge to proselytize, Fr. Peter let it pass.

After a few minutes of the obligatory, meaningless chit-chat, Dombrowski opened a badly weathered, brown leather briefcase. The gumshoe pulled out a pad of paper and pen and his cell phone, lightly depressing the "record" application as he got down to the purpose of his visit.

"Let's go back to the earliest days of your life, Fr. Kearns, and please tell me everything you know about those days: the places you lived, the people you lived with, any foster homes you know anything about…. I need to know everything that you know about the early years of your life."

Fr. Peter related essentially the same sketchy biographical

information that he had provided to Margaret in the early days of their friendship. Peter knew absolutely nothing about his birth family. He knew that he spent most of the first decade of his life in several different foster homes, until Sam and Barbara Curtis, his last foster parents, took him into their home. He lived with the Curtises from the fourth grade until his sophomore year in high school, when he entered the seminary. Both of the Curtises had been dead for several years, but Peter said the last he had heard, Sam Jr., who was fifteen years older than Peter, had moved to Arizona. Francine Curtis, a year older than Sam, lived in Baltimore, and the eldest Curtis child, Ronald, who was twenty-nine when Peter came to live with his parents, still lived in Chicago.

"What do you know about how you came to be a foster child in the first place," Dombrowski asked.

"Nothing, really, apart from surmises," answered the priest. "The only thing I ever remember being told was that I was burned while in the home of my birth parents. I never knew how it happened, or whether it was accidental or intentional. But I figured in either case, that was most likely what landed me in my first foster home."

The detective momentarily studied the burns on his host's face, feeling excused from the constraints of propriety which, in most circumstances, place a taboo on staring at another's unsightly defects or deformities.

"Well, Chicago's a big city, but I can start with the newspapers and see if there was any article about a young boy being burned and placed in foster care. How old were you when that happened?"

"I think I was an infant. But I never thought to probe into the subject much. I remember Mrs. Curtis telling me one day that I was burned really badly when I was little and that I was lucky to be alive, but I never asked if she knew how old I was when it happened and she never mentioned it again. I assumed that I was either abused or neglected and I felt lucky to have been taken into the Curtises' home. They were really wonderful people and I came to consider them my parents, even though I never was adopted."

"Did you ever get an idea of how long you had been in foster care before you went to the Curtises?"

"I know that it was years rather than months, but I don't know how many years."

"Do you have any recollection of other, earlier foster families or of your birth family?"

"I would say that I moved around to at least four different homes, but I don't remember much about them. It seems like in one of them I had an Asian foster mother. She had a strong accent, but I don't think I was there long." The priest paused momentarily and then added, "I also remember a foster father who smoked cigars and never talked. I kind of grew up thinking that cigars take a voice away from their smokers. The foster mother in that home was nice, as I recall, and talked plenty. I sure don't know any of these people's names, though."

The detective probed a bit further, asking what the priest knew about the location of any of the homes he had lived in. Unfortunately, it seemed that Fr. Kearns knew next to nothing about his life before the Curtises.

"Well, I guess I need to talk to the Curtis children and see what they know," said Dombrowski, as he turned off the recorder on his phone and put the pen and paper back in his briefcase.

Deciding to start with the child who was closest to Peter's age, the detective asked, "So where in Arizona might I find Sam Curtis, Jr.?"

**46**

Robert Waite stood at the end of the conference table where his team of attorneys for the Fannie Williams defense had assembled for one of their final meetings before the trial. Each lawyer had his and her own separate files in front of them, along with water glasses and coffee cups. As the lawyers filled their cups, Waite adjusted the blinds in the conference room to shut out some of the morning's glaring sunrays, which reflected off the water glasses in a prism of color and light.

As required by the court's pretrial conference order, with the trial just two weeks away, pretrial discovery was now completed. The lawyers discussed motions *in limine* that they needed to draft as well as those that they needed to respond to from the other side - motions to raise issues for the court outside the presence of the jury before the start of a trial. Then they reviewed the proposed jury instructions that Paul Erickson flashed on a large pull-down screen as part of a Power Point presentation. The lawyers suggested a few minor changes here and there, but this well-oiled legal machine was revving up and just about ready to go.

# 47

The engine of the Boeing 737 was shifting down as its landing gear rumbled out of its compartment and the plane prepared to land at the Phoenix Sky Harbor International Airport. The female flight attendant with a strong southern accent picked up the coffee cups and other beverage containers from the passengers as the captain had informed them that he would be landing the plane over the mountain just this side of the approaching horizon. Ten minutes later the plane descended onto the desert runway, first braking softly and then more loudly as the plane settled firmly onto the asphalt landing strip and the pilot put more of the runway behind them.

Len Dombrowski pulled his large frame upright in his seat and rubbed his eyes and yawned, in an effort to rouse himself from his flight-induced torpor. Fortunately, since the person paying his tab purchased a first-class ticket for him, he was among the first to rise from his seat when the plane stopped. He reached into the overhead storage compartment and retrieved his only bag for the short stay and disembarked the plane.

After following the signs outside the terminal to taxi cabs and buses, Dombrowski hailed a passing cab and found himself sitting down again, with his small suitcase on the seat next to him behind the cabbie.

"Where we going?" asked the Moroccan cab driver in a friendly tone.

Dombrowski looked at the address in his cell phone. "3130 Oleander Lane."

Twenty minutes later, the large detective paid his fare, but asked that the cabbie hang around for a little while in case no one was home or in the event that he had the wrong address or was shown to the door more quickly than expected.

"Please give me fifteen minutes. If I'm not back by then, you can take off."

Realizing that he was detaining the cabbie beyond the fare he'd paid and the accompanying tip, Dombrowski pulled out another ten dollars and handed it to the grateful, smiling cabbie.

"No problem, sir."

Dombrowski lumbered up the driveway of the attractive, tri-level home in this upper-middle class neighborhood. A mailbox, affixed to the outside of the house, proudly announced the names of the home's owners: "Curtis." Dombrowski rang the doorbell and seconds later heard footsteps approaching the door. The door was opened by an attractive woman about forty years old with short, blonde hair and a beaming four-year-old "mini-me" in tow. The detective displayed his credentials for Mrs. Curtis through the glass storm door. Expecting her hesitancy until he explained his presence, Dombrowski informed the slightly suspicious homeowner that he was an investigator from Chicago who was looking for Sam Curtis and needed to talk to him about his foster brother, Peter Kearns.

Speaking through the still-closed storm door, Sylvia Curtis told the detective what he half-expected to hear: that her husband, Sam Curtis, was at work. Sensing her discomfort, Dombrowski pulled a business card out of his wallet and started to reach out with it, thought again and said, "I'll just stick this in your mailbox. I'd really appreciate it if you could have Mr. Curtis call me so I can talk to him as soon as he gets home."

"I hope everything is alright with Peter," responded Mrs. Curtis with an air of burgeoning concern.

"He's very sick, Mrs. Curtis, and I'm hoping your husband can give me some information that might help me track down someone from Peter's biological family for an operation that is needed to save his life. He's going downhill fast, so time is critical."

"Oh my. OK then. I will have Sam call you from work. Is your cell number on the card?"

"Yes. Thank you. Where does Sam work?"

"Downtown. He takes a lunch break about noon. Maybe he could get free to meet with you."

"I hope so. Thanks again."

Dombrowski walked back to the waiting cab. As he opened the door, "Amir Adediran," as the cabbie's passenger-side visor identified him, turned back toward him in his seat and asked, "Where now?"

"Downtown. And I hope that ten gets me at least halfway there."

**48**

Although he was not a formal member of St. Michael's parish council, as pastor of the church, Fr. Peter had the power to veto any action of the council, though he had never yet done so in his time at the church. Still, Fr. Peter attended every monthly meeting of the parish council, as well as every executive committee meeting and budget committee meeting. On this Monday evening meeting of the St. Michael's parish council, nine voting members plus Fr. Peter and the pastoral assistant were in attendance.

Mrs. Betty Cordova, a widowed, sixty-year-old, lifelong member of the parish was currently serving as council president. She was kind and widely loved in the parish, but the one fault that she was commonly perceived to have as council president was her tendency to allow debate and discussion to carry on longer than necessary, thereby frequently resulting in three-hour meetings where sixty to ninety minutes had been the norm prior to her tenure.

As the discussion over the last item on the agenda, the hiring of a new director of music, dragged on for nearly an hour, Fr. Peter furtively stole a glance at his wristwatch below the surface of the conference table. It was 10:05 p.m. and the pastor felt increasingly ill as the meeting wore on.

"I apologize to you all, but I have a terrible headache and feel a fever coming on. I think I'd better get to bed and keep my germs to myself."

Fr. Peter rose from the table, exchanged his "goodnights" with the council members and walked out of the room on the first floor of the parish office building and outside toward the rectory on the opposite end of the parish complex. The distance to the rectory was about one city block, but as he made his way in a diagonal path across the church parking lot, the priest felt his head pounding harder, causing him to feel nauseated, and, at the same time, he was nearly overcome with fatigue. After opening the back door of the rectory and heading through a short hallway toward the living room and the stairway up to his bedroom, Fr. Kearns made a last-second detour into the first-floor restroom and vomited into the stool. He immediately began shivering uncontrollably, which added to the pain in his head. He walked up the stairs, climbed into his bed and slid under his covers without removing any clothing other than his shoes.

Moments later, the priest realized that he should have taken some aspirin before trying to go to sleep, but felt frozen to his present spot by his throbbing head and chill. Deciding the headache wasn't going to get better without some help, after about five minutes the ailing clergyman marshalled his energy for a quick burst out of bed and walked, shivering all the way, to the upstairs bathroom, where he opened the medicine cabinet and located an expired bottle of Ibuprofen. Knowing that the usual adult dosage was one or two pills, Fr. Kearns took three with a quick gulp of water and returned, still shivering violently, to his waiting bed. Eventually the shivering and pain subsided and Fr. Peter fell asleep, thereby escaping this, the worst-yet episode of his disease.

## 49

Since she was now the sole breadwinner of the Montoya family, Juanita had asked for, and received, extra shifts at the Gas-N-Shop. She enjoyed her job for the most part, and had a couple of co-workers with whom she had become fairly close, although she never socialized with any of them outside of work. While she was grateful that her boss was able to accommodate her request for more hours, this resulted in less time with her three young children. In each of the last two weeks, Juanita had worked close to sixty hours. Juanita's sister, Vada, generously arranged to schedule the hours at her own job at a refrigerator factory around Juanita's need for child care so that she had the children much of the time. While they continued at their child care, Vada was generally with them for the extra hours that Juanita had picked up.

Although Juanita wasn't able to get to the jail on as many visiting days as she'd like, and on fewer still when she could bring the kids, she was determined to handle the added load on all fronts and to maintain regular correspondence with Antonio until they were reunited. As she got busier, she noticed that the days were starting to go by faster. Day-by-day she would get through these four years and get her family back together. It certainly could have been a lot worse. And Fr. Peter's friend, Margaret, had put Antonio in touch with a drug and alcohol counselor who was permitted to come and meet with Antonio regularly in the jail. While abstinence from alcohol naturally came easy for Antonio in his present state of incarceration, they both hoped that this counseling, and the forced abstinence, would give Antonio a good start on his recovery from alcohol dependency when he got out.

On a couple of recent occasions, including today, Vada gathered up the Montoya children and took them to see their father. When they arrived at the jail and Antonio was led to the visiting room, the two boys ran up to the window with excitement when they first caught sight of their dad. Antonio was equally excited to see them. Although the visit that day, like always, was far too short, Antonio made sure to give some individual attention to each child in turn, however fleeting and inadequate. Vada did her best to stay in the background as much as possible while Antonio interacted with his kids. At the end of the visit, Antonio thanked Vada warmly for bringing the children to see him. She smiled and offered a few words of encouragement.

"You look good, Antonio. You are starting to look better than you've looked for a long time."

"Thanks Vada. I have to look better than I did an hour ago, thanks to you. I miss these guys so much!"

He then turned a final time to the children and thanked them for coming to see him. As he watched them exit the visiting room, Antonio realized that this was the first visit where none of the children were crying when they left.

Since Nita was due to get off work at just about the time Vada and the Montoya children were leaving the jail, Vada decided to go straight to the Montoyas' house so the kids could be waiting for their mother when she arrived.

**50**

As the taxi drew nearer to the approaching downtown skyline, Len Dombrowski felt the vibration of his cellphone in his right, front pants pocket. With his large frame crammed uncomfortably into the back seat of the cab, the big man half stood as the ring finger on his right hand fumbled inside his pocket to position the phone toward his waiting palm, hopefully before the ringing had stopped.

Bringing the phone up to his face, Dombrowski was relieved to see that this unfamiliar number had a Phoenix-area area code.

"Hello. This is Len Dombrowski."

"Mr. Dombrowski," began the male voice on the other end. "This is Sam Curtis. How may I help you?"

"I suppose your wife told you what's going on, didn't she?"

"Yes. I understand it's about Peter Kearns."

"That's right. I'm hoping you can make yourself free at lunchtime today, Mr. Curtis." This in no way resembled a question.

"Sure. How about a few minutes after 12:00 at a little café around the corner from where I work?"

Dombrowski wrote down the name and address of the restaurant. "I'll head there now and have a table waiting," said the detective as he ended the call. Turning now to the cab driver, Dombrowski repeated the name and address of the restaurant. Ten minutes later, he paid the cabbie the additional three dollars and ninety cents of the fare, along with a tip, and exited the cab.

"You don't have to wait for me this time. Thanks."

The detective entered the café and looked at his watch. He was forty minutes early, but went ahead and got a table and an iced tea with lemon. The detective sat in his booth and reviewed his case notes until his reverie was interrupted by the male voice he'd heard on the phone earlier that morning.

"Hello Mr. Dombrowski. I'm Sam Curtis. The waitress told me where you were seated." Sam Curtis wore a friendly expression as he reached out to shake the larger man's hand. The mammoth paw of the detective swallowed up the hand of his lunch mate.

"Thanks for meeting me Mr. Curtis. Please call me "Len.""

"Fair enough. Then I'm Sam."

After ordering a Diet Coke and being handed a menu, Mr. Curtis asked what the detective would like to know. The detective again pulled out his cellphone and opened the recorder app and asked Sam Curtis to tell him everything about his family's history that he could remember. Then he honed in on the arrival of Peter Kearns to the home.

One of the questions that Peter Kearns himself was unable to answer was whether "Kearns" was his birth name or was given to him later. Peter said that if it wasn't his name from birth, it was his name as long as he could remember, and he had no recollection of ever staying with a family named Kearns.

"I think my parents assumed that Peter's birth name was "Kearns," said Sam Curtis "I remember them referring to the Kearnses when referring to Peter's family of origin, although they never knew them, I'm sure."

"Well, I'm going to start out with the assumption that that was the name of Peter's birth family. But, unfortunately, that's a fairly common name, especially in a big city like Chicago, and we don't know for certain that Peter was born in Chicago, or in Illinois for that matter."

Dombrowski probed the deepest recesses of Sam Curtis' faded memory throughout the hour-and-a-half lunch. It was clear that the youngest of the Curtis children was not going to be a source of much information, and he opined that the oldest child, Ronald, was likely to know the most about what his parents knew of their rather mysterious, long-term foster child. Before parting, however, the detective did have a final question for Sam Curtis.

"Do you know whether your parents ever considered adopting Peter?"

"Well, I think my parents treated Peter as if he were one of the family. I know they loved him and felt that he loved them. But I think I remember my mom talking about it after we were grown. I believe that there was a financial advantage at the time for them not adopting Peter. They got some help with his expenses as long as he was in foster care and they weren't sure that they would continue to get that help once he was adopted."

Dombrowski picked up the tab for both men's lunches and stood to leave. "Thank you for your time today, Sam, and if you think of absolutely anything that might help, please give me a call, okay?"

"I certainly will, Mr. Dombrowski. And I'll try to brainstorm with my family to see what else they know about Peter."

Within three hours of landing, Dombrowski was hailing another cab and heading back to the airport.

## 51

It was a cold, windy morning in the "windy city," as the bells in the clock tower of the Cook County Criminal Courts building on South California Avenue, chimed eight times to signal the start of the new work week. In one hour, the trial that would determine the fate of Fannie Williams was set to get underway.

Fannie was finishing breakfast in a meeting room with Robert Waite and her son, Jarrod, when a jailer pressed the buzzer outside of the room.

"Ms. Williams, it's time for me to escort you to the Courthouse."

Fannie took a final drink of orange juice and wiped her mouth with her napkin and then reached out for her son's hand.

"Jarrod, give me a hug."

Mother and son held each other in an emotional, extended embrace.

"Momma, I love you. You're going to be alright."

"I love you too Jarrod," smiled Fannie. "You make me proud."

Jarrod Williams discreetly wiped a tear from his cheek and promised to meet his mother in the courtroom. The jailer then escorted Fannie and her attorney out of the cell where they were joined by a second jailer. The pair signed Fannie out of the jail and headed for a white Ford van in an adjacent parking garage that was warmed up and waiting for them with a third jailer at the wheel.

For the first time in months, Fannie was dressed in civilian clothes or "civies" as the jail staff called them.

Her attorneys had planned her attire with her carefully for each day of the trial, even picking out some new clothes to add to a couple of Fannie's favorite dresses. They had explained to Fannie's amazement that the trial was about "being yourself," but with the lawyers acting as directors as well as legal specialists. Today, Fannie was wearing one of her new outfits, purchased for the opening day of trial. It was a powder blue skirt and jacket combination, with a white blouse and a set of small, silver hoop earrings. Her attorneys stressed the importance of making the right impression on the jurors the first time they laid eyes on her.

Noticing the growing cadre of escorts, the smartly dressed defendant quipped, "You fellas must think I'm really bad."

"Just following our standard protocol, Ms. Williams," responded the first jailer with a smile.

Within minutes, the van pulled into an underground garage below the Cook County Criminal Courts building and Fannie and Robert Waite were ushered through a series of underground tunnels to an elevator that ultimately deposited them outside of the courtroom where Fannie's trial was to take place.

The area around the courtroom was crowded with people. "Are all of these people here to watch my trial?" Fannie inquired with astonishment.

"No," Waite answered her. "Most of these people were summoned here for jury duty."

"Okay, let's go on in," ordered the jailer, as he held the door for Fannie and her lawyer.

As the pair entered the cavernous courtroom, Fannie's eyes panned the room. The courtroom was divided approximately in half by a golden rail that ran across the width of the room and had gates at each end as well as in the middle to allow passage between the areas separating the spectators from the courtroom participants. Fannie looked at the enormous bench where the judge sat, behind which were American and Illinois state flags. Inscribed in the stone wall behind the judge in italic print was the famous motto, "In God We Trust."

For the first time since nervously entering the room, Fannie smiled and thought to herself, "Yes, we most certainly do!"

**52**

Today's visitor to Whispering Willows sported a major league team's ballcap and carried a wooden baseball bat as he approached Room 132. When the visitor rapped on the doorframe of the opened room, its sole occupant coughed and then responded.

"Yeah, who is it?"

Walter Midland was sitting up in bed, reading a newspaper with the assistance of a pair of glasses. He peered over the glasses to make the identity of his unexpected visitor.

"Kearns, isn't it?" snarled Midland.

"Why yes, Mr. Midland. Excellent memory."

"Not all that excellent. You were the last person to come in here without poking me with a needle, shoving a thermometer in my mouth or waking me up to make sure I'm getting a good night's sleep!"

The young priest laughed out loud at the older man's response.

"Well, I brought you a couple of gifts," said Fr. Kearns, still wearing a broad grin. The priest removed the Chicago Cubs hat from his head and tossed it onto Mr. Midland's lap from an arm's length away. As Midland picked up the hat for a closer inspection, the priest spun the baseball bat and extended it, handle first, to the bedbound man.

"Somebody owed me a favor and got the players to sign this bat," said the priest sheepishly.

"Well, if that don't beat all," blurted Midland with barely suppressed excitement. The elderly man held the bat close to his face and spun it slowly as he deciphered the autographs of nearly forty current members of the Cubs. Fr. Kearns sat quietly several minutes until Midland finally looked back up at him and spoke.

"I could probably hit better with this bat than half that team, but I appreciate the gesture. Very nice of you Father."

The two talked Cubs baseball for about twenty minutes, after which Fr. Peter excused himself and left the room without broaching the subjects of God, faith or the elderly man's impending death. Still, the priest was encouraged by the fact that he left Midland smiling.

Fr. Kearns turned from Walter Midland's room and stopped at the front desk. He spent the next thirty minutes talking to a woman at the desk and then walked out of Whispering Willows and headed back to his car in the parking lot, putting his right hand to his left lower rib cage as he opened the door and climbed in.

**53**

Len Dombrowski sat at his desk. While waiting for return calls from several people with whom he'd left messages in his quest for information on Peter Kearns' background, the large man flipped on the outdated computer on his desk and started exploring the matter from a different angle.

Dombrowski began by searching for any Chicago newspaper stories regarding house fires where people were reported injured for the years representing the first five years of Peter Kearns' life. After quickly realizing that the scope of this search was excessively broad and unwieldy, Dombrowski picked up the phone again and placed a call to the Illinois State Fire Marshall's Office.

After being transferred three times, the detective finally found himself speaking with a young man from one of the offices deep within the Fire Marshall's Office. The young man identified himself with a civilian title that Dombrowski didn't catch. But what the detective did understand from the pubescent-sounding voice on the other end of the line was that all manner of records are maintained and preserved relating to fires, including the amount of property damage caused by fires in the city and state each year, the number of fire-related deaths and injuries, and a wide variety of other data. The young man also said that while much of the fire data is open to public inspection, certain data is protected by law, such as the names of minors killed or injured in fires.

Dombrowski was starting to feel that the more he worked the matter from this angle, the more convoluted and confounding the information became. Within minutes of ending his conversation with the Fire Marshall's Office, the detective's phone rang. His receptionist was running errands so the investigator answered the phone in his office.

"Len Dombrowski. May I help you?"

"Hello, Mr. Dombrowski. This is Ron Curtis returning your call." Given the information about the Curtises' ages that the detective got from the youngest Curtis child, Dombrowski estimated Ron Curtis to be about 50 years old now.

"I understand you are trying to help Peter Kearns," continued Curtis. "My brother, Sam told me you would probably be calling me. How is Peter doing? Is it leukemia that he has?"

"Yes, Mr. Curtis. I'm afraid so. He has a very rare form which requires him to get a bone marrow transplant from a blood relative. No other donor will do the job, I'm afraid."

"Well, I will do anything I can to help. I'm sorry I've kind of lost touch with Peter. He is a special kind of guy."

"That's what I understand," replied Dombrowski. "Do you have some time right now to tell me everything you can remember about Peter's past? And, of course, if anything else occurs to you later, you could always call me back."

"Sure," said Ron Curtis. "For starters, I remember that Peter came to us when he was 8 or 9 years old."

"Do you know anything about any other names he may have gone by at any time?" probed the detective.

"He came to us as 'Peter Kearns,' and I never heard anything about him having any other name.

"Do you recall ever meeting or hearing of anyone else connected to Peter, such as a caseworker from Child Services or anyone at all?"

The eldest Curtis paused on the other end of the line, trying his best to resurrect long-dormant memories. After several quiet seconds, Mr. Curtis spoke with a start.

"Yes, I *do* remember something that might be useful. There was a couple who got my parents interested in being foster parents. I think it was a woman who Dad knew from work and her husband. What were their names....? Everly! Mr. and Mrs. Everly, I believe. I couldn't possibly tell you their first names, but I'm pretty sure their last name was Everly. I don't know if they themselves were foster parents or what the connection was, but I feel certain they persuaded Mom and Dad to become foster parents for Peter. I remember my parents referring to that several times in later years."

During the telephone conversation with Ron Curtis, Dombrowski found out where Sam Curtis, Sr., had worked during the time period in question and spent another thirty to forty minutes trying desperately to plow the largely fallow field of the eldest son's memory, in hopes of jarring some further recollections. When he was satisfied there was no more information to be had from Curtis, the detective set out to track down Mrs. Everly, if that was indeed her name.

# 54

When Antonio was first informed by jail officials that he was to be transferred to Stateville to serve his sentence, he had images of one of America's most notoriously dangerous prisons; the home to many of the city's most vicious gang members. As it turned out, his particular offense and sentence made him eligible for the Stateville Minimum Security Unit.

Today was the day. Antonio lay awake in his cot. It was not yet five and he had been awake since about three. It was still dark, except for the small lights that ran along the hallways at about knee height that were always illuminating the inside of the facility, day and night. Antonio decided that he'd rather get up now and rouse himself with some light exercise, rather than to potentially fall into a deep sleep right before he had to get up anyway.

He had started a daily exercise regimen the day after he had entered his guilty plea. Before that day, Antonio had been so burdened with self-loathing that he cared nothing for himself. But with the help of Fr. Peter's encouragement and the realization that he had a family on the outside that would be waiting eagerly for the day of his release, Antonio understood that he still had a life to live. A minute of jumping jacks to get the blood moving, followed by fifty pushups and then one hundred sit-ups.

"Good, you're already up," barked Tomkins, a jailer who was

never among Antonio's favorites. "Get cleaned up and dressed. They're taking you out of here in twenty minutes."

When he was shaved, showered and dressed, Antonio sat on the side of his bed. He looked around the confines of the small cell that had been his home for the past several months, wondering what awaited him in the next phase of his incarceration. As he looked down at his knees, his peripheral vision saw a single drop of blood fall onto his shirt, just above the belly. Antonio stood up and walked over to a small mirror above the sink in his cell. In his rush to get ready, he had nicked himself shaving, just above his lip. He tore a piece of toilet paper off the roll, wetted it under the faucet, and pressed it firmly over his lip.

As Antonio was standing at his sink, Tompkins came back to his cell.

"Let's go, Montoya."

Antonio was placed in handcuffs and shackles and led by Tompkins to the reception center where they were met by two burly security officers from the Department of Corrections. They took him outside and had him climb into the back of an unmarked, gray van. As Antonio sat alone in the back of the van, he saw the backs of the two guards' heads through a steel mesh screen that separated him from the driver's compartment of the van.

There were no windows on the side of the van, but Antonio was able to watch the progress of the van through the windshield, although the screen partially obstructed his view. Before long, the van was ascending a ramp onto I-55 South. As he watched the world passing by outside the van, Antonio longed for his family. He didn't know what kind of visitation he would be allowed at Stateville, but he had been told that he would be checked in and instructed on the facility's rules upon his arrival.

About an hour later, the van pulled into a garage reception area at the institution where Antonio would be spending an uncertain period of years. He was told that he'd learn of the possibility of receiving credits against his sentence for good behavior and by taking advantage of educational opportunities and self-improvement programs.

As Antonio was led from one area into the next, he was relieved to see that this particular facility did not much resemble the maximum security prisons that are typically portrayed in the movies. He was further relieved when he was informed during orientation that he could earn more liberalized visitation with his family based upon his behavior within the facility. If Antonio was calculating correctly, he might be eligible for release in about two years and nine months, after credits and time served in jail.

**55**

The jury of eight women and four men, including three African-Americans, one Hispanic, one Asian-American and seven Caucasians, was selected by the attorneys in just under three hours. The judge then recessed the proceedings for lunch and just completed the court's preliminary instructions to the jury. Now, the trial itself was finally getting started. Each attorney was given an opportunity to make an opening statement. The judge explained to the jury that the opening statements are not themselves evidence and should not be considered evidence. Instead, they are more in the nature of a roadmap, with each side explaining to the jury what they believe the evidence will show.

The prosecutor laid out the "bare, ugly facts," as he called them, surrounding the Defendant's "brutal bludgeoning" of "the victim." It appeared to be an uneventful evening, with no drama of any kind leading up to the attack. He led the captivated jury right up to the beating with the baseball bat and the Defendant leaving the victim for dead. Fannie almost found herself persuaded of her own callousness by the time the prosecutor sat down.

Interestingly, because Fannie was claiming she acted in self-defense, Robert Waite did not substantially take issue with anything that Garrison Blaze said in his opening statement. He simply told a different story, focusing not on the incident that the Assistant State's Attorney expounded upon with meticulous detail, but on circumstances extending back to the beginning of Fannie and Maurice's relationship forward, culminating in the incident described by the prosecutor. Waite's obvious strategy was to persuade the jury that, far from being an inexplicable, uncharacteristic explosion of brutal fury, Fannie's seminal act of aggression was a rather natural, predictable response to a pattern of abuse over a period of years, arising from the basic human instinct for self-preservation.

Garrison Blaze called Chanelle Riggy, Maurice's niece, as the state's first witness. After providing some basic biographical information and explaining her relationship to the victim, Ms. Riggy was led, detail by detail, through the events that took her to Fannie and Maurice's house, where she found Maurice lying bloodied on the living room floor. Although she had remained stoic throughout her testimony, the witness became visibly upset when she described the scene at her uncle's home. Fannie's attorney knew from Ms. Riggy's deposition that she was unaware of the often volatile nature of her uncle's relationship with Fannie, so he passed when offered the chance to cross examine the witness.

The State's next witness was the city police officer who had responded to the 911 call that Ms. Riggy had made upon the discovery of Maurice lying in the living room of the home that he had shared with Fannie. The police officer, dressed in his bright, blue uniform, recited the particulars of his involvement with the scene in an understated manner, which contrasted sharply with the significantly more charged language employed by the Assistant State's Attorney. Officer Connelly, a witness clearly practiced in providing testimony in criminal courts, provided short, succinct answers to the state's attorney, answering no more than called for by each question.

Arriving within minutes of the ambulance that had also been dispatched by the 911 operator, the police officer explained how he had parked his "commission" on the street in front of the Williams/Thompson residence, directly behind the ambulance. By the time Officer Connelly approached the front door, the usual crowd of curious, neighborhood onlookers had begun to gather on the sidewalk and front yard.

Connelly told of how he entered the front porch and found the front door opened, presumably left that way by the paramedics who were in the front room attending to the victim on the floor. Maurice was already on a gurney and was being administered oxygen when the officer approached him. The officer explained that he quickly assessed that this was a serious crime scene and radioed the dispatcher to send for a forensics team. The officer was approached by Mr. Thompson's niece, Chanelle Riggy, who advised that she had just come to the home to borrow some card tables and then found her uncle, nearly dead, with no one else present in the home. As the officer completed his statement from Ms. Riggy, the crime scene technicians arrived and began taking photographs and gathering evidence. The baseball bat was tagged and placed into a large evidence bag. Officer Connelly testified that he finished his report in the kitchen as the techs performed their job in the living room. When Maurice Thompson was whisked away by the paramedics, the officer told the jury that he didn't know whether the victim was dead or alive.

When the State finished its direct examination of Officer Connelly, Robert Waite informed the court that he had no cross-examination for the officer and thanked him for his testimony.

The next witness was a crime scene technician, Officer Shania Jones. Officer Jones was the witness through whom all of the tangible items at the scene were officially placed into evidence, except for the bat, which was initially identified and presented through Ms. Riggy. Officer Jones had taken a number of photographs and made measurements at the scene and, upon exhaustive questioning by the Assistant State's Attorney, covered the minutia at the scene until the jurors eyes glazed over. However, the jurors' attention was re-engaged as the prosecutor began introducing enlarged glossy photographs of the victim and the crime scene. The final picture put into evidence was a close-up of the baseball bat in the foreground, with Maurice

Thompson's head behind it on the floor. This perspective caused the bat to look enormous and out-of-proportion to the head that had been struck with it.

When Garrison Blaze sat down, Robert Waite stood up. The photographs of the crime scene had been published to the jury, which had been passing them around during the testimony of the officer. Duplicates of the photographs had been provided to the defense. Picking up one of the sixteen-by-twenty inch photos from the defense table and allowing the prosecutor to see the photo he was holding, Waite directed his attention to the witness.

"Officer Jones. Directing your attention to State's Exhibit Fourteen, I'd like you to tell the jury what that glass item on the coffee table next to the couch is."

The witness looked at the photograph and answered promptly: "That is a bottle of Jack Daniels whiskey."

"And what, if anything, can you tell us about the quantity of whiskey that was found in this bottle at the scene?" inquired Fannie's attorney.

"The bottle was empty," answered the witness.

"Thank you Officer Jones." Waite turned to the judge and said: "The Defense has no further questions of the officer."

**56**

Margaret Millington had stayed in daily contact with Fr. Kearns over the past weeks as his condition worsened. After the latest report from two separate workers in the St. Michael's rectory, Margaret was alarmed. She called Detective Len Dombrowski to get a report on his progress. The detective explained to Ms. Millington that he was pursuing several leads at once and, since he was aware that time was becoming more precious, he was sacrificing the usual advantages derived from face-to-face contacts and was now conducting almost all of his investigation electronically and by telephone.

Margaret listened attentively but a bit despairingly to the open-ended information that had been unearthed by the detective so far. Peter had confided to Margaret that his doctors had told him that his overall health was declining at an accelerated rate, and, while he seemed at peace with whatever fate was in store for him, Margaret was determined to do whatever she could do to get Peter a bone marrow transplant from a blood relative. In the conversation with Dombrowski, she satisfied herself that he understood that she expected his entire attention to be devoted to this case and that, if he needed help, she would be happy to get him some assistance.

He finally admitted that, in this race against the clock, more manpower might be useful. When Margaret offered to find him help, Dombrowski told her that he knew investigators that he could enlist in the cause. So as soon as they ended their conversation,

Dombrowski was determined to get back on the phone until he had two other investigators agreeing to drop all that they were working on to try to help him save Peter Kearns' life.

Because of the nature of this particular search, Dombrowski's first call was to Jerome Cheatham. Like Dombrowski himself, Cheatham was a private investigator. Cheatham was a career Army officer, who, upon his honorable discharge with a Purple Heart, spent fourteen years working as an investigator for the Illinois Department of Children and Family Services. Then just five years ago, he opened his own private security firm. Dombrowski hoped that Cheatham might be able to use his contacts to open a few doors that were shut to most others.

It was getting late in the day and Dombrowski had not taken time to eat. He asked Cheatham if he would meet him to discuss some urgent business over a sandwich and a beer. The duo found themselves in an Irish sports bar just thirty minutes later.

"Jerome, like I told you on the phone, I really need your help on this thing," Dombrowski began, after a short exchange of badinage.

"I gathered that. So you've got an orphan priest who needs to find his birth family to stay alive? Is that what you said?"

"Almost. We don't really know if he was an orphan or what exactly happened. It seems more likely that the state took him from his parents due to abuse or neglect. He grew up with the understanding that some nasty burns on his face and body were suffered when he was with his birth family. And he ended up in the foster system in the mid-to-late '80s. Unfortunately, the foster parents who had him through most of his childhood are deceased and their kids have very limited information."

"So what *do* we know about this kid?"

The aging waitress detected this transition in her patrons' conversation and came forward to take their orders. Dombrowski then spent the next hour bringing Jerome Cheatham up to speed on the case, as he devoured an oversized breaded pork tenderloin sandwich and fries. When they'd finished, Dombrowski picked up the other man's tab and they agreed they were going to start back to work early the next morning on their agreed upon spheres of concentration.

As the two men left the bar and went their separate ways, Dombrowski pulled out his cellphone again and punched in a seldomly dialed number in his contacts list – Annalise Stollmeyer. Stollmeyer specialized in computer-aided searches. Her background was in computers long before she began offering her services for investigations. An MIT computer science engineering graduate who had tired of the corporate rat race, decided shortly after marrying her orthodontist husband that she would join the ranks of the self-employed. She was now helping police and private investigators conduct internet-based investigations from her home, while caring for her three-year-old daughter.

Dombrowski had consulted with Stollmeyer on one other case a couple of years earlier and found that her expertise was well worth the money. He figured there was even a greater premium on efficiency here, where time was truly not his friend. After explaining the nature of his case and the time commitment he needed from her, Stollmeyer at first balked. Dombrowski then displayed his practiced power of suasion and told her about some of the ways he had heard that Fr. Peter had spent his life as a priest helping others. Stollmeyer finally agreed, stating, "I'm going to have to risk losing one particularly demanding client if I have to place him on the back burner, but that's a chance I'll have to take."

The detective expressed his sincere gratitude. She, in turn, told him to scan and email her all of the information he had so far and gave him an encryption code he could use to protect the data. He was beginning to feel confident that he would find where Peter Kearns came from, and just hoped it would be in time for the information to help the young priest.

**57**

It was a beautiful Sunday afternoon, so Margaret decided to drop in on her friend, Fr. Kearns, for a social visit. She hoped to persuade him to enjoy the weather with her and take a drive to a nearby park. She reached Peter by phone on the way to the rectory and, although he had planned to make a visit to the hospital that afternoon, she persuaded him to change his plan and join her on her impromptu trip to the park.

As she neared the rectory of St. Michael's parish, Margaret reminisced about the afternoon, not so very long ago, when Fr. Peter persuaded her to go to the patio outside of the hospital, where they had their first meaningful conversation of many. Margaret was astonished to think back to the miraculous transformation she had undergone since that time. She remembered enjoying Fr. Kearns' company for the first time, but she still wanted a drink desperately then. Today, she found herself experiencing only fleeting thoughts of drinking and her depression felt like a thing of the past.

To her surprise, Peter was already waiting outside of the rectory as she pulled up. He was standing beside the front door and, as he spotted her, he smiled and slipped a rosary that he was holding into his right pocket. By the time her car had come to a complete stop, Peter was at her front passenger door and climbed into Margaret's silver Mercedes Benz.

It had been a week and a half since Margaret had seen Peter.

She observed immediately that he had continued to lose weight. This observation led Margaret to ask Peter about his ongoing symptoms and his general strength.

"I am doing okay, Margaret," Peter answered unconvincingly. "I'm still able to do just about all of my duties, so I'm happy about that."

"What's Dr. Cappel's current thinking about treatment?"

"Well, she says that she likes to be finishing chemotherapy when she is ready for the bone-marrow transplant. What makes this particular variety tricky," the priest continued, "is that the donor has to be selected and ready for surgery before they finish with the chemo. She can't finish the chemo treatments and then put me on hold. If she does, she says the benefits gained from the treatments are quickly lost by the delay and the patient is usually too weakened to undergo further treatments and then endure the bone marrow transplant."

Margaret glanced over at her passenger and imagined that he betrayed an arched eyebrow of inquiry. She pulled into a parking spot close to a duck pond and put the center console gear shifter into park. She squared her body in her grey leather seat and faced Peter.

"So what does she want to do while we're looking?"

Peter broke eye contact, turning his head to look straight through the windshield as he answered his concerned friend.

"Dr. Cappel feels that the cancer is too aggressive to delay the chemo any longer. I started last week and have had two sessions already."

Margaret understood the dire meaning of Peter's words. If he were to survive this disease, a donor had to be lined up by the time the chemotherapy treatments were completed. She swallowed hard and pressed on.

"Uh, so how long is…. how long are your treatments supposed to last?"

"Well," Peter replied, "She wants to hit it hard since I'm relatively young. After two more outpatient treatments next week, she wants to have me go into the hospital for a week of sustained chemotherapy. After that she'll need to check my bone marrow cells to see how much progress we've made."

Margaret got out of the car and opened the back driver's side door and retrieved a half of a loaf of bagged bread from the backseat. Peter alit from the passenger's side and Margaret hit the autolock on her key fob as the pair walked to an unoccupied bench which sat just feet from the near end of the pond. A small paddling of ducks recognized the bag in Margaret's hands and swam eagerly toward her. She opened the bag and offered several slices of bread to her companion on the bench.

Peter gently steered the conversation to less distressing topics and asked Margaret about her sister, AA, and a movie that she had watched with a friend after a meeting a couple of evenings earlier. Before long, when there was a brief lull in their conversation and Margaret noticed that her bag was empty and that the ducks had left them in their solitude, she stood up and stretched and they walked lazily back to her car.

**58**

All three investigators were used to chasing leads into a dead-end. But with the increasing urgency of their present assignment, the frustration with each new dead-end became heightened. While Ms. Stollmeyer remained stationed at home on the computer, the two other investigators set out again on foot with separate, but related goals. Jerome Cheatham spent the better part of the afternoon gathering information from people he knew at the Department of Children and Family Services. After doing an online search through the Illinois Secretary of State's Office, looking for the former employer of Peter's foster father, Sam Curtis, Sr., Stollmeyer concluded that the "Printer's Workshop" was no longer in business. She texted Dombrowski the name and address of "Perfect Copy" print shop. It turned out that this was the same business that Sam Curtis, Sr. had worked for but it now operated under new owners and a different name and location.

Dombrowski went into the shop to see if anyone knew anything about a Mrs. Everly.

"Is Mrs. Everly in?"

The young boy manning the desk near the front door looked up from his work and gave the response that Dombrowski feared but expected.

"Who is Mrs. Everly?"

"Well, I was kind of hoping you might tell me," the detective shot back. "She worked here a number of years ago, but I don't know how long ago she might have last been with the company."

Dombrowski slowly scanned the faces of the people he could see working at their desks and tables in the large open room. Most of them appeared to be under thirty-five. The detective realized that few, if any, of these current employees were old enough to have worked even at the time of Sam Curtis' death, let alone at the much earlier time when Peter came to live with the family.

"Could you tell me who here has been with the company the longest? Anyone more than twenty or twenty-five years?"

The kid he had spoken with before looked annoyed and answered him. "This is a small shop. I don't think anybody's been here ten years."

As the detective felt another door about to figuratively shut in his face, he had an idea.

The large man cleared his throat and spoke to all before him in a voice intended to overpower the machines that were chattering.

"Excuse me. My name is Len Dombrowski. I am a private investigator. I'm looking for a woman named 'Everly.' She or her children might be heirs to my client's very large estate. I am going to leave several of my business cards here on this desk and hope that someone might call me with information about how I might find Mrs. Everly or any child of hers. A finder's fee might apply to anyone who can help us find her."

The detective waited and watched to see whether anyone moved. The kid had a noticeably more interested expression, which Dombrowski thought he tried to hide. He picked up one of the cards, put it in his pocket and went back to his work. Slowly, several other employees made their way to the front to get a closer look at their unexpected visitor and to pick up one of his cards. Satisfied, Dombrowski turned and exited.

**59**

Under Illinois law, a defendant commits aggravated battery when, in committing a battery, other than by a discharge of a firearm, he or she knowingly or intentionally causes great bodily harm or permanent disability or disfigurement. Therefore, the nature and seriousness of the injury inflicted upon the victim by the defendant is an essential element of the crime. The State's next witness was the neurosurgeon who was called in by the emergency room staff to deal with the trauma to Maurice Thompson's head. After taking the witness through his impressive credentials, the assistant district attorney asked the doctor to explain the condition of the patient upon his initial examination.

Dr. Ahmed Mansour testified that the patient was unconscious at the time of the examination, having been brought to the hospital in an ambulance approximately twenty minutes before Dr. Mansour's arrival. He observed a cut behind the patient's left ear, with blood matted to the back of the head. According to the emergency room chart which was reviewed by the doctor, the patient was bleeding out of his nose upon arrival. The ER staff had stopped that bleeding and cleaned the blood from the nasal cavity. The doctor also observed slight bruising bilaterally under the patient's eyes. CT scans of the patient's brain revealed a four-centimeter, closed lineal fracture of the occipital bone. The witness patted the back of his own head as he spoke to direct the jury's attention to the area of the fracture.

Finally, and perhaps most dramatically, the doctor described the injuries to his patient's brain. Before doing so, Dr. Mansour explained to the jury the process of taking an MRI and how the "magnetic resonance imaging" works. In this case, Garrison Blaze had Maurice Thompson's brain MRI projected onto a large monitor connected to a laptop on the table in front of the D.A. Holding a pointer as the doctor testified, the D.A. helped the jury see the significant findings in the MRI as the doctor discussed them.

Of particular note, according to Dr. Mansour, were two areas on opposite sides of the brain where lesions could be seen. The doctor explained that the medical term for these lesions is a French term, "coup contrecoup."

"Could you please tell the jury what this means and why the lesions appear to be on opposite sides of the brain?" asked the prosecutor in his most helpful-sounding tone.

"Yes," replied the doctor, who, as if on cue turned his body in his chair to face the jury directly. "The coup injury is at the site of the trauma. In this case, it would be just below the skull at the site where the bat came into contact with the victim's head."

"And the contrecoup injury?" asked Blaze.

"That is a bruise on the opposite side of the brain, caused by the brain bouncing off the other side of the skull from the impact."

The assistant state's attorney looked for a reaction from Fannie's lawyer, but he was stone-faced. The inscrutable Robert Waite.

The doctor remained on the stand for another fifteen minutes, as the prosecutor led him through the procedure of inserting a VP shunt into Maurice's brain to drain cerebrospinal fluid to relieve pressure that had built up within his skull. Fannie noticed that of the state's first four witnesses, her attorney had chosen not to cross-examine three. She had spells of anxiousness during the trial, but whenever she looked out into the gallery and made eye contact with her son, his confident smile gave her courage.

# 60

Jerome Cheatham called Len Dombrowski with what he thought was a major discovery in his area of the investigation. He had found the name of the couple that first had Fr. Peter in their home as an official foster child. While this might prove to move the investigation closer to Peter's birth family, it was also problematic in and of itself. It turned out that Peter's first official foster parents were Frank and Maureen Floyd. But when Peter came into their home, he was already five years old.

So, Dombrowski asked, "Had Peter already been abused when he came to them?"

"Well, that's another curious thing," answered Cheatham. He was not placed into the foster system as a result of any reported abuse or neglect."

Dombrowski looked dumbfounded. "Then how did he come into foster care?"

"Apparently, he was an abandoned child."

"Abandoned? When? By whom?"

"I don't know yet. I'm afraid this is as far back in Peter's life as my contacts are going to be able to get us," Cheatham admitted with a marked decrease in enthusiasm.

Not wanting to react too negatively to potentially useful information, Dombrowski said, "Let's look at everything the Floyds would have received on this kid when he was first placed into their home. Surely there's a record of that," the detective offered.

"Yes. I am holding it in my hands as we speak," Cheatham replied.

"Okay, great," answered Dombrowski. Can you email it over to me right away?"

"You got it," said the former investigator for the Department of Children and Family Services. "It's on its way!"

Looking at the image on his cell phone, the detective quickly read the bits of information provided at the time of Peter's entry into the Illinois foster care system. He then called Cheatham back.

"Jerome. I'm going to try to meet with the Floyds right away. Could you do me a favor and see if you can track down the DCFS employee who filled out this intake sheet and find out what else she might be able to tell you?"

"Absolutely. I'm already on it. I left a message with the head of the department who now handles assessments for the department. I'm going to see if the assessment worker who filled out this paperwork would have any notes or reports that went along with this summary sheet."

"Perfect," Dombrowski answered. "Please let me know as soon as you hear something."

**61**

"Please raise your right hand to be sworn," intoned the bailiff, who led the People's next witness to the witness chair.

"Do you swear to tell the truth, the whole truth and nothing but the truth, so help you God?"

"I do," responded the witness, obediently.

"Tell the jury your name, please," instructed the Assistant State's Attorney.

"Maurice Thompson."

Margaret Millington, who had been present throughout the trial, was now seated in the back row of the gallery. She briefly made eye contact with the witness as he took his seat on the witness stand. He did not know her, but she knew who he was and she wanted to be angry at him for Fannie's predicament. But Thompson, sporting a navy blue suit, made a pitiable picture as he hobbled to the stand with the aid of a wooden cane. Thompson looked broken and old, his white hair contrasting with his ebony skin. Margaret thought he looked more like an elderly grandfather at a wedding than the abusive brute that Fannie had described.

Fannie's attorney noticed that, as Blaze took the witness through the preliminaries, the latter's right eye occasionally appeared to wander. The medical records which had been provided to the defense team in pretrial discovery indicated that this was a result of the brain injury Maurice had sustained in the attack. The longer the victim was on the stand, feared Waite, the more deeply was this handicap likely to be embedded in the minds of the jurors.

"And so," continued the state's attorney, bringing the witness to the day of the domestic dispute, "tell the jury what you did that day from the moment you woke up.

"Well, I…, I ate breakfast and watched TV. Then I went out and ran some errands."

"What time did you get back home, Mr. Thompson?" the prosecutor inquired.

"It must've been around five, because I was home at least a couple of hours when Fannie came in."

"What happened when Fannie came home, sir?"

"She got on me right away. Bickering and riding my …, riding my back, like she did."

"What were you arguing about?" asked Blaze.

"I don't have no idea. And it never mattered. Then she just snapped!" belted the witness, in a line that Waite was certain had been rehearsed.

"What did she do, Mr. Thompson?"

"She picked up a baseball bat and came flying across the room at me." The witness stopped.

"What happened next?"

"I honest-to-God have no memory after that," answered the witness, believably. "The next thing I remember, I was in the hospital and it was three weeks later."

In order to buttress the testimony of Dr. Mansour, the neurosurgeon who had testified about the nature and extent of Maurice's injuries, the assistant state's attorney spent the next half hour going over how the witness' injuries had affected his life. By the end of it, there was certainly no question that his injuries were profound. It was up to Robert Waite to do what he could do to avoid bleedover; in other words, to prevent the jury from being overly demanding in its requirements to find self-defense in order to punish Fannie for the severity of the victim's injuries.

When the state concluded its questioning of Maurice Thompson, Mr. Waite got up from the defense table and took several steps in the direction of the witness.

"Good afternoon, Mr. Thompson. My name is Robert Waite and I am Ms. Williams' attorney. I have a few questions for you, if you don't mind."

The witness stole a quick glance at Fannie at the mention of her name. Fannie was focused on her attorney and did not catch this.

"Yeah, sure," answered the witness as he sighed and anticipated what might be coming.

"You told Mr. Blaze that you left the house for a while and ran a few errands that day, is that correct?"

"Yes," answered the witness without hesitation.

"And where was Ms. Williams during this time?" asked Mr. Waite.

"Uh, she was at work."

"How long had she been at work that day?" pressed Waite.

"She left the house at four-thirty to get to her first job at five..."

"Is that 4:30 a.m., Mr. Thompson?"

"Yes. And then she leaves there at 12:30 and goes right to her next job at one," continued the witness.

"And would you please tell the jury about the errands you ran that day, Mr. Thompson?"

"I got my check in the mail and had to buy some groceries and things," Maurice replied, provoking a searching look from his inquisitor.

"Isn't it true, Mr. Thompson, that Ms. Williams does all the grocery shopping?"

"She does most of it, yeah," acknowledged the witness.

"So what did you do for the five hours or so that you were gone?" demanded Fannie's attorney brusquely.

"I went out," said Maurice, in an assertion that began as an introductory clause, but which the witness hoped to convert to a complete response.

Fannie's attorney wasn't about to let it happen. "Yes, Mr. Thompson. The jury now understands that you went out for several hours while Ms. Williams worked one job and then the next. My question is, 'Where did you go?'"

Since the defense team had taken a wide-ranging discovery deposition of Maurice Thompson, this line of questioning was anything but a shot in the dark. Robert Waite knew exactly where Maurice had been, and Maurice knew that he knew.

"I went out and had a couple drinks," answered the witness, as innocently as he could muster.

"Where did you go, sir?"

"I went to Sandy's."

"And what exactly is Sandy's?" asked Mr. Waite, turning now from the witness and facing the jury to await the witness' answer.

"Uh, it's a bar," replied the witness.

"And did you run a tab for the couple of drinks you had at Sandy's bar that day?"

"Yes," answered the witness, realizing the futility of evading the truth.

"And what were you drinking that day, Mr. Thompson?" asked Waite, making the victim feel like a defendant.

"I was drinking whiskey," answered the witness, now with a bit of an edge.

Waite picked up a document from the table where his exhibits were arranged and pre-marked and asked the judge for permission to approach the witness.

"You may," answered the judge.

Robert Waite walked slowly to the witness and handed him the paper. "Mr. Thompson, would you be so kind as to identify the document which I just handed you and which is marked as "Defendant's Exhibit A?"

"This is a copy of my bill from Sandy's that day."

"I move for admission of Defendant's Exhibit A into evidence," announced Fannie's lawyer.

"No objection," replied the Assistant District Attorney.

"Defendant's A is admitted," ruled the judge.

"And we're talking about the day of the incident that led to Fannie's arrest, are we not, Mr. Thompson?"

"Yes," acknowledged Maurice.

"Can you tell the jury the amount that you spent at Sandy's bar that day?" asked Waite.

The witness looked down at the document, squinted momentarily and answered, "Thirty-six dollars."

"And with that thirty-six dollars you purchased how many whiskey drinks, Mr. Thompson?"

"Six," said the witness.

"And where did you go after you left Sandy's?" asked the attorney, with a bit more drama in his voice to ensure that the jury stayed with him.

"I stopped at the liquor store," answered Maurice.

"How long were you home before Fannie got back from work?" asked the attorney.

"I guess about two hours," Maurice said.

"Did anyone else come to your house that day between the time you got home and the time Fannie came home from work?"

"No. I was home alone," said the witness as he unconsciously gave his questioner a quizzical look.

Robert Waite walked slowly and purposefully back to his counsel table and ran his right index finger down the notes on his legal pad. He then looked up and said to the judge, "May I please have State's Exhibit Fourteen, Your Honor?" The judge had the exhibits in front of him and pulled out the photograph that showed the crime scene with the bottle of Jack Daniels in the background.

Waite strode back across the courtroom toward the witness, placing the photograph before him and asking, "Mr. Thompson, is this the bottle of liquor that you bought after you left Sandy's?"

"Yes," Maurice admitted.

"I have no further questions of this witness, Your Honor."

**62**

Peter sat in a soft leather recliner, with his left arm extended on the armrest, palm up. An IV tube joined his arm to the medication bag which was hung above his head. A television was on to help patients pass the time during chemotherapy treatments. A game show was playing, which Peter recognized from his childhood, although the new host of the old show was noticeably younger and hipper.

The young priest held his cellphone in his right hand, and checked and responded to emails for about thirty minutes. Then he picked up a book that he had found on a bookshelf in the parish rectory. Peter read the book, which was a meditation on the Confessions of St. Augustine, for another thirty minutes, but he found himself dozing. After having to read the same paragraph three times, Peter decided to give in to his fatigue and shut both the book and his eyes and lie back in his recliner.

A short time later, Peter was awakened by an unfamiliar voice. "Excuse me, sir," began the young female standing in front of him. "Are you watching this channel?"

Upon opening his eyes, Peter looked around the room and saw that, of the three patients, including him, who were in the room when he fell asleep, he was the only one left. The young girl appeared to be about ten and was with a woman, apparently her mother, who was just getting situated for her own chemo treatment.

Peter answered the girl, "No, young lady. Help yourself." Peter smiled warmly at the girl and her mother, who he guessed to be about his age. As Peter turned toward the girl, she noticed the scars on the right side of his face for the first time and her own face revealed her sudden fear. The girl's mother kept up the conversation in an effort to smooth over the awkward situation created by her daughter's obvious distress.

"What are you getting treatments for?" asked the girl's mother tentatively.

"I have leukemia," answered Peter. "How about you?"

"Breast cancer. This is my first treatment," she confided. "They tell me the treatments don't actually hurt, but kind of make you sick sometimes. Have you been getting treatments long?" she inquired.

"A while now," Peter replied. "Sometimes I feel nauseated, but not all of the time. For me, the worst part is usually the day following a treatment."

Peter looked back at the woman's daughter. "What is your name?" he asked.

The girl looked at her mother who smiled and nodded her approval.

"I'm Brooklyn," she replied with no further signs of trepidation.

The trio carried on a conversation about the child's baby brother and her school, as well as the woman's recent diagnosis with breast cancer. Presently, the nurse walked in and announced that Peter's treatment that day was concluded.

Peter turned sideways in his chair to face his new friends again. Although they had not spoken of religion, Peter asked the woman, whose name he learned was, "Gloria," if they would like to pray with him quickly before he left. She said that that would be fine, but looked a bit surprised at the invitation. Peter reached out and grabbed the hands of the young girl and her mother, forming a small prayer circle. He closed his eyes and softly asked the Lord for a blessing upon their doctors and nurses and themselves, as well as their families. At the conclusion of the brief prayer, Fr. Peter opened his eyes and, still holding the hands of the woman and child, told them that the woman's name came from the prayer recited by the multitude of angels that appeared at the birth of the Savior. The prayer, Peter explained, is known as, "*the Gloria*."

Closing his eyes again, Peter concluded the prayer by asking that the heavenly host of angels that sang the original Gloria at Jesus' birth, now pray to that same Lord for this mother. Peter opened his eyes, smiled at the mother and child and told them goodbye. As he walked out of the large room and rounded a corner, the mother continued to hold her daughter's hand. The young girl, whose head reached to her mother's chest, stepped closer to her mother and hugged her from the side.

**63**

Although Jerome Cheatham had hoped to find the caseworker who originally filled out the intake sheet on Peter Kearns when he entered the foster care system in Chicago, he was informed that that caseworker had passed away several years before. Therefore, his investigation was going to require him to engage in his least favorite part of investigations - digging into records.

According to an assistant archivist at the Chicago Office of the Illinois Department of Child and Family Services, records of their department from as far back as Dombrowksi and his fellow investigators needed were stored on microfiche. Many of the more commonly referenced records were later digitized from microfiche. The intake sheet filled out by the caseworker when Peter Kearns entered foster care was in a category of documents that had been digitized and was capable of fairly quick retrieval. Other accompanying documents, including notes, were not, and they proved much more difficult to track down.

After a couple of telephone calls, Jerome Cheatham was on his way to a state office building that was primarily used to store records for a number of state agencies. A meeting was arranged there between Cheatham and the state's chief archivist, Alberta Moravia.

Stepping out of the cab and walking briskly to the entrance, Cheatham compared the address he had written in his notebook to the numbers embossed in large, faded gold lettering on the front of the building. Cheatham was immediately struck by the contrast between the state-of-the art DCFS headquarters and this late nineteenth century relic that was fittingly used to store old records. As he passed through the revolving doors at the entrance of the building, Cheatham half expected the foyer to be in black and white.

The investigator glanced around the dimly lit reception area, looking for someone to help him find Ms. Moravia. At just that moment, an extremely thin, middle-aged woman with jet-black hair pulled back in a bun with retro, black-rimmed glasses came around the corner and approached him as an old friend with her hand extended in greeting.

After making their introductions, Cheatham commented on her correct assumption regarding his identity when she saw him.

"I guess you don't get many visitors in here?"

"We don't get *any* visitors in here, Mr. Cheatham. In fact, I don't recall the last time I had to come out here to meet someone. The few people who do come here are employees of the state and I already know them. So it's a pleasure to meet you."

As she spoke, Cheatham noticed that the identification tag that Ms. Moravia wore on a cord around her neck was in serious need of updating. The same woman with the same type of glasses frames and the same smile was beaming at him from the identification tag. But the woman on the tag had unnaturally bright, red hair. And the frames on the glasses in the picture were of a shade of red that almost perfectly matched her hair.

The archivist led her visitor to a bank of computers in a small, first-floor office. A man nearly as old as the building was sitting at one of the computers. He peered up over his glasses at Cheatham as the duo entered the room. Cheatham smiled and nodded. The old man ignored him and looked back at his computer monitor.

Ms. Moravia pulled up a chair at a computer at the opposite end of the small room from the man who was the only other occupant of the room at the time. She pulled out the chair next to her and signaled for Cheatham to sit beside her.

Within seconds the oversized computer monitor was humming and coming to life.

"Okay, Mr. Cheatham. So you need the records on a Peter ...."

"Kearns. Peter Kearns," he said helpfully.

The archivist was evidently a speed reader. After trying to focus on the monitor as Ms. Moravia scrolled forward and backward and opened one computer file after another in rapid succession, Cheatham began to feel dizzy and looked away from the computer screen to give his eyes a rest. He inadvertently made eye contact again with the elderly gentleman, who scowled at him.

"Here's something interesting," Ms. Moravia said. "I just stumbled across some notes which indicate that an interpreter helped to provide information for the intake."

"An interpreter?" replied Cheatham with interest.

The archivist leaned closer to her monitor and squinted. "Yes. A Korean interpreter, to be precise."

"Well, now we may be getting somewhere. We do know that Peter Kearns remembered being cared for by an Asian woman. That must be her. I wonder how long Peter was in the care of someone who didn't speak English?"

"Maybe the interpreter can tell you. If he's still alive. His name and phone number are right here."

"Is there anything else?" Cheatham inquired.

"Just that the name of the person that the translator was getting the information from was redacted, or removed, for privacy."

"Well, I'll take that name and phone number and thank you then," said the investigator as he rose from his seat.

The sound of Cheatham's chair legs scraping against the old wooden floor as he pushed himself away from the table obviously irritated the old man. Before he had a chance to express his further disapproval of the interloper, the former Army officer breezed past the man, patting his back like an old chum and saying loudly,

222

"It's all yours again, buddy." He thanked the archivist, gave her a card in case she happened to find out anything else that might be helpful, and hurried to get back to Dombrowksi with this promising information.

**64**

Ginger Wolfe had been trying to get her sister, Margaret, to come and visit her and her family for weeks. Margaret had been putting her off, despite every intention of paying her sister a visit, as she had become more and more preoccupied with Peter's declining health and the fast-paced investigation that she had launched. She hated to be away from town in the event an emergency matter required her attention in Chicago. So on this Saturday afternoon, Ginger made arrangements to go back to Chicago to spend the day with Margaret. The ladies had made plans to have lunch and then do some shopping together downtown. Ginger packed a bag in case Margaret ended up inviting her to stay the night before returning home.

When she arrived at Margaret's home, Ginger was immediately struck by her older sister's appearance.

"Margaret, you look terrific," beamed Ginger, when she appeared at the front door to let her in.

Margaret smiled broadly. "Thanks, honey. I feel even better."

"I guess life is treating you well, huh?" pressed Ginger.

Margaret invited her sister to come inside and have a seat in the living room.

"Can I get you something to drink before we go to lunch?" asked Margaret.

"No, thank you. I can wait."

"Okay, Ginger. Well, here's the deal. Life has not been all

smooth sailing here by any means, as you know. But I've found that I have an entirely different outlook on life these days. Some days are more difficult than others. I'm really worried about Peter. Then, to be honest with you, there are still a lot of days I fantasize about drinking. It's not even that I really want to drink anymore. There's just an occasional longing that I can't explain. Some days, it's no problem at all. Other days, well, it's a different story."

Ginger had a question she wanted to ask, but she was reluctant for fear of offending her sister, which used to be all-too-easy to do. She decided to try it.

"Margaret, do you mind if I ask, have you managed to avoid drinking altogether so far?"

"Yes. So far. I take it 'one day at a time,' as they say. I'm still focusing on today and not worrying about tomorrow until, well, tomorrow," Margaret said with a laugh.

"What accounts for the difference in you then, Margaret? Is it just that you're not drinking?"

"That's an important part of it," Margaret admitted. "And it's a necessary part. But I think the even bigger change is my overall attitude. Having the faith that we really matter and can make a difference in the lives of those around us makes me *want* to live. I *want* to help other people experience the changes that I have experienced. I know it can happen for them. I think I know how to do it too," Margaret concluded.

The sisters spent a few more minutes on that subject and then shifted into lighter topics for about twenty minutes. At a pause in the conversation, Margaret finally said, "Let's go eat. I'm starving." She then drove them to a Chinese restaurant and enjoyed the rest of the day together. Ginger did spend the night, and the sisters had the best time together that they had shared in many years. By the time she got back home to Carl and her sons, she was convinced that Margaret truly had undergone life-altering, and hopefully permanent, changes for the better.

**65**

As Peter descended the elevator of the medical office building after his chemotherapy treatment, he was overcome by a wave of nausea. He fought the urge to vomit and watched the lighted numbers over the elevator door appear to slow down. The elevator doors opened on the 3$^{rd}$ floor to take on two more passengers, making a total of eight, with Peter stuck in the back corner.

Watching the floor numbers go from three to two and then, finally, to one, Peter wrestled with a dilemma: whether to rudely push his way to the front so he could dart out as soon as the doors opened, or to wait several seconds longer and increase the chances of an accident that would surely disgust all aboard. He opted for a hybrid of these two options and remained where he was until the doors started to open, at which time he nudged his way forcefully past the others, managing a single expression of apology before yielding helplessly to his body's response to the nausea. As he exited the elevator, Peter spotted a trash can with a plastic dome cover and hinged flap. He pulled the entire dome top off and began retching uncontrollably into the can. His fellow passengers gave him the widest possible berth and scampered past.

One of the passengers, an older nurse, while maintaining a safe distance, stayed in the area to make sure the young priest didn't require any assistance. When, at last, the deed was done and Peter stood erect and wiped his mouth and chin with the back of his hand, the nurse took a couple of steps forward.

"Are you alright, Father? Is there anything I can do to help?"

At first, Peter thought that he felt better since he had vomited. But just as he started to smile and thank the kind nurse, he suddenly became dizzy and fainted, falling to the floor. The nurse knelt beside him and checked Peter's vitals; the priest's black clerical suit and black leather shoes juxtaposed against the bright, white tile. Moments later, other medical personnel surrounded him. Eventually Peter was taken by ambulance to the hospital.

**66**

When Jerome Cheatham left the state records building he had tried to pass his new information onto Len Dombrowski, but had to leave a voicemail. He then tried calling the number that the archivist gave him to the Korean language translator. Although the listing of the number may not be current, assuming the translator was still alive, Cheatham hoped he could at least reach someone who might be able to put him in touch with the translator who had that phone number over twenty-five years earlier.

"Hello," came a male voice on the other end of the line. The detective was disappointed that the man who answered had no trace of an accent as one might expect from a man named "Lee" who served as a translator of the Korean language.

"Hello," Cheatham replied. "I am looking for a William Lee."

There was a short pause on the line and the man said, "I'm sorry. You must have the wrong number."

Cheatham felt his heart sink momentarily. He realized it was probably unreasonable to expect the number to belong to the same man all of these years later. But that phone number was the only connection he had to the man who had at least met the Korean woman who had once had Peter Kearns in her care. And "William Lee" was hardly a unique name, especially in a city the size of Chicago.

The investigator immediately called Len Dombrowski again

to tell him about the translator who he was unable to locate. Dombrowski thanked him and tasked Stollmeyer with tracking down the translator. He had already asked her to try to find the Floyds, who evidently got Peter from DCFS after the Korean woman turned him over to them. He was feeling frustration with all of the potential leads that were leading to people they couldn't find. Just then, Dombrowski's phone rang.

"Hello, Dombrowski," answered the big man.

"Mr. Dombrowski. This is Margaret Millington. Any news?"

"We are following up on several leads as quickly as possible, Ms. Millington."

"Well, I hate to sound impatient, but I just found out that Peter's condition is worsening."

Dombrowski waited for her to continue. When she started speaking again, it was clear that her voice was beginning to break.

"He has been rushed to St. Francis Hospital." Fully struck by the irony that this was the very place that she and Peter had met, Margaret struggled to maintain her composure. After allowing a few more seconds to pass, Dombrowski resumed the conversation.

"What do you know about his condition, Ms. Millington?"

Margaret cleared her throat and answered, "I guess he's stable right now, but I'm on my way over there. I just left the courthouse where a friend of mine is on trial."

"I promise you Ms. Millington. We will get to the bottom of this mystery."

"I believe you, Mr. Dombrowski. But please hurry. Do whatever you need to do. If he continues to weaken, I'm afraid that none of this will matter."

Just as this conversation was ending, Dombrowski's phone rang again. Annalise Stollmeyer had a current phone number for Maureen Floyd, Peter's first foster mother. She told the detective that Frank Floyd had died and that Maureen Floyd was alive and well in a retirement community in St. Petersburg, Florida and texted him the number. The big man felt his pulse quicken and he suddenly felt very warm. He pulled a handkerchief out of his pocket and wiped his brow.

Momentarily, Dombrowski's cell phone beeped, indicating that a text message had come through. He opened the message and saw the phone number for Maureen Floyd that Ms. Stollmeyer had sent him. He placed his right thumb on the telephone number, causing his phone to dial the number.

An elderly woman answered the phone. "Hello, Mrs. Floyd. I'm a private investigator in Chicago named Len Dombrowski. I am trying to save the life of a young man that you once had in your home as a foster child."

Dombrowski heard the woman sigh and then she was silent. "Mrs. Floyd?"

"Yes, I'm still here. I don't know how I'm in a position to save anyone's life. What's going on?"

"Do you remember a young boy you had in your home about twenty-eight years ago named Peter Kearns?"

"Peter? Why yes, I certainly do. What has happened to him?" she asked with evident concern.

"Peter is very sick. He needs a bone marrow transplant from a blood relative. I'm hoping you can help me figure out who that might be."

"That poor, sweet boy was always a mystery to us. My husband and I would have adopted him, but we were afraid of what horrible things may have happened to him. We had other children we had adopted in the home, and..." her voice trailed off incoherently.

"Mrs. Floyd, can you tell me who had Peter before he came to you?"

There was another interminable pause on the line.

"There was something else about him," resumed the woman, ignoring Dombrowski's question. "I don't even know if he came from Chicago originally."

Dombrowski felt sick. "What do you mean, Mrs. Floyd?"

"Well, when we were considering the possibility of adopting

Peter, the people we met with at the child welfare department said that they had searched all of the records in all of the states and they couldn't ever find a birth certificate for him."

The detective's head was reeling. He was trying to comprehend what this meant to his investigation. When the woman on the other end of the line started talking again, the detective almost wasn't listening.

"Ms. Koo wasn't sure where he got the name, "Kearns," since they couldn't find a birth certificate that could have possibly belonged to him.

"Wait a minute, ma'am. Who did you say?"

"Ms. Koo. She's the Korean woman who told the child welfare people that she found Peter."

**67**

It was finally time for Fannie's defense team to present their case to the jury. Robert Waite rose from the defense table and faced the judge.

"The Defense's first witness is Fannie Williams," announced Fannie's lawyer.

During the presentation of the state's case-in-chief, Fannie was referred to impersonally as, "the Defendant." But over the course of the next several hours, Waite took pains to familiarize the jury with Fannie's name and to make sure that they came to know far more about the on-again, off-again relationship between her and Maurice Thompson.

Today, Fannie was wearing her favorite blue dress. Her attorney made arrangements for her hair to be redone by the beautician she saw before the first day of trial. Although he cautioned Fannie about not sounding too rehearsed in her answers, she knew every question that her attorney would be asking her.

Waite laboriously took Fannie through her earliest dates with Maurice, overcoming numerous objections from the prosecution based on an alleged lack of relevance. Waite patiently explained how all of this background information was critical in order for the jury to understand Fannie's claim of self-defense, based on being a battered woman. The prosecutor clearly wanted to minimize the amount of sympathetic detail that the defense would be allowed to present. The judge overruled each and every one of the objections during this line of questioning, allowing Waite to put all of this information before the jury.

Next, Fannie's lawyer began weaving into his examination questions designed to demonstrate to the jury the many small ways in which Maurice came to exercise control over Fannie. He had Fannie tell the jury Maurice interfered with her plans to spend time with friends and later limited even her phone calls with them. Gradually over time, Fannie's world became smaller. She worked; she came home; and she worked some more.

After they had been together for about a year, Maurice began to make belittling, cutting comments to Fannie, occasionally at first and then more frequently. Maurice drank daily and the more he drank, the more verbally abusive he became, especially when he was drinking whiskey.

At this point, for the first time in her testimony, Fannie's eyes filled with tears.

"Can you tell the jury some of the names that Maurice would call you?" asked Waite.

"Do I have to?" Fannie replied sheepishly.

Waite smiled patiently at his client's spontaneous deviation from script.

"Yes, please," answered her attorney.

It was obviously painful for Fannie to recount for the jury a half dozen or so of Maurice's most commonly used insults. As she repeated these words in front of a courtroom full of strangers, Fannie made fleeting eye contact with her son and quickly looked back at her attorney.

Fannie's attorney then segued from verbal and emotional abuse to Maurice's emerging pattern of physical abuse.

"Did Maurice ever hit you?" asked Waite.

Fannie suddenly felt an unexpected pang of fear as she was asked for the first time to talk about these matters in front of so many people. Despite her attorneys' efforts at preparing Fannie to testify, she now found herself on the verge of forgetting all that they had told her to ensure that her testimony was clear and audible. With her chin resting on her chest and her eyes downcast, Fannie answered her lawyer.

"Yes," mumbled the clearly uncomfortable witness.

"Tell the jury about the first time you remember Maurice hitting you," continued Waite. As he made eye contact with Fannie, her attorney tapped his own chin to remind her to keep her head up while testifying.

"Objection, relevance!" shouted Blaze, jumping out of his seat. "Judge, these questions have to be closely tailored to the incident in question. Mr. Thompson is not the one on trial here."

The judge turned toward Waite for his response to the objection. Waite stood across from the assistant district attorney with his hands folded in front of him and said, "Your Honor, the history of the parties' relationship as a whole and certainly the history of physical abuse that was established before the events on the evening of Ms. Williams' arrest are most crucial for the jury to determine whether Ms. Williams had reasonable fear that her life was in danger when she struck Mr. Thompson."

"Overruled," bellowed the judge. "You may continue Mr. Waite."

**68**

After being unconscious for over an hour, Peter woke up. He was now alone in a small cubicle in the emergency department at St. Francis Hospital, separated from the surrounding cubicles by a three-sided curtain rack up against a tiled wall. Peter was already connected to an IV and was awakened by the increasing pressure caused by the inflation of an automatic blood pressure cuff on his arm. He immediately was aware of an intense headache. As he considered his final conscious moments, he vaguely remembered vomiting into the trash can after his chemotherapy, but nothing thereafter.

Within moments of coming to, a nurse opened the curtain to his room and walked in. Seeing him awake, the nurse spoke to Peter.

"How are you doing?" asked the twenty-something female nurse.

Peter made a brief, vain effort to reposition himself in the bed to sit up a bit. "I was hoping you could tell me," he answered with a hint of a smile.

"Well, we're waiting for the doctor to check on you, but you are stable right now," said the nurse. "By the way, I'm Dana. Let me know if you need anything."

"Thank you Dana. I will," replied the priest, who noticed that his black priest suit had been replaced with a light-green hospital gown. When the nurse again left the cubicle, the priest pulled back the thin piece of fabric that was imitating a blanket and peeked down the front of his gown. He was somewhat relieved to find that he was still wearing his own underwear.

Within a couple of minutes, Dana was back with some instructions for her patient.

"If you need to use the restroom or want to get up for any reason, you need to push this button and get assistance, okay?" admonished the nurse.

"I understand. Thank you, Dana."

The next time the curtain was opened, it was by a tall, very dark man wearing a traditional white doctor's smock.

"Hello. You are Fr. Kearns?" asked the doctor, whose eyes fell from Peter back down to the chart in his hands.

"Yes," Peter answered.

"I am Dr. Quashee," said the physician extending his hand to his patient in greeting.

Peter shook the doctor's hand.

"How you feel?" asked the doctor with an accent that Peter assumed to be either from Africa or a Caribbean island.

"Well, I have a headache, but other than that I don't feel too bad," Peter replied.

"We are going to run some tests and find out why you pass out," said the doctor, with his head tilted to the side.

Peter had no recollection of passing out, but it made sense, since he had no recollection of being taken by ambulance to the hospital in the first place. He was put through a battery of diagnostic tests in the E.R., including CT scans, an EKG and some lab work. About two hours after introducing himself to Peter, "Dr. Q.," as the nurses called him, came back in.

"Okay Fr. Kearns. We are going to have you as our guest, but we'll be moving you to a room for the night very soon, alright?"

With so little information being offered, Peter didn't even have any questions for the doctor, so he simply thanked him and closed his eyes in hopes of obtaining a bit of relief from his continuing headache.

## 69

It took Annalise Stollmeyer less than one hour online to track down Koo Seo-Yun, the woman that Mrs. Floyd reported had found an abandoned Peter Kearns many years ago. The investigation team knew that an interpreter was needed nearly three decades earlier, when Ms. Koo provided information for the intake at the Department of Children and Family Services. After forwarding the woman's current phone number to Len Dombrowski, Stollmeyer went back to the computer to search for telephonic interpreters, in case Ms. Koo had still not learned English.

On the fourth ring, a female voice answered.

"Hello," said the woman on the other end.

"Hello," replied Dombrowski, afraid to let himself be too hopeful about the identity of the woman he was speaking with.

"Is this Ms. Koo?" Dombrowski asked.

There was a pause on the line. Dombrowski thought about his client's desperation to solve the mystery of Peter Kearns' birth and the clear fact that he really could not afford any more dead ends. He needed to solve the mystery right now, and he literally held his breath momentarily as he waited for the woman's reply.

"Yes. This is she. How may I help you?"

The detective was nearly dumbstruck. This is actually her! And her English is now impeccable.

"Ms. Koo, my name is Len Dombrowski. I am an investigator

and I am hoping that you can provide some simple information that could allow me to save a young man's life."

"Yes. What do you need to know?"

"I believe that you took a young boy into your home about twenty-eight years ago. He ended up in foster care afterwards and is a fine, upstanding adult now. He's actually a Catholic priest. But I'm afraid he is critically ill. His doctors say that he needs a bone marrow transplant from a blood relative, and I am hoping maybe you can help me find out who Peter's parents or siblings might be."

"Hmmm... ."

The woman sounded as though she were processing all of this, or perhaps recalling details that she may not have thought about for decades. The detective finally interrupted her reverie.

"Ms. Koo, how and where did you find Peter Kearns? You did find him, didn't you?"

The woman finally responded, "I did take that young boy into my home for a couple of years. But my sister is the one who asked me to take care of him. She got him from a family that had employed her."

"Was it the Kearns family?" interjected an audibly excited Dombrowski.

"I don't remember. I'm really sorry. It has been so very long ago..."

"Well Ms. Koo, I would really appreciate it if you could give me your sister's phone number. You could call her first if you'd like to let her know what we need."

"I would love to be able to help, Mr......"

"Dombrowski," offered the detective.

"My sister used to live in Chicago. We came here together as young college students. I would love to help, Mr. Dombrowski, but my sister moved back to South Korea several years ago after we had some disagreements. I don't have a current telephone number... ."

"What is your sister's name?" pressed Dombrowski, with desperation seeping into his voice.

"My sister is Koo Jae-Sung. I last spoke with my mother about six months ago and she told me my sister was in Seoul then. I believe she is still there."

"Ms. Koo, would you do me a favor?"

"Yes. Certainly," answered the woman, politely.

"Could you see if your mother or any other family member knows a phone number for her or where she works?

"Yes, I will be happy to see what I can find out."

The detective gave Ms. Koo his telephone number and confirmed her address while she was feeling cooperative, so that he could track her down if that suddenly changed.

**70**

"The first time that Maurice hit me was a year or so after we started going out." Fannie looked over at her attorney for reassurance.

"Go on, Ms. Williams," urged her attorney patiently.

Now Fannie found herself looking over at her one-time lover. Waite followed her eyes and also stole a glance at Maurice, who was now slouching in his seat and looking down toward his lap. Waite hoped the jurors noticed his guilty demeanor as they waited for Fannie to continue.

"We ate a nice supper I fixed for us. I just finished with the dishes and was going to sit a piece with Maurice on the couch in our family room. He saw me coming in and hollered to me. Told me to get him a beer from the fridge."

"What happened next, Ms. Williams?" said Waite, continuing to encourage his client.

Fannie now fixed her gaze convincingly on Maurice, who looked up in time to make eye contact as she continued.

"I says to Maurice, 'Are you sure you need another one right now?'"

"Why did you ask him that, Ms. Williams?" inquired Waite.

"Cause he done been drinking all day before that. He was getting that sloppy look he gets when he's drunk."

"What did he say to that?"

"He says, 'I don't need nobody countin' my beers,'" Fannie replied.

"Go on, please," urged the attorney.

"So I went back to the fridge and got out a beer for him. I opened it and was walking over to where he was sittin'. I didn't see one of his boots on the floor and I tripped on it. Made me spill it out all over my hand and Maurice's leg. He got up and slapped me across the face."

"Did he say anything to you when this happened?" asked Waite.

Fannie glowered. "I remember this like it was yesterday," Fannie answered calmly, belying the anger she felt in recalling the incident.

"He says, 'Watch out, you... He cursed. Do I have to say it?"

"No, Ms. Williams. That's not necessary," replied Waite. "But did he call you a bad name?"

"Yes," Fannie answered.

"How is it that you remember this incident so clearly, Ms. Williams?" Waite inquired.

"Because it was the first of a whole lot a beatins' I got from Maurice after that," Fannie answered.

"Tell the jury about that, Ms. Williams."

**71**

"Knock knock. Anybody home?"

Although Peter was feeling extraordinarily weak and achy, his spirits were lifted when he looked up and saw Margaret step inside his room, carrying a large potted plant with three balloons collectively carrying the message: "GET-WELL-SOON."

Margaret had not gone more than two or three days without seeing Peter in recent weeks, knowing that his condition was worsening rapidly. Still, she was somewhat taken aback at his pale and gaunt appearance today. Margaret set the planter on a table in front of the window and walked over to Peter's bed. She leaned over and, for the first time since they had met, pulled him close to herself and held him in an extended embrace. Unexpectedly, Margaret was overcome with emotion and began to cry as she held the thinning young priest against her body. After weeks of maintaining a façade of unshakable confidence and optimism, Margaret was embarrassed at her loss of composure, which inadvertently revealed the true level of her concern.

Margaret stepped back and quickly wiped the tears from her eyes, making a transparent effort at reassembling her more sanguine demeanor. Peter acted none-the-wiser, smiling at Margaret and thanking her for the gift.

The two began talking about life, including the activities at St. Michael's Parish, a mutual friend's struggles with sobriety, and

Margaret's growing involvement in the ministry to the confined. Forty minutes or so into their conversation, a tall, stately woman in a white doctor's smock stepped into Peter's room, followed closely by a nurse. Peter introduced Margaret to Dr. Cappel, who was holding Peter's medical chart in her hands and frowning. Barely taking time to acknowledge Margaret, the oncologist addressed her patient curtly.

"Fr. Kearns, I would like to speak with you alone please."

Margaret, looking suddenly uncomfortable, backed away and turned towards the door. Peter stopped her by announcing in reply, "Doctor, Ms. Millington is a very dear friend and confidante. It would be far easier for her to hear what you have to say than for me to try to accurately update her right after you leave."

"Very well, Father," Cappel replied, yielding to her patient's wishes as Margaret stepped back to the wall to give more space to the doctor and her patient.

"I need to get you to our cancer center right away. Your immune system is seriously degraded right now."

"What would I do then?" asked the priest.

Dr. Cappel pulled the chart to her chest as she folded her arms, striking a matter-of-fact pose.

"We would keep you in a sterile environment to try to keep you alive."

Peter looked from the doctor over to Margaret and back to the doctor.

"And I suppose that will not improve my actual disease to any degree, is that true?"

"Well," answered the doctor, not sure where the priest was going with this, "you are in a very critical stage of this disease and ....."

Peter interjected, "But if I do not have the transplant we are hoping for, I have reached the end of my other treatments, correct?"

"Fr. Kearns, I am trying to give you the best chance to live that I can," answered the leukemia specialist.

"And I appreciate that very much, Dr. Cappel. But as I

understand it, nothing can be done for me without a transplant beyond maintaining my life for a marginally longer time without any possibility of actually curing the disease, isn't that true?" asserted Peter. It was clear the priest had spent some time thinking about this subject.

"Well, we don't want you to contract an infection of some sort which would greatly complicate any effort to cure the disease," she replied, in a tone that acknowledged the accuracy of Peter's conclusion.

Interrupting the dialogue between the doctor and her friend, Margaret asked a question, "How long does Peter have to get his transplant, doctor?"

Dr. Cappel looked at Margaret briefly and then made eye contact again with her patient. Peter raised his eyebrows and nodded to her, indicating that he would like the doctor to answer Margaret's question.

"We are now at the critical point where your body could become too weak to survive a successful transplant. It needs to be performed imminently."

Peter nodded his head as he took in the doctor's dire reply. "Okay then," interjected Margaret. "We are going to find that bone marrow donor right now."

Margaret crossed the room briskly, telling Peter to rest as she exited his hospital room. As Margaret raced out of the room to make a phone call to Dombrowski, Peter's conversation with his doctor continued. The upshot of the conversation was that it was Peter's decision alone as to whether to be transferred to the cancer center or not. So long as he were kept in a sterile environment, he could really only be kept comfortable until he either had his bone marrow transplant or died waiting.

**72**

Len Dombrowski pulled the vibrating cellphone from his right front pocket and saw that his prized client was calling for another update. He was eager to tell her about the exciting progress that was being made in the investigation. But it wasn't long into the conversation before he realized that the exigent circumstances of Fr. Peter's health prevented Margaret from sharing his satisfaction with the investigators' efforts. The panic in Margaret's voice alarmed the detective, who knew of no way to effect any shortcuts in the investigation that was fully consuming the time of three experienced specialists working on overdrive.

After a brief conversation aimed at reassuring Margaret that everything humanly possible to locate Peter's family was being done, Dombrowski promised to provide real-time updates to her until the mystery was solved. Developments were now unfolding in hours and minutes rather than weeks and days and the detective excused himself to get back to work. Just as he was hoping to avoid personal phone calls and other distractions to avoid missing a call back from Koo Seo-Yun, his phone again began vibrating again with a number that he did not recognize. Before he had a chance to ponder the matter, the detective realized by the large number of digits on his display screen that this was an international call.

In his haste to push the "answer" button on his screen, the detective nearly hung up on the caller.

"Hello?" said the big man as calmly as he could muster.

"Hello," replied the soft-spoken female voice on the other end. "I am trying to reach a Mr. Dombrowski," continued the unknown caller.

"This is Len Dombrowski."

"My name is Koo Jae-Sung," replied the woman. "My sister tells me you believe that I may be of some assistance to you."

The detective was struck by the similarity in the voices of Koo Jae-Sung and her sister. If it weren't for the fact that he had just spoken with Koo Seo-Yun in much less time than it would take for her to travel to South Korea, he might easily have believed it was she.

After explaining further the emergency that her sister had outlined for the caller minutes earlier, Dombrowski began to unearth everything that this woman knew about Peter Kearns. She told Peter that when she and her sister arrived in the United States nearly three decades earlier to attend college at the University of Chicago, they both had partial scholarships and some financial support from their family back home. But both women found it necessary to supplement these resources by part-time employment, due to the unexpectedly high cost of living in this densely populated metropolis. While her sister had dabbled in a variety of jobs, Koo Jae-Sung lucked into a relatively lucrative position as a housekeeper for a young professional couple.

The husband was a dentist and his wife was a nurse. As it turned out, their names were, in fact, Dennis and Muriel Kearns. Ms. Koo explained that Mrs. Kearns was very attentive to her infant child. Due to Dr. Kearns' work schedule and the hours of Ms. Koo's employment in the home, she rarely saw or spoke to him. As best she could recall, the boy was less than a year old when she went to work for Dr. and Mrs. Kearns and he had already suffered the incident that caused his burns, though he continued to be treated for them. She was never told the details of that incident, although she

246

confessed she had often wondered about it. She confided that from her experience diapering and dressing the child, virtually no area of the boy's body was entirely spared by the fire.

"How was it that the Kearns gave their son to you, Ms. Koo?"

"Because I was new to this country, I originally thought that perhaps Americans were more…. *casual* about putting their children up for adoption. I was very young and naïve. But to answer your question, Mr. Dombrowski, there were no formalities involved in it at all. The offer caught me completely by surprise."

"So please, how did this happen?" pressed the detective with growing astonishment.

"One evening, shortly after Dr. Kearns came home from work, I heard him and Mrs. Kearns arguing in another room. I couldn't tell what they were saying. Shortly after they had become quiet, Mrs. Kearns came into the family room where I had been reading to Peter. She was obviously very sad. She sat down next to me. Mrs. Kearns held my hand in her lap and told me I was very good with Peter. She began to cry and told me that she and her husband could not keep him and asked if I would care for him."

"If you would care for him?" asked the detective.

"Yes. That confused me at first, because I had been caring for him for many months by this time. But she made it clear to me what she meant by this. She wanted me to keep Peter."

"How did you react to this?"

"Mrs. Kearns was clearly very sad about what she was asking me to do. After hearing the argument right before she came and talked to me about this, I had to assume that Dr. Kearns was making her do this. I asked her why she would want to give her baby away and she wouldn't tell me. She just cried. But she was very insistent."

As he was discussing all of this with Ms. Koo, Dombrowski began to wonder if there was a connection between the boy's injuries and his parents' decision to give him away outside of the normal adoption process. And if that were indeed the case, they may have no interest in stepping forward publicly now to have their names associated with Peter. But the detective knew that that was a bridge he would have to cross when he got to it. In the meantime, his focus was on getting to that bridge; in other words, finding Dr. and Mrs. Kearns.

**73**

Robert Waite took Fannie through the ensuing years of her relationship with Maurice in painstaking detail. She told the jury about the typical pattern where Maurice would come home drunk and if something set him off in that state, he would often fly into a rage. He would curse at Fannie and throw things at her. On about a dozen instances where she could recall the specifics, he physically abused her. She told the jury about him choking her until she passed out, pushing her over a coffee table, punching her in the eye, twisting her arm behind her back, dislocating her shoulder, and even trying to push her out of a moving car when he was driving drunk.

Fannie explained that she had tried to leave her abuser repeatedly. A couple of times, she had actually left him and had considered getting orders of protection to keep him away. He would come and literally beg her to take him back, promising that he loved her and that he was determined to change. Fannie admitted that she should have left Maurice after the first time that he even threatened to hurt her, but she said she had no idea what the future would hold and always found his apologies convincing.

"So, Ms. Williams, tell the jury, please, how you would know when Maurice was likely to hurt you?" asked her attorney.

Fannie fixed her eyes on Maurice and he again looked down. Fannie then looked over at the jury box and into the faces of each juror, from her left to right. She told the men and women on the jury that if he drank whiskey before she got home and started cursing at her, she either had to leave or take a beating. It had happened many times before and most recently just a few weeks before the fateful evening that led to this trial.

Upon further questioning from her attorney, Fannie told of how, on the evening in question, she knew there was going to be trouble when she saw the empty bottle of Jack Daniels in the living room. She tried to tread softly and avoid him, but Maurice seemed to sense this and force exchanges with her. She felt that he was taunting her like a cat with a mouse. This was his way of provoking a fight with her. She had become pretty good at not taking the bait. Sometimes Maurice would pass out before any fireworks occurred. If he did not, it usually got ugly.

Fannie had been on the witness stand for an hour and a half. Waite paused and looked at his watch. He told the judge that the next part of his direct examination was likely to take a while and he knew that it was already 4:30 in the afternoon. The judge pushed his leather chair back from the bench and turned to face the jury.

"Ladies and gentleman, we'll go ahead and break for the day. I would remind you that you are not to discuss this case with anyone until after your deliberations. Please return here at eight o'clock tomorrow morning. We stand adjourned."

Fannie had been trained by her attorney to stand any time the jury was entering or exiting the courtroom, so she dutifully stood at the jury box even before her own lawyer had risen. The jury filed out of the room in single file before anyone in the gallery made a move for the doors.

# 74

Walter Midland was not one who took well to change. He had been married to his Becky, who Walter called "Beck," for thirty-nine years when she died of an excruciatingly painful brain tumor. She had learned during their marriage to never surprise Walter by rearranging furniture in any room in their house without getting his expressed approval in advance. Otherwise, she had found that he would obstinately convince himself to hate any such change, just because it had been made without his say-so. She knew Walter had to be conditioned to get used to any new idea gradually in order to weaken his instinctive resistance.

But today, Walter was angry because a change was being imposed upon him without his say-so. In fact, he was given no input into the decision made by Whispering Willows at all. True, he had been placed into his current bedroom at the facility at the single room rate, but that was just because he had been lucky that their numbers had been down a bit during his stay thus far. But all of that was changing. Today. Without warning. Like it or not, the center's administrator, Ms. Wagner, who, upon making her introduction to patients seemed to exaggerate the Germanic pronunciation, "Vogner," had informed Walter just two days earlier that his time for enjoying his single room was coming to an end. And it was coming far too abruptly for Walter. So this was the day that he was going to meet his new roommate and Walter had decided he wasn't even going to feign a welcoming reception for this intruder upon his privacy and solitude – whoever he may be.

Chicago was and is, of course, a big city. It is a very big city. There are between two and a half and three million residents in the city at any given time. Walter and Beck never had children and didn't really get out and socialize much. Beck had worked at a school library and Walter had worked for an auto parts manufacturer. He generally came straight home from work and spent a lot of time watching TV. As a result, Walter was only acquainted with an extremely small percentage of the city's residents, including those within walking distance of Whispering Willows. Therefore, from the time that Ms. Wagner had delivered the bad news about the roommate that he would be getting, it had never occurred to Walter that he might actually know his new roommate.

Ms. Wagner informed Walter that a nurse who was an independent contractor and not affiliated with Whispering Willows was going to come in and sanitize the room and establish a hyper-sterile environment in the room. Evidently, she explained, his new roommate's physician demanded that this protocol be followed as a condition of his continuing treatment of the patient. While the room was thus being prepared, Ms. Wagner explained that Walter would need to be moved to another room. She didn't expect it to take more than an hour or so.

When he got back to his room, Walter was relieved. It did not look drastically different than before he'd left. One difference was that there was a clear sheet of plastic dividing the room in half between the beds, with a zippered door at the far end of the partition. Walter was hoping that he would still get lunch, as it was one o'clock and he had not yet been fed. It wasn't the greatest food in the world, but Walter admitted to himself that it beat starving. To his further relief, his lunch tray was brought to him within minutes of being returned to his room. And he saw that the baked chicken and broccoli that he had ordered was still steaming, although the dinner roll's appearance on the corner of the tray left something to be desired.

Since being diagnosed with pancreatic cancer, Walter, who was by nature a bit of a grump, had adopted a demeanor that was morose. Therefore, it would not take a drastic change in his normal personality at the facility to make sure that his new roommate got the point that he was not welcome.

Midland's narcotic dosage had recently been increased to help him deal with his increasing pain. As a result, after lunch on this particular day, he was fading in and out of consciousness. The television on the wall aired a game show followed by a soap opera. Walter totally ignored both. As the soap's closing theme began to play, Midland opened his eyes to the sound of his door being pushed against the door stop and squeaking wheels rolling into the room. Walter frowned as he observed the detestable Ms. Wagner leading a pair of paramedics into the room. He saw by their uniforms that they were employees of an ambulance company. The stretcher was inclined to about a 45 degree angle. That made it easy for him to see the patient who was coming to join him. Midland's jaw dropped and he let out a phrase that was both blasphemous and vulgar. He was immediately embarrassed at his lack of self-control in light of the identity of the roommate, which was none other than the young priest, Kearns.

"You?" demanded the older man, incredulous.

"Why not? I needed a bed somewhere. The first guy they wanted to stick me with was a White Sox fan," grinned the priest impishly.

The older man's first thought after recovering from the shock of finding out that the priest would be staying in his room was his concern that he might continue to curse in front of him. He decided he would warn the priest about that possibility later, after he got settled in.

**75**

The conference call between Detective Len Dombrowski and his two associates did not last long. Everyone knew his assignment, and this time there was no separation of responsibilities. All were independently going to use each and every investigative technique that they knew or could think of to track down Peter's parents or any brothers or sisters that he may have out in the world. To his delight, finding an online listing for the dental office of Dennis Kearns, previously in Chicago but now in Oak Park, Illinois, was simple. As he was assembling his thoughts, he got calls from each of the other two investigators in succession. First, he was called by Annalise Stollmeyer who also had found the listing for Dr. Kearns. Before he could clear the line after informing her of his own success in tracking down the dentist, Jerome Cheatham beeped in. He allowed Cheatham to join in the conversation that was underway.

"Okay, Annalise, I'm going to talk to Dr. Kearns. Why don't you track down any children he might have in the meantime. Jerome, maybe you could be looking for Mrs. Kearns, in case Dr. Kearns isn't at work today."

"I should be able to handle that," replied the computer ace with a growing confidence that was shared by her two teammates. "No problem," chimed in the career soldier.

Dombrowski got into his car and sped south and then due west toward Oak Park. It was a drive that would normally take twenty minutes, but, despite traffic, the detective reached his destination in eighteen minutes.

Dr. Kearns' office was located in a shopping plaza, next to a Mexican restaurant. According to the sign out front, he was in practice alone. Dombrowski walked through the front door and into the waiting room of the dental office. The reception area contained several chairs, a lightly padded leather couch with metal legs and three end tables. The receptionist sat behind a wall that was glass from about four feet off the ground to about eight feet high. A sliding window allowed the receptionist to speak to patients. It was closed as the detective approached the counter. He looked to his right and saw that a large tooth with a smiling face adorned the wall. The tooth was holding the obligatory toothbrush and reminded patients to brush at least twice a day.

As the large man reached the receptionist window, he looked down to his right and saw a bell on the counter. The receptionist noticed his hulking frame towering over her and opened the window. Smiling, she asked Dombrowski if she could help him. The detective informed the receptionist that he was a detective, intentionally omitting the modifier, "private," in hopes that he'd find the dentist more cooperative than might otherwise be the case.

"Please tell Dr. Kearns that Detective Dombrowski from Chicago is here and that I have an urgent matter to discuss with him."

As the receptionist rang somewhere back in the dental offices, the private investigator wondered if his misleading identification qualified for the crime of impersonating a police officer.

About two minutes later, a man who appeared to be in his mid-sixties, with silver hair and silver, round glasses came to the window. He wore a stern, unwelcoming expression.

"Yes, detective. What can I do for you?" inquired the dentist, impatiently, in his white dental smock.

"Could we speak somewhere in private for a minute, doctor?" replied Dombrowski.

The dentist peered out into the waiting room and saw four patients waiting. He looked more carefully at Dombrowski.

"I don't see a badge. Do you have any identification?"

"I am a private investigator, Dr. Kearns," explained the detective, holding out his identification.

"What's this about?" demanded the dentist, without hiding his irritation.

"I am trying desperately to save someone's life, and I think you can help me."

The dentist's countenance softened ever so slightly. "Okay, but just for a minute. As you can see, I have a waiting room full of patients out here."

The dentist led Dombrowski through a small maze to his private office. It was small, but appeared to be well-organized. The detective glanced quickly at the diplomas, certificates and awards that indicated he had the credentials for a dental practice. The dentist seated himself behind the desk and indicated for his visitor to have a seat.

"What's this about saving somebody's life, Mr., I'm sorry, what is your name again?"

"Dombrowski. I'll make this as simple and straightforward as I can, Dr. Kearns. I know you had a son, Peter, about thirty years ago. I don't care why you gave him up for adoption or anything, but he needs a blood relative to donate some bone marrow or he is going to die very soon."

The dentist's expression grew dark. After barely settling into his seat behind the desk, the dentist jumped up again, clearly irate.

"I'll make this as simple and straightforward as I can, Mr. Dombrowski. I don't appreciate strangers coming into my office under false pretenses and making crazy accusations!"

"Doctor, I …"

"Get out. Now!" The dentist's face was purple and contorted and he pointed to the door of his office.

"But doctor, please…."

"Get out before I call the police," screamed the irate dentist.

"But, Dr. Kearns," continued the detective.

At that moment, the dentist reached into a desk drawer and pulled out a 9 mm Sig Sauer handgun and laid it on the desk in front of him.

"Now you're a trespasser. Goodbye Mr. Dombrowski."

For a split second, the detective thought he was about to get shot and contemplated reaching for his own weapon. However, at the same time that he realized he would be too late, he understood by the dentist's tone and body language that he was just telling him to leave; not that his life was over.

The detective didn't need any more convincing; he walked out of the door sideways, keeping an eye on the dentist. He could not believe that this agitated maniac ever had anything to do with the kind and gentle Peter Kearns.

As soon as he reached the doorframe, Dombrowski felt slightly panicked about his investigation. Momentarily putting his own personal safety aside, he turned fully back toward the dentist, who was now holding the gun down to his side.

Dombrowski made a final, desperate plea.

"I understand you aren't interested in what I came to talk to you about. But do you know of any brothers or sisters or anyone else who might be able to help me?"

The dentist smiled darkly. "You can go talk to his mother."

"Where is Mrs. Kearns, doctor?"

"I don't know. But she hasn't been Mrs. Kearns for over twenty-five years now."

Knowing that he was pushing it, Dombrowksi asked if the dentist might know where to find his ex-wife or what name she used now.

"Try Joliet. And I don't know if she's married or what her name is, but her family is in Joliet. Their family name is "Tucker.""

The detective hurried out of the dentist's office and drove back toward the city, calling his associates to update them along the way. He was beginning to get a hunch as to who was most likely responsible for Peter's burns. But he was surprised that, adamant as he was not to get involved in the matter, the dentist didn't seem to mind directing him to Peter's mother.

## 76

At 8:10 a.m., Fannie was back in the witness chair for the second day. Her attorney took her through each minute detail of the day of the assault on Maurice that he had scribbled on his legal pad shortly after he had been retained for Fannie's defense. He had Fannie describe Maurice's slurred speech, giving examples of how he was pronouncing specific words differently than when he was sober. He had Fannie tell the jury about seeing the bottle of Jack Daniels in the living room and noticing that it was empty when she got home. She explained that there were no bottles of Jack Daniels or any other whiskey in the house when she left for work that day and that Maurice must have consumed the entire bottle in one day.

The attorney had Fannie tell the jury about how, after she had worked two jobs that day, she was greeted at home by a foul-mouthed, angry, red-eyed, visibly intoxicated and obnoxious housemate.

"So Ms. Williams," began Waite, "do you acknowledge that Maurice had not tried to hit you that day before you hit him?"

"Yes," replied Fannie firmly.

"Well, had he said anything threatening to you?"

"Objection," interjected Garrison Blaze, rising out of his seat. "That question calls for a legal conclusion."

"Sustained," ruled the judge.

But Robert Waite was not concerned. He actually set up the prosecutor for that objection in hopes of drawing to the jury's attention the inescapable conclusion that his rephrased question elicited.

"Okay, Ms. Williams. Please tell the jury if anything was said that caused you to fear for your safety."

"Maurice told me that he got on a good drunk and would probably have to whoop my ass later."

"Did that concern you, Ms. Williams?" asked Waite.

"Yes, sir," Fannie answered.

"Why was that?" pressed her attorney.

"Because the week before he said the same thing. Then he done punched me in the face."

"Were you injured, Ms. Williams?" continued Waite.

"Yes, sir, Mr. Waite," Fannie replied. "He broke a bone by my eye." Fannie reached up and touched her left temple as she spoke.

Waite then offered into evidence a set of certified medical records from the hospital exactly one week before the incident for which Fannie was on trial. The records indicated a hairline fracture of the left orbital bone.

"By the way, Ms. Williams, is Mr. Thompson right-handed or left-handed?" asked the defense attorney.

"He use his right hand for everthing."

"And Ms. Williams, it says in these medical records that you told the hospital staff that you hurt your eye by having a vase fall from a high shelf while you were dusting. Is that what you told them?"

"Yes," answered Fannie.

"Was that true, Ms. Williams?" asked Waite.

"No," admitted Fannie.

"Then why did you say that?"

Fannie made eye contact with a petite Hispanic woman on the front row of the jury box and answered, "Because Maurice said he'd take me to the hospital if I told them that, but he said he'd make the other eye match it if I told them what really happened."

Waite surveyed the faces of the men and women of the jury and knew from Fannie's recitation and from their expressions that he'd hit pay dirt. He deliberately paused in his questioning for fifteen seconds, but in the courtroom it felt like an eternity. Although the prosecution knew the defense case through the pretrial discovery process, the impact of the presentation was substantially stronger than Garrison Blaze had anticipated. He had the opportunity to cross-examine Fannie a bit later in the morning, but didn't relish it, because her testimony rang true and was compelling.

As if to emphasize the weakness of the assistant state's attorney's cross-examination, Waite waived the opportunity to ask any follow up questions after the cross was concluded.

He then called his second witness to the stand, who identified herself on the record as Dr. Eloise Hunter. Waite asked the witness about her impressive educational credentials, her research into the subject of "battered spouse syndrome," and her vast experience working with victims of domestic abuse over the course of her career of thirty-five years. Dr. Hunter explained to the jury the well-recognized pattern of victims of abuse staying with their abusers, lying to others to cover up injuries inflicted by their abusers and being ostracized from friends and families as the victim's circle of support shrinks. The average abuse victim, according to Dr. Hunter, finally leaves her abuser, if at all, on the seventh attempt to get away.

Although early use of "battered spouse syndrome" in defense of murder or battery cases seemed to be presented as a sort of psychological defect among the defendants on whose behalf the defense was asserted, later research, according to the witness, indicated that the woman's violent responses, after being subjected to well-established patterns of aggression, were perfectly rational and not indicative of any psychosis. Therefore, if a victim of repeated acts of abuse is in the midst of this sort of recurring pattern, she may reasonably perceive that she is in danger well before the interaction between the partners would appear to an outside observer to present an imminent threat.

On cross examination of the expert, Garrison Blaze got Dr. Hunter to admit that not all jurisdictions recognized battered spouse syndrome. She also had to admit that she had never examined or evaluated Fannie and that she had no idea whether she was an abused spouse or not.

The defense's third and final witness was Jamika Smith, Maurice's ex-wife. Through a series of open-ended questions, Waite had Ms. Smith tell the jury about the pattern of drunken abuse that she was subjected to during her short marriage to Maurice Thompson. Many particulars matched the pattern previously described by Fannie.

When it was his turn to question Ms. Smith, Blaze got the witness to acknowledge that they had a nasty, contested divorce, during which she had tried unsuccessfully to get a share of her husband's retirement account. "Would it be fair to assume that you were angry with Mr. Thompson at the time of your divorce?" She nodded her assent.

"Would you answer out loud for the record, Ms. Smith?" urged the prosecutor.

"Yes," replied Jamika, obediently.

"And would it be fair to assume then that you were angrier still after the divorce when you were not awarded any part of the retirement plan that you felt entitled to?" The witness admitted that she was angry at the time, but pointed out that that was many years ago and that she had put all of that behind her. Robert Waite then announced that the defense rested.

## 77

"Really, Father. Why in the world did you come here? If you somehow got the impression during your visits here that this place is loads of fun, I hate to be the one to disappoint you."

The priest smiled, but didn't speak immediately. He was in immense pain at the moment, which was as intense as he had experienced, and was trying to put it out of his mind before answering. Fr. Kearns then replied to his new roommate.

"To tell you the truth, I think these cancers are pretty scary. I knew you were someone who had been dealing with it for a while, so I thought maybe you could help."

Midland looked at the priest skeptically, so the priest expanded on the matter.

"It seems like we are both battling versions of the same animal. Maybe we can kind of help each other deal with whatever comes our way."

The older man smirked. "I get it, you're wanting me to show you how to deal with cancer with a cheery disposition." The priest chuckled good-naturedly at Midland's sarcasm.

"I hate to tell you this, Father, but most people come here to die. You're still a young man with a possibility of being cured. Shouldn't you be in a hospital?"

Peter was struck by this more talkative version of Walter Midland so, despite his present discomfort, he didn't dare throw a wet blanket on this rare occurrence. The priest explained that there was nothing further his doctor could do unless they located a family member to donate bone marrow for him. He thought that in the meantime, he and Mr. Midland could try to support each other in their common struggle.

While talking to Midland, Peter did his best to hide the increasing pain, which was particularly pronounced in his side around the ribs. The older man started talking about baseball. Then he began speaking tenderly of his deceased wife. It was the first time Peter had seen this soft side of the man and was reassured to confirm that he had one.

After figuratively taking a walk down memory lane with his roommate, Peter asked him why he had become so bitter. When Midland scowled at the young priest, Peter feared that he had taken the conversation a step too far. But then Midland sighed and explained that he was angry at God for taking his wonderful wife prematurely.

"I have to admit," confessed the older man, "I have never been the most charming guy in the room, but it was really hard to watch such a beautiful, innocent gal as my Beck be put through so much suffering. I mean, if the Lord wanted to take her, there's nothing I can do about it, but no one should have to go through what she did. Tell me how I'm supposed to feel about that, Father?"

The priest nodded his head slowly in understanding. Midland wasn't sure he was going to answer him after a longer-than-expected pause by the cleric.

"I don't think there is any easy answer to that, Mr. Midland," acknowledged Peter. "It is amazing what people can endure, isn't it?" Midland nodded his head in agreement. The priest continued, "You mentioned that you weren't always the most charming guy in the room. Did Becky ever complain about that before she got sick?"

The older man admitted that she had. "I am who I am," offered Midland by way of an excuse.

"Obviously, I didn't know your wife, but did she come to rely pretty heavily on you in her sickness?" inquired Peter.

"She got so bad," replied Midland, "that I eventually had to do everything for her. I dressed her, bathed her, and even fed her near the end."

Peter noticed that the older man looked more angry than sad as he spoke these words.

"So much for our loving God," concluded Midland bitterly.

"We know, Mr. Midland, that our lot in this life is to suffer. Thank goodness there's a lot of joy along the way too. But, like everything else in life, our suffering isn't scattered evenly. I'd wager that despite your wife's pain, she very much appreciated your loving assistance in her final weeks."

"I think she did," he admitted.

Out of the blue, Midland steered the conversation in an unexpected direction.

"If you don't mind my asking, how does a guy avoid sex his whole life?"

This is something that Peter had discussed with friends and others over the years on a number of occasions, but he didn't see it coming from Walter Midland. Peter admitted to the man that he began each day by praying to the Holy Spirit to help him keep his vows and to avoid temptation in general.

"One thing that I remember when I feel especially weak, is that our Lord himself prayed fervently throughout his life, and especially in the Garden of Gethsemane on the night before his crucifixion when he faced intense temptation. He took his friends, Peter, James and John away from the rest of the disciples and asked them to pray with Him that none of them fall into temptation. I have also learned to change what I'm doing if physical urges creep upon me. I pray, but I also get moving. Often I have gone for a walk. Eventually, the moment passes and I always try to remember to immediately thank the Lord. Thinking of Jesus and all of his sacrifices helps bring me out of the carnal feelings that tend naturally to afflict us all.

"I just can't imagine never having sex," Midland confessed.

"Well, I'll bet that, unless you're Superman, if you added up all of the actual time you've engaged in that enjoyable activity, which is a gift from God when used properly, it wouldn't be more than a year or so. I'm just cutting out that year and spending it in different ways." Now Peter was smiling broadly.

The pair's conversation was interrupted by a nurse, who came in to hook up some IVs with medication ordered by Dr. Cappel. She had a number of medical issues to discuss with Peter, so Midland turned back toward the television and mused about the life of his celibate roommate.

## 78

It was the first Saturday of the month; the day that would soon become the favorite of the Montoya family since Antonio had been transferred to Stateville. This was the day when, for two hours, Antonio got to see, touch and hold his family and they got to see, touch and hold him. The first part of the reunion on this day was devoted to A.J. excitedly filling his dad in on all that was going on in his six-year-old world, including getting to go to Six Flags Great America on his birthday and riding his first roller coaster. He explained with pride how he wasn't quite tall enough to ride it, but he was close when he stood on his tip-toes, so the coaster operator had winked and let him on. Juanita smiled and nodded her head to confirm A.J.'s story.

Antonio was holding Inez in his arms and kept staring into her eyes and kissing her, as if to ensure she remembered him until next month. Finally, after giving Johnnie a few minutes to render a typically embellished version of his past few weeks, Juanita asked Antonio how he was getting along. The first thing he mentioned was that he had been sober for one hundred and twenty-seven days. Although he was just taking it a day at a time and his task was made easier by the lack of access to alcohol in the prison, Antonio explained to Juanita that he was learning the tools to help him maintain sobriety when he got out and that he was progressing through the steps of Alcoholics Anonymous, which he was dedicated to continuing upon his release.

"How are you holding up, honey?" Antonio asked, as he tenderly placed his hand on his wife's shoulder, next to her neck. Juanita looked into her husband's eyes and assured him that she and "the team" were adjusting, but that they were counting the visits until "Daddy" came home.

Antonio then told Juanita that he had maintained regular correspondence with Fr. Kearns. Together, they had decided upon a sort of voluntary penance that Antonio was going to undertake when he was out of Stateville. In addition to his regular job, he was going to work a part-time job of just five hours a week for the rest of his working life to contribute those earnings to a scholarship that would be set up in the names of Vicky Bunch and Erica Benning. Although he realized he could do nothing to bring them back, Antonio explained that this was one small way to help make sure that the girls' names lived on in a way that could bring some small measure of good to other young people.

At the end of the too-short visit, the young family hugged and kissed and said their goodbyes, and Juanita left the visiting room feeling confident that in the not-too-distant future she would be getting back the Antonio that she loved.

## 79

As it turned out, Dr. Kearns' information about his ex-wife's family living in Joliet, Illinois was correct, and it didn't take Annalise Stollmeyer long to track down the ex herself, and she immediately relayed the information to Dombrowsi by phone. Muriel Kearns was now Mrs. Muriel Beatty. She had been remarried to Mark Beatty for twenty-seven years. She and Mr. Beatty had four children, who had all grown and moved out on their own. Two of them remained in the area and the other two had moved out-of-state. Muriel Beatty, still a nurse, now only worked part-time in an obstetrician's office. Her husband was a successful realtor in Joliet. In fact, as Dombrowski approached the home at the address his assistant had found for him, he was quite impressed with both the neighborhood and the home. As he looked at the massive house, Dombrowski considered that Mrs. Beatty must have continued to work only for enjoyment of her job.

The detective saw a car in the driveway and nearly felt like skipping. He had called Margaret as he had promised and she was thrilled with his news. If Mrs. Beatty herself was unable or unwilling to serve as the bone marrow donor, there were four potential donors in the half-siblings that Peter had never met. For this particular contact, Dombrowski and his team agreed that a face-to-face meeting was imperative.

The detective lumbered up the long sidewalk from the driveway

.o the front door. The oversized wooden front door, which looked like it had been taken from an old church, was surrounded by a beautiful stone portico. Dombrowski pressed the doorbell. He listened to the chimes of the doorbell sounding throughout the inside of the large home. Momentarily, he heard the pitter-patter of footsteps approaching the other side of the great door.

Peter Kearns' mother opened the door and greeted the unexpected stranger. He identified himself as a private detective, but was not invited inside the home. It didn't take a detective to see that Mrs. Beatty was cautious in dealing with him and he didn't blame her.

"I want to assure you that I am not here to try to sell you anything, Mrs. Beatty. I do have extremely important business to discuss with you. May we sit here please?" asked the big man, motioning to a couple of chairs on a patio extension off the front porch. He assumed that would allow them to be seen from the street and hopefully make the woman less apprehensive about talking to this rather imposing stranger.

"Ma'am, my name is Len Dombrowski," he said, holding out his identification badge for her to see. I have been looking for you for some time."

"Really? Me?" asked the woman, obviously surprised and confused. "Why have you been looking for me?"

"It has to do with your marriage to Dr. Kearns."

"Oh my goodness. What's happened to him?" asked the woman, placing her hand over her mouth in surprise.

"Nothing as far as I know, ma'am. But it has to do with the child you had with Mr. Kearns – Peter."

"Oh, I can't believe someone's coming to ask about him after all this time. What's the problem, detective?"

Dombrowski was stunned by the woman's nonchalance. It was as if she were being confronted with a long-neglected parking ticket, not a baby that she had inexplicably given away to a foreign housekeeper.

"Well, Mrs. Beatty. Peter has a very rare form of leukemia...."

"Where does he live?" Beatty interjected. "He must be thi‍‍years old by now!"

The detective was starting to think this woman was as crazy as her husband. Kind of a shame the marriage didn't work out, mused the detective.

"I guess that's probably about right. But however old he is ma'am, he's not going to get any older unless he has a life-saving surgery right away, and that's why I'm here."

"What can I do for you, detective? I'll tell you whatever I possibly can."

"Well, it's not so much what I want you to tell me, Mrs. Beatty. As I was saying, Peter has a very rare form of leukemia. With most forms of the disease, I guess they can do all sorts of treatments, but with what he's got, he needs a biological relative to donate some bone marrow for a transplant."

"And?" asked Mrs. Beatty, with not a hint of maternal concern evident in her tone.

"Well, Mrs. Beatty, I was hoping you'd want to donate some bone marrow to save your son's life." The detective was now visibly upset. How could this woman be so cold?

"There must be some mistake...... Oh, I get it. You thought I was Peter's mother!" exclaimed the woman in astonishment. That makes perfect sense, I guess. Does he still go by "Peter Kearns" then?" she asked.

"You're not Peter Kearns' mother?" asked the detective, flabbergasted.

"No," answered the woman, now regretfully. "And I don't think you'll ever find her."

## 80

After a brief recess, the attorneys and the judge conferred a final time about the jury instructions that would be read to the jury. The attorneys then came out and made their closing arguments, with the State going first and last, as the judge explained, since the state has the burden of proof. Following the closing arguments, the judge told the jury that he would read them the applicable instructions on the law and then send them to the jury room for deliberations.

The jury sat attentively in the courtroom for the trial's final act. Garrison Blaze had left the comfort of his counsel table, where the lead detective on the case had been seated beside him throughout the trial. He was now standing directly before the jury, preparing to deliver his closing argument. The assistant state's attorney had a large television monitor arranged in plain view for the jury, so that he could bring specific items to their attention, providing visual aids to the oral argument that he was going to advance in the effort to obtain justice for Maurice Thompson.

The prosecutor began his argument to the jury by explaining that, after the attorneys had concluded their final pitches to them, the judge would be instructing them on the law that was to be applied to the evidence that they had seen and heard throughout the course of the trial. It was up to them to determine the credibility and weight to be given to each and every bit of evidence presented. It was up to them to consider the motives that various witnesses may have

had to be truthful or otherwise. Yet, argued Blaze, there were certa
facts that were not in dispute. Facts that really spoke for themselve.
These facts, which the prosecutor enumerated and displayed in a
Power Point presentation, included the following:

1. On the evening in question, Maurice Thompson was beaten
   severely with a baseball bat, causing a loss of consciousness
   and injuries to both his skull and his brain.
2. Fannie Williams is the person that inflicted these injuries
   on her unarmed victim.
3. Maurice Thompson had made no move toward Fannie or
   any threat of imminent harm at the time of her assault.

These facts, said the state's attorney, are each unquestionably
true. None of them require that the jury choose among competing
statements or theories. Each is uncontroverted by the defense and
must be taken as true by the jury.

On the other hand, argued Blaze, the defense rests solely on
the self-serving testimony of the woman who has every incentive to
lie; to avoid the punishment she deserves and the punishment that
the Illinois legislature has prescribed for such a violent offense. She
claims that there was a history of physical abuse in the relationship
she had with Mr. Thompson. And yet, argued the prosecutor, not a
single witness could corroborate any such abuse in the history of her
relationship with the victim. And, in fact, Blaze continued, the only
medical records introduced by the defendant herself contradicted
the testimony she is giving now about an earlier injury. He pointed
out that Fannie's trial testimony differed what she told the doctors
and nurses at the time, the very doctors and nurses she was relying
upon for treatment of her injuries. But now, in an attempt to escape
justice, he argued, she told another story – a story which conveniently
attempts to make Mr. Thompson appear to be the violent one. "And
again, she claims this without a shred of corroborating evidence,"
stated the prosecutor.

Blaze reminded the jury about the extent of the victim's injuries, s testified to by Dr. Mansour. He said that justice demanded that this brutal attack not go unpunished.

In response, Fannie's attorney told the jury that the reason that trial by jury had endured over the centuries is that the public recognized that, despite its faults, juries brought together the varied experiences of people from all walks of life who, collectively, can generally discern the truth about conflicting evidence better than the smartest single person, whose own experiences are necessarily far more limited.

Waite said that the men and women on the jury had the opportunity to look in the eyes of the witnesses who testified and to judge their credibility for themselves. He also pointed out that, since Illinois allowed alleged victims to be present in the courtroom during the trial with certain exceptions, the jury also had the opportunity to see the person who is supposedly the victim react to the testimony in the courtroom. He said that the jury could use its common sense in considering those reactions as well.

The defense attorney reminded the jury that, in order to convict Fannie Williams, the state had the burden of proving each and every element of the crime charged. He also explained how, when the defense of self-defense is raised, the state must negate that defense beyond a reasonable doubt.

Since he had reserved a few minutes to respond to Waite's argument, Blaze then got to talk to the jury a final time, thanking them for their service and urging them to "do the right thing."

Lastly, the judge read the final instructions to the jury and they followed the bailiff out of the courtroom into the jury room to begin their deliberations. When the jury was gone, Fannie realized that the back of her dress was saturated with perspiration. She made eye contact with Maurice as the attorneys gathered their files. Although she wasn't sure, she thought her former boyfriend looked sorrowful for the first time since the trial had started. She wondered, if it were so, whether it was because he felt bad to hear his treatment of

her spoken out loud, or simply because he still had feelings for h
Walking out of the door to go wait for the jury's verdict, Fann
realized she absolutely didn't care which, if either, happened to be
the case.

**81**

When Walter Midland awoke from a nap, he looked over at the bed next to him and saw that his roommate was reading the Bible. He closed his eyes again and pondered momentarily the different ways that people occupied their minds. After a short while, Midland heard the leather-bound book being laid softly on the table between them. He took the opportunity for another frank discussion with the priest.

"Do you really believe in heaven, Father?" asked the man.

Peter, who had been unable to sleep due to his continued pain, sat himself up slightly in his bed and turned partially toward Midland.

"Yes, I do," replied the priest, speaking through the transparent, plastic partition.

Looking thoughtful, the older man confessed to the priest that he saw no reason to think heaven was real. He believed that heaven was created by man so that he would not fear death. This familiar argument had long troubled Peter and the suffering priest put his pain out of his mind and engaged Midland in a practiced inquiry into the topic.

"Have you been to the Grand Canyon?" asked the young priest.

"Yes," answered Midland. "It is magnificent."

"And have you sailed on an ocean?" continued the priest, conjuring energy from the deepest reservoirs of his being.

"Ha-ha. Many years ago," reflected a smiling Midland, who

was thinking back to a time when he was much younger and remembering the feeling of the warm sun on his skin and the wave splashing into the small boat he was on as part of a fishing group.

As though sensing he could be in danger of losing Midland at sea, the priest continued. "And Mr. Midland, have you ever looked up at the stars at night and wondered about the vastness of the universe?" Midland acknowledged that he had done so many times.

"Well, so have I," replied the priest. "And I am amazed at the awesome power of the Creator of all of this. It would be very difficult to describe any of these things to a blind man, would it not? I mean, I think you would have to have seen all of this to believe it, don't you?" Peter asked.

"I suppose so," admitted the older man.

"And yet, our Lord, who obviously loves to create wonders for our benefit, has promised us that he has something much greater prepared for us in the life to come. Is it so hard to believe that the Creator of all that we can see is capable of creating much more that we only see later?"

Midland remained silent and the priest continued.

"When you look in the mirror, Mr. Midland, what do you see?"

"A dying old fart," replied the man with a chuckle.

"Well, do you remember being a young boy?" Peter asked.

"Of course. Some memories are as sharp as if they were yesterday."

Peter scooted his body fully onto his side so he could better see his roommate. "Wasn't that boy who experienced those things that come to your mind from your childhood, you?" asked Peter. The priest did not wait for the obvious answer and continued. "So is Walter Midland that young boy? Or is Walter Midland the older man lying here today? Or is Walter Midland that man who spent much of his life in between with his loving wife?"

Midland stared intently but without comment as the young priest continued.

"Well, here's what I'm getting at. The essence of your being is not determined by the state of your physical body throughout your life.

ou are you at every stage of development, from before your birth, through adolescence, during middle age and even now. I find that a common obstacle to faith is that we all have difficulty conceiving of a soul living apart from our mortal bodies. The concept appears to be beyond our experience. But I'm not sure that's completely so."

"I had an interesting conversation with one of our now-deceased parishioners at St. Michael's that I will never forget. Mary Nolan, who had been a science teacher for fifty years until she retired, lived to be 105 years old. She told me that she recognized her soul in the later years of her life. Obviously intrigued by this, I asked Mary how she came to do that. Here is what she told me. Mary said that she had very distinct memories of being a little girl during World War I. She remembered things she thought about back then and she remembered looking at her face and hair in a full-length mirror in her parents' bedroom."

"She said that when she was one hundred and living her final years in an assisted living home, she would still look at herself in a mirror. Although her eyesight was badly deteriorated, Mary could see that nothing in her appearance looked much as it did as a child. She had a pacemaker to help her heart keep its rhythm. She had two artificial hips. A bit of senility had set in and Mary knew it. But she said that the inner self in that old woman observing her reflection was the same exact being, apart from the old and deteriorating body, that remembered her mother talking about the war her father was fighting in over in Europe so many years ago - the exact same person. Well, Mary explained, 'If I am both that long-gone child and this old shell of my former self, the only constant is that timeless inner being that watched as the century took its toll on my outer body.' Mary was convinced that that was her soul."

"So, Mary explained, if the passage of time and the aging of her body while she was alive failed to change that inner being or soul, why should the mere stopping of her heart and the further deterioration of her body be assumed to do so?" Peter smiled inquiringly at his roommate, who was clearly deep in thought.

Peter concluded the story. "As Mary pondered this, ˸ considered that maybe what she saw as her soul was just her brai˸ She ultimately decided though that her brain was what allowed he˸ to recognize the separateness of her inner being or soul, but that her soul was not her brain; that it was independent of every bodily function and separate from the body itself."

"So I believe that when our earthly body dies, that frees our soul or essential being to go to the place our wonderful Creator has promised that He has prepared for us."

The older man spoke for the first time in several minutes. "Do you really think our souls just go to a whole new world?" asked Midland, earnestly considering the matter.

"Imagine being a baby in the womb, Mr. Midland. After you've been in that secure world for the first nine months of your existence, the only world that exists for you is that dark universe that you have known. You are surrounded by amniotic fluid and you get your nutrients through the umbilical cord. Then, suddenly one day, following a violent passage through the birth canal, you are surrounded by an overwhelming bright light, suck in your first breath of air and come face-to-face with your human 'creators,' your parents. I imagine our passage into heaven being something like that; simple yet sublime.

The priest then concluded this thought. "Like Mary, I think that our faith is really consistent with our human observations, if we dare to think with the eyes of faith rather than the pessimistic eyes of the unbeliever."

When Peter finished, Midland, appearing transfixed, replied:

"I don't know if heaven is real or not, Father," said the older man, "but that is beautiful and worth thinking about."

Peter winced again and Midland caught it. "Are you sure you're okay Father?" he asked.

The priest shrugged it off. He then told the older man, whom he knew had himself been suffering greatly, that his Catholic foster parents taught him to offer up life's difficulties to the Lord. Midland

d he didn't understand what he meant by that, so Peter explained
ore fully. He told him that when he was growing up, it was not
unusual for him to be stared at by other children or teased due to
the scars on his face. His foster parents told him that Jesus suffered
while he was on the earth and that he did it willingly for our sins.
"They told me that any difficulty we face can be offered as a silent
prayer to our Lord and our suffering joins us to him. Now, whenever
I experience pain, I think of our Lord's suffering and death and feel
that he is with me. If he could handle so much pain for me, I figure
I can take much less for him."

Peter then asked Walter if he would join him in prayer and he
prayed the "Lord's Prayer," followed by a short invocation: *"Dear
Father. Thank you for this life you have given us on earth. We know
that everything that proceeds from your mouth is true and that you
have promised an eternity of joy in your heavenly kingdom for all who
believe in you. Please accept our unworthy souls into your kingdom
when our days here are done, and allow us to see you face to face, with
all of our loved ones who have preceded us and all of your angels and
saints. Amen."*

**82**

Fannie had spent three and a half hours in a small room in the basement of the courthouse. Her son, Jarrod; her daughter, Veronica, who had flown in from Seattle for the last day of the trial; and her entire defense team were with her, awaiting the call from the court. They ate, talked and even played cards to help pass the time. Finally, Waite received the call from the court that the jury had reached a decision. They quickly went upstairs and re-entered the courtroom for the final time. As she had been throughout the trial, Margaret Millington was seated in the back of the spectators' gallery to observe the proceedings. Several minutes later, the jury filed back into the courtroom, with the Hispanic woman that Fannie focused on during her testimony leading the way, indicating that she had been selected foreperson.

As the jurors walked single file past the counsel table toward the jury box where they'd spent most of the past week, Fannie was prepared to acknowledge any who might look her way. Not one of the twelve or the alternate juror who was with them looked her way. They all appeared focused and ready to finish their duty. Fannie gulped and took in a deep breath. When the jurors were all in their places, the judge asked them if they had reached a verdict. The jury foreman said that they had and the judge asked her to read the verdict. The gathering din that greeted the return of the jurors quickly subsided. The woman stood and, for the first time, glanced at

Fannie and then looked back toward the judge. She then announced in a surprisingly powerful voice that rang through the crowded courtroom: "We the jury find the Defendant, Fannie Williams, not guilty of aggravated battery."

Gasps and cheers combined to create a clamor. Fannie's son, Jarrod, leapt over the small wall that separated the parties and their attorneys from the gallery. He grabbed his mother and held her in a close embrace, tears flowing freely down both of their faces. Fannie's daughter, Veronica, and Margaret joined the brief celebration. Although they didn't hear it, the judge banged his gavel, proclaiming that the case was dismissed. Before Fannie could express her gratitude to her benefactor, Margaret slipped away from the group and headed directly to Whispering Willows to check on Fr. Peter.

**83**

When Margaret arrived at the convalescent center, she was informed by the staff that Peter had had a very difficult night and was now sleeping. After scrubbing her arms and hands and donning the green hospital gown, per protocol, Margaret unzipped the doorway into Peter's part of the room and entered. She pulled her chair up next to his bed and picked up the young man's hand and held it in hers. Peter's hand felt cool to the touch. She looked at his hand and thought the skin had a bluish tint. Margaret gave Peter's hand a quick squeeze. He opened one eye and squeezed back. She sat there with him and let him sleep, engaging Midland in quiet small talk.

As she watched her visibly weakened friend sleep, she noticed some irregular breathing that she thought may have been sleep apnea, but it concerned her. She also noticed that one of Peter's arms, exposed by the gaping, pushed-up sleeve of his hospital gown, was covered in a number of bruises she had not noticed before, from the wrist to the elbow.

Margaret casually asked Midland if Peter had complained about feeling any worse today. Peter's roommate replied that he had been in a lot of pain all over his body. "Oh, and he said he hasn't had the urge to use the bathroom for a couple of days, but he didn't particularly complain about it."

Margaret was now really frustrated with Peter for being taken to Whispering Willows rather than to the hospital. Dr. Cappel had certainly made her recommendation clear in that regard. She had no way of knowing whether any of these symptoms were serious or not. Although the hospital may have been unable to cure Peter, there would have been superior treatment of his symptoms and complications. But Peter was unyielding in his determination to spend time with Midland, even if it were to be his final days.

About an hour after she arrived in Peter's room, Margaret's phone rang. She reached into her purse with her free hand and picked it up. She saw Len Dombrowski's name on the screen. She had not even had a chance to say "hello" when the detective began speaking in a rush. Dombrowski explained that he had gone to meet with Muriel Beatty, formerly Kearns, and that it turned out she was not Peter's actual mother. Beatty had explained that she was persuaded by her husband to give up the child because he was afraid of losing his dental license over this child that had been brought to them in a very mysterious way.

Pausing from time to time only long enough to catch his breath, the detective told Margaret the story that had just been related to him by Muriel Beatty. Evidently, about thirty years ago, when she was married to Dr. Kearns, she had a friend, Amy, from nursing school. Amy had sat for her boards twice and had failed to pass them both times. Therefore, while Muriel and others in their class were beginning their careers, Amy had to find something else to do until she was able to become licensed.

Margaret's attention was momentarily diverted as Peter made a strange choking sound and then resumed a more normal breathing pattern.

"So," continued the detective excitedly, "Amy heard about a job for a doctor who needed an assistant. He wasn't worried about credentials, so she applied for the job. She was hired immediately after the interview. Amy was sketchy, according to Mrs. Beatty, about the type of work she would be doing for the doctor. She evidently got busy with the job and several months went by where Muriel didn't hear from her. Mrs. Beatty said that she was so preoccupied with her own new job and her new marriage that she didn't think much about it."

"Then, according to Beatty, one night in the middle of winter, someone rang the Kearns' doorbell at two in the morning. Doc Kearns, I guess, has a thing for guns. He grabbed a gun and went to the door to see who it was."

Peter made the choking sound again. "Hold on a second, please, Mr. Dombrowski," Margaret interjected. Before she could hear his protests on the other end of the line, she had put her phone to her side and stood over Peter's bed. "Peter, are you okay?" she asked, no longer worried about waking him.

Margaret lifted the phone to her face and started to tell the detective that she was concerned about Peter, but now the detective was the one interjecting.

"So when the dentist answered the door, there was Amy. But Dr. Kearns had never met her and didn't know who she was. She was holding something small and apparently alive up against her chest. It was wrapped in blankets."

Peter made a choking sound again. Now Margaret was truly alarmed. She pushed a button next to Peter's bed for assistance. It took a minute for someone to respond and in the meantime, Dombrowski was continuing his frenetic tale.

"As Dr. Kearns was staring at her, Muriel came to the door and saw Amy and explained to her husband who she was. Muriel said that she asked if she could come in. The three of them sat in the living room around the Kearns' coffee table," continued Dombrowski. "Amy, holding the wrapped creature and rocking back and forth, was very emotional and went on to explain that her job for the doctor was to assist him at an abortion clinic in the city."

Margaret was only half listening as a nurse entered the room. "Could you please check on Fr. Kearns?" she asked the nurse. "He sounds like he's choking."

As Margaret watched the nurse tend to Peter, the increasingly excited detective was literally yelling into the phone at her. "Amy said that most of the abortions her boss performed were done in the first trimester or early in the second trimester and were generally done with a suction machine. He called that procedure 'dilatation and evacuation,' or' D & E.' But sometimes, and more often lately, the doctor was doing later term abortions – sometimes into the second trimester and beyond. The doctor's preferred method for the late-term abortions was by saline injection, which involves a caustic, chemical mixture being injected into the womb. Margaret heard the detective trying to tell her about Amy's work at an abortion clinic, but that was about all she was getting from this, as she watched the nurse place a stethoscope on various areas of Peter's chest while wearing a worried expression.

Oblivious to Margaret's distractions on the other end, Dombrowski continued. "The doctor called Amy at home that night and needed her to come in for a procedure. When she got there, it turned out to be another late-termer. After delivering the dead baby, he handed it to Amy for disposal as he always did. Only this little baby that Amy thought was about six and one-half months gestation was not dead! The eyes were open and looking right at her!" yelled the detective, incredulous.

"So Amy panics, I guess. When she takes the baby out of the room, the doctor thinks she's going to put the fetus in an incinerator. Instead, she finds some blankets, wraps the baby up and drives away in her car with the baby on her passenger seat! She didn't know where she was going, but she left the abortion clinic and never went back. Then she thought about her friend, Muriel, who graduated from nursing school at the top of their class and was married to some sort of doctor."

At this point in the detective's hyperventilating monologue, two more staff from the hospital joined the nurse in tending to Peter. Midland watched the scene silently from the other bed. As this was transpiring, the detective continued with his story.

"Amy unwrapped her bundle on the Kearns' coffee table and there was a tiny, premature baby boy. It was a miracle that he was alive. His skin was peeling off all over his body. But apparently, this little guy had the will to live and, by God, he was still alive!"

"Muriel said Amy started crying and told the Kearns that she didn't know what to do with the child. She was afraid she would get into trouble if she took him to a hospital, but she was pretty sure what her employer would have done if he had realized the baby was alive, and she couldn't bear the thought."

"The Kearns helped Amy get the baby into the bathroom and laid him on a towel in the bathtub. They filled it with warm water, just to the point that it came up over the baby's shoulders to keep him warm and to try to rinse off the remaining chemicals. When they finished cleaning him off, the baby was still alive. He seemed to be having trouble breathing now, so Dr. Kearns gave him oxygen, placing an adult-sized mask over his entire, miniature face.

Margaret listened dazedly as the detective's narrative continued. At the same time, she watched as the nurse began performing chest compressions on Peter. "No, no, no, detective, I can't do this right now," Margaret said with an excitement that rivaled Dombrowski's. "Peter, I love you! Hold on!" Margaret yelled from the bedside.

But the detective insisted that she hear him out. So, while watching the frantic scene before her, Margaret heard the detective say something about getting ahold of financial records belonging to the abortion clinic to try to learn the identity of the boy's mother.

"As it turned out," Dombrowski continued, "there were five abortions at the facility that day. An 'M' by the name of the customer who paid the bill indicated that a male child was aborted and an 'F' meant it was a female. According to these records, Margaret, there were four females and one male that day!"

Margaret could see that the nurses were trying to resuscitate Peter, and she opened her mouth to say something but found she couldn't speak. She had an unimaginable thought that she tried unsuccessfully to push from her brain. "Is this the reason the detective is in such a delirious state?" Margaret wondered. Suddenly she did not want to hear any more, but the detective concluded his tale in a full-throated scream, "Margaret! The customer who paid for the abortion for the male child was *Alfred Millington*!!!" Margaret gasped and held her head between her hands with her mouth agape. Her body shuddered involuntarily and she felt nauseated.

Just then, the movements of the medical personnel lost their urgency. The facility physician looked at Margaret and shook her head slowly and unmistakably. Margaret, in utter disbelief of what she had just witnessed and of what she was just told, dropped her phone on the floor and flung herself on top of the young man who was now lying lifeless before her. She began to moan unrestrainedly.

"Ms. Millington? Did you hear me? Ms. Millington?" It was Dombrowski, unaware of what had happened, coming from the phone on the floor.

One of the hospital staff who had been helping with Peter picked up the phone. "I'm sorry. I'm afraid Ms. Millington can't talk right now," and ended the phone call.

After giving her some space for awhile, the staff eventually tried to comfort Margaret, but she was inconsolable. At first they moved her to an area of the convalescent center away from the other patients. They eventually called for a cab, as she was clearly in no condition to drive. Forty minutes after her phone call and about an hour after Peter died, Margaret was dropped off at her house.

As she exited the cab, she felt disembodied. Without even thinking about where she was going, Margaret turned in the direction opposite her home and began walking aimlessly. She eventually ended up a mile away at a pharmacy. She walked in and mindlessly purchased a bottle of scotch. She then walked the mile back to her home. Grief-stricken, Margaret sat on the sidewalk in front of her townhouse and stared straight ahead, the bottle still unopened in the bag beside her.

Margaret spent the next couple of days in bed. She didn't eat or drink. Her phone rang a few times, but she ignored it. The bag with the bottle of scotch ended up on her kitchen counter, untouched.

**84**

It was 9:55 a.m. and St. Michael's was packed with people who had come to pay their final respects to their pastor and friend. The congregation spilled from the pews into the side aisles along the walls. The choir loft, perched high in the back of church, was filled with so many people that the ushers had to come up and ask about thirty people to come back downstairs to avoid overloading the structure.

Cardinal Umberto Malaya, a bishop who had emigrated from Honduras around the time of Peter Kearns' birth, stood upon the altar, facing the congregation and gazing past them to the large wooden doors at the back of the church. A pair of undertakers slowly opened the doors and kicked down the metal stands that propped the doors into place. Seconds later, the plain wooden casket was carried in by eight pall bearers and placed on a metal cart with wheels so it could be easily rolled up toward the altar.

A soprano soloist burst into song, accompanied by the lively strains of the pipe organ. The funeral home employees now directed the movement of the casket, with the pall bearers trailing immediately behind the casket. As the casket was slowly rolled forward down the center aisle, a Franciscan choir joined the soloist, creating an uplifting, celebratory processional.

When the casket was just a few feet short of the altar, a couple of adult altar boys gently draped it with a glossy, white cover, bearing a large gold cross. Two younger altar boys then circled the casket with incense and the cardinal greeted the standing-room-only congregation and began the funeral mass for the repose of the soul of Father Peter Kearns.

After a reading from the Gospel of Matthew, the cardinal turned over the duty of the homily to Fr. Ben Stura, a priest who had long been a friend of Peter Kearns. Fr. Stura spoke about the promise of salvation offered to all believers and shared a few memories of his late friend. He then invited anyone who felt so moved to share a memory of Fr. Kearns. Several people accepted the invitation and in their turn spoke briefly to the congregation. When the last of this group sat down, there was a pause, and Cardinal Malaya sat up in his seat to make sure no one else was preparing to come forward before he moved into the next part of the mass. But just then, the cardinal noticed a slight commotion about three-quarters of the way back, as a woman was making her way past the people seated in her pew toward the center aisle.

The woman who was now walking up toward the lectern on the altar had reddened eyes, hardly making her unique at that moment, and she was holding some tissues in her hand. Only those who had not been around Fr. Kearns in the past year were unfamiliar with Margaret Millington.

She stood before the lectern, still clutching the tissues in her left hand, which now could be seen by those seated nearby, to be trembling, blew her nose softly, cleared her throat, and addressed the crowd.

"My name is Margaret Millington. I, like many of you, had the good fortune of crossing paths with Peter Kearns." Not being trained at public speaking, Margaret's eyes were fixed on the people in the first two rows directly in front of her. Still, the sound system effectively amplified Margaret's voice throughout the cavernous sanctuary.

"I was one of Fr. Kearns' difficult projects." Margaret allowed herself a hint of a smile at these words. "When I met Fr. Kearns, I was at the lowest point of my life. I had just been divorced and, not feeling like a soul in the world would miss me, had attempted to kill myself. Why Fr. Kearns came to my hospital room, I never knew. But I will be forever grateful that he did. Because Peter Kearns saved my life. But more importantly, he saved my soul."

Margaret now had the attention of every person in the church as she continued.

"I have come to realize over time that I'm just one of countless hurting people touched by Fr. Peter's love."

"Before meeting Peter Kearns just about ten months ago, I was lost. I thought that growing old and losing my looks was the worst thing that could happen to me. That thought bothered me more than losing my husband, whom I knew hadn't loved me for years. But this young man who lies here today told me about the beauty that really matters; the beauty that lies beneath a person's exterior and rests in their heart. That is why I can stand here today and tell you without hesitation that Peter Kearns, with his pitifully scarred and disfigured face, was the most beautiful person I have ever known."

Margaret bit her lip and forced back the tears that were welling up in her eyes.

She continued. "You know, when I first met Peter, I kind of felt sorry for him. What a lonely life, I arrogantly thought. How can a celibate, single man like this really enjoy his life? But what I have come to learn in my time with Peter Kearns is nothing less than the key to happiness on earth. Loving others. Yes, it is really that simple. The key to happiness on earth is to follow our Lord Jesus' command and love one another."

At this point, all of the people in the pews that were close enough for Margaret to see were visibly stirred. But her voice grew stronger.

"We know that the Ten Commandments were laid down not for God's benefit, but for ours. But Fr. Peter Kearns' life demonstrated to me that the command of Jesus to love one another is likewise not for His benefit, but for ours. To love others provides an obvious benefit to the recipient of our loving actions. But the joy that emanated from Peter made it obvious that the love he shared was returned to him in spades."

"Most of us," she continued, "limit our experiences of love to a handful of close relatives: our spouse, children, parents and siblings, maybe a few close friends over the course of our lives. But Peter's secret was that he loved literally every person he met, even strangers. As a result, he was filled with more joy than anyone I have ever known."

"And what is amazing," Margaret said, now speaking more comfortably and with a still stronger voice, "is how contagious love is. People responded to Peter. Maybe not at first, and maybe not all the time. But the vast majority of people respond well to a sincere person who is kind to them."

"Peter Kearns' capacity for love has been the greatest source of faith that I could ever imagine."

At that moment, the cardinal rose to his feet and began clapping. The other clergy in the church followed suit. Shortly, the entire congregation was on its feet, enthusiastically joining this tribute to the memory of the young priest.

Margaret was moved deeply, and the tears now flowed freely down the face of the priest's proud mother, who herself joined in the applause. Eventually, the spontaneous celebration tapered off and Margaret concluded her eulogy.

"For me, what is most exciting about the power of love is that all of us have the ability to love generously. We, too, can experience the same joy that our friend Peter had." "God bless the soul of Peter Kearns and God bless each one of you."

As Margaret walked back to her seat, her eyes met those of many of Peter's other friends and admirers among the crowd. Many of these nodded their approval to her. An elderly gentleman in a wheelchair seated in the aisle gave her a thumbs-up sign.

The funeral mass continued from that point forward in rather ordinary fashion. But long would people remember the extraordinary young priest who served them and the essence of his being that Margaret distilled so clearly that day.

Just ten months after trying to take her own life, Margaret had attained an amazing resilience. As she lay in bed immediately after Peter's death, Margaret was unable to sleep. Instead, she thought deeply about the heaven that Peter longed to see. She thought about the transformation in her life over the past ten months and about the meaning of all of our lives.

In the early years of her marriage, Margaret very much wanted children. To think that her child was actually walking around in the same city all these years, growing into an amazing young man, initially made Margaret resentful. Although she knew it was ultimately her decision not to keep her baby, she could have been Peter's mother and enjoyed his presence for the past thirty years. But then she wondered how Peter would have turned out if he hadn't been raised by the Curtises, where he developed an impeccable character and an unusually strong faith.

After going back and forth in her mind, Margaret finally concluded that for Peter, his life was rich and full as it actually unfolded. She could not be sure he would have made the same impact on the world around him if she had raised him. Considering all these things, Margaret eventually came to peace with all that had happened. She felt more strongly than ever that heaven was real and she was certain that Peter was there now. Moreover, she truly believed that she would be reunited with him again one day. And rather than blaming herself for trying to snuff out the life of this beautiful person, Margaret thanked God for intervening and allowing her effort to fail. She thanked God for Peter's short, yet abundantly fruitful, life.

She also thought about all of the good that she and each of us are capable of doing in the course of our busy, fleeting lives. All we have to do is open our eyes and love all of those that we see. Ironically, the son she never knew existed taught her that, despite our flaws, we are all special to our Creator and meant to be together in eternity.

Though we can't always see it, Margaret now believed that we are *all* connected, through space and time, now and forever.

As she was walking to her car after mass, Margaret received words of appreciation from a number of people, both friends and strangers alike. Some dark rain clouds had formed in the sky outside the church, and Margaret felt the beginning of sprinkles escaping onto the crowd, which started to disperse quickly to their cars. Despite the change in weather, Margaret thought to herself that it was still a beautiful day, and she looked forward to many more to come.